Swept Away

TONYA SHARP HYCHE

ISBN:1-4609-9053-6

ISBN-13:978-1-4609-9053-7

LCCN:2011904384

TO THE FOLLOWING PEOPLE:

Butch and Paula,
who inspired me and gave me courage to write my first novel.

Steve and my boys, Dustin and Dylan,
who continue to love and support me.

Kathleen and Teresa,
the sound of your voices always brighten my day, and
you can always make me laugh.

In memory of my father, Pat Sharp III.
I have strived to live my life to the fullest with no regrets.

I Dream...

I Explore...

I Pray...

I Love...

Part One

CHAPTER 1

Kathleen Bishop was standing in the front of the classroom with a marker in one hand and a dry eraser in the other. She looked at her students' faces as she rambled on about World War I. She could tell they had reached their limit for the day. It was seventh period; in only two minutes the bell would ring and end their day. She continued on, "There were three major reasons why the Great War started in Europe in nineteen fourteen. One, militarism, two, nationalism and—"

Riiinnnnggg...

"Really? Are they ever going to ring the bell consistently at this school?" she thought. She quickly realized her students were packing up and said, "Okay class, we will pick up tomorrow. Don't forget to read pages four hundred eighty-one through four hundred eighty-four tonight, class dismissed."

"Bye Ms. Bishop, see you tomorrow."

"Good-bye, Jillian. Be safe!"

'Be safe' were words that were spoken more often than 'cute outfit' or 'did you go to the basketball game last night?' This is Bellview High, a public high school located in downtown Chicago on the wrong side of town. Here we count how many kids we lose to drugs, gunfire, stabbings, and dropouts instead of points on a scoreboard.

A beautiful sixteen-year-old Hispanic girl was walking toward the door, one of the last to leave. Lisa sat in the back beside Eddie, the father of her child, who hasn't been to class all week.

"Lisa, where is Eddie? He has not shown up now for three days."

"Ms., you know Eddie. Eddie is just being Eddie. Eddie don't answer to nobody. He chooses when to come to school, and when he got to work. Look, Ms., you're really sweet for asking, and I know you truly care, not like some of the others, but we are running low on fuel, and Eddie has to be able to pay up on some things, you know?"

Lisa was smiling and waving her hands around while she spoke. Always giving the impression that life was all good and nothing bad could touch her. A dangerous assumption for a single mom who was forced to take care of herself, thanks to her no good mom who had set the ball rolling for another cycle of broken home and family. Lisa and Eddie's life was typical of most of her student body. Mom was a single parent, and father had either left, died, been to prison, or even worse—mom doesn't know who dad was.

The question that always crossed Kathleen Bishop's mind was how could I possibly expect them to care or learn world history, when they live each day just trying to survive? Most of her colleagues had replied, "You don't. Get your years in, get your loan paid, and leave." Six years ago that was the goal. Teach in a high school that served a lower socioeconomic neighborhood for five years and the government would pay your student loan. After last year, Kathleen had decided to stay on, shocking the head of administration. Over 90 percent of the staff left after five years. Mr. Potter, the principal, was overjoyed to hear that Ms. Bishop was happy and felt that she belonged there and could make a real difference in the lives of her students.

"Thanks, Lisa. Take care of yourself and baby Mia. Oh, and Lisa, do your math homework first before history. Mr. Muehsler informed me that you are in danger of failing math this six weeks."

Rolling her eyes, she smiled and replied "Just for you, Ms."

Kathleen walked over and sat behind her uneven desk and punched in her computer password. She clicked on the Internet and then patiently waited for her school's home page to appear. As she waited, she looked around the room. The gray paint was starting to peel on one wall and there was a new hole a few feet down on the adjoining wall. Toward the back of the classroom she noticed a gray Bellview High sweatshirt lying under a desk. She knew someone would miss it dearly when he or she stepped outside into the freezing winter temperatures. She frowned, no one was going to come back and chance missing the bus. At this school, if you missed the bus, you walked. Her attention turned back to her computer screen when she heard the ding noise. Once online, she looked up Eddie's information under her school's grade book system. Under name, she typed Eddie Jones. A few moments passed and then information slowly appeared. The phone number read unlisted number—no surprise there. There was however, an emergency contact number. She pulled her personal phone out of her top desk drawer and dialed the number. After two rings, she heard the all-to-familiar message to most teachers on this campus.

"The number you have dialed is no longer in service..."

Feeling frustrated but not surrendering to defeat, Kathleen scrolled down to the address. Taking out a pen, she wrote down the address 3800 Wilson Street, Unit 323. As she was laying down her pen, the overhead PA system beeped and then announced, "Teachers, at this time please begin to pack up for the day. Our officers will be conducting a final walk through in five minutes. Teachers please have a safe drive home and see you bright and early in the morning for a six forty-five faculty meeting."

Taking the hot pink sticky note titled teacher's notes, with the address neatly written on it, she packed her papers to grade in her satchel and shut down her computer. She quickly took one more look around, and then made her way to the door and locked up her classroom. She glanced down the hallway but saw no one. Most teachers she knew packed up five minutes before the bell rung and then stood by the door with their students, ready to leave with them.

As she walked down the empty hallway, she could only hear the clatter of her high heels against the tiles. She had to keep her eyes to the floor to make sure she didn't step in a spilled drink or trip over tossed textbooks. After a few more turns she finally reached the exit door that led into the parking lot. She easily spotted her ninety-eight Tahoe because there were very few cars left. Shaking her head, she was not surprised to find that she was one of the last to leave.

The temperature outside had dropped significantly since midday. Chilled, she tucked her satchel under her arm and began to run the remaining steps in two-inch heels. Due to her height of five feet three inches, she wore heels every day, along with a jacket and skirt. Kathleen felt that it was important for her students to see her dressed as a professional each day. Somehow that would inspire them to graduate, go on to college, and make something of their life. Aiming her key toward the lock, she heard a noise and jumped, dropping her keys to the ground. Spinning around nervously, she was glad to see that it was only Officer McKinney.

"I'm sorry Ms. Bishop, here let me get the keys." He bent down and picked up the keys and then handed them over to her and asked, "Is everything alright?"

She smiled back and said, "Yes, thank you. Man is it cold!"

He said, "Yeah, I bet you miss Florida this time of the year."

"Oh, we won't even talk about that," Kathleen said as she quickly got in her car.

He laughed and then closed her car door. He motioned through the window for her to lock her door and waved as she started the engine. Opening her satchel, she gathered her GPS and typed in Eddie's address. Waving again to Officer McKinney, she pulled out of the mostly empty parking lot and headed toward the street, directed by the voice command system.

CHAPTER 2

Eddie Jones was hanging out in unit 411 on the fourth floor of the Benedict Housing Complex. High as a kite, he was visiting a customer about a potential job opening on the West Coast. Eddie knew his time here was up, and it was time to move on. Joe Banks's unit was no different than the one he shared with Lisa below. As Joe talked on his phone, he glanced around the place again just to make sure they were alone. He had been on edge for the last few days. Lisa had asked questions but only once. She knew her boundaries and didn't push him when he refused to answer. That is why he liked her and decided to keep her around. It surprised him last night when he made the decision to take Lisa and the baby with him. He would move out to the West Coast first, and when he got established, he would then send for her and baby Mia in a few months.

Joe hung up his phone and said, "You are set man. Leroy will expect you in two days."

For the first time in several days, Eddie felt a sense of relief. It didn't last long though; the family he was tied up with was dangerous, very dangerous. He finally said, "Great. I'm leaving as soon as Lisa gets home."

Joe asked, "You really like that bitch?"

Eddie turned to face Joe with his red eyes and stumbled a little, "Yeah, the baby too."

"Huh, is she going with you?"

Catching his balance with an old, worn-out faded recliner he said, "Eventually, just not now. Look I need to go, but thanks, man."

Joe walked over and placed a hand on Eddie's shoulder, "Don't disappoint, Leroy. It will make me look bad man."

Eddie just smiled and then turned toward the door and stumbled out unaware of the evil that lurked below in unit 323.

Lisa arrived home from school and was making her way up the three flights of stairs when another girl commented, "Well, look at the little schoolgirl. You really shouldn't leave your man all alone, honey."

Lisa just shrugged her shoulders and kept climbing the stairs. She was in no mood to entertain any discussions with Sybil, who was a complete loser. She just wanted to get home and see her baby. Sybil didn't stop though and kept mumbling behind her. Lisa didn't care. After she made the last flight of stairs, she could no longer hear Sybil. She opened the door to the third floor and smiled as she closed it behind her. As she walked along the hallway she managed to pull out her unit key from her hip pocket. She found the door marked 323 and unlocked it with her key. Lisa stepped in and then locked the door behind her. As she was making her way back toward the bedroom, she heard a thud in the kitchen. Lisa called out to her Aunt Ella who watched Mia while she was away at school. Not too alarmed, Lisa assumed Ella had let herself in the apartment while she was at school. When Ella babysat, she would move around with Mia between her apartment in unit 144 and unit 323.

Lisa continued to walk toward the kitchen even though there was no answer. Slowly pushing the swinging door inward, she called out once more, "Ella? Mia? Are my baby girl playing hide and seek?" Just then a hand wrapped around Lisa's mouth and another around her waist, and dragged her into the living room. Thrown down hard against the couch, Lisa was stunned speechless as a large white man was leaning down on her with his hands wrapped around her throat squeezing her breath away. Out of the corner of her eyes, she saw another man appear from the kitchen and slowly make his way over to her. The man was known as Patch, and he was coming closer carrying a knife with a long shiny blade.

"Lisa, this kind man is going to allow you to breathe, if you lay still and don't move a muscle," Patch said.

Billy Joe slowly released his hands and stepped around Lisa toward the front of the couch. Gasping for air, Lisa curled up into a ball and held one hand on her throat and the other around her waist.

Patch continued, "Now that we have your undivided attention, where is Eddie?"

A raspy sound slowly made its way out of Lisa's mouth. Shaking her head she responded, "I don't know."

The man slowly moved the knife closer to Lisa and gently pressed it to her cheek. Lisa felt the sting of the cut but kept staring into his cold dark eyes. She knew that look before and instantly knew he had tasted of death before. With moist eyes, she watched him closely as he leaned down and spoke softly into her ear. She could feel his hot breath on her face as he said, "How unfortunate for you."

At that moment Patch froze and turned around as he heard a baby whimpering and keys jingling on a chain. Opening the door with one hand and looking down talking to Mia, Ella never knew what hit her. In one quick moment, Patch had sliced through Ella's stomach and was holding Mia as Ella doubled over and fell to the ground. Kicking the door shut, Patch turned around to see Billy Joe holding Lisa face down on the couch, muffling her screams. Placing Mia on a chair near the couch, Patch sat down beside Lisa and wiped the blood off his knife on her legs. Billy Joe released her then as Patch placed the blade of the knife to the back of Lisa's neck as she began crying and shaking uncontrollably. Patch continued demanding more answers that Lisa didn't have.

"Tell us where Eddie is hiding the money, and we will make your death painless."

As if the baby was aware of the drama unfolded in its home, baby Mia let out a deafening squeal. Still holding the knife on Lisa, Patch stretched out with his other hand and lifted a pillow off the couch and covered Mia. All sound stopped, and Lisa was pitched into a slow trance with shadows dancing all around her.

She whimpered, "Not the baby! Oh Mia! Please, please, don't hurt her."

The other man appeared from behind Patch and continued to hold down the pillow. Now with both hands free, Patch grabbed Lisa's hair and yanked upward with the knife still pressed to her neck. Blood began to leak around Lisa's neck and down her back.

"One more chance—where is the money?"

Lisa's mind couldn't take the shock and horror of her child's lifeless body beneath the pillow. She felt as if she was sinking and water was slowly moving over her body. She tried to cry out once more, but no sound emerged. The knife had continued around her neck cutting her voice off forever.

Travelling along Bruce Street at a creeping speed, Kathleen began to think about how different life would be if she had left Bellview High School. Home is south Florida, where the weather would be a pleasant, sunny seventy-five degrees for mid-November. She could be teaching in one of Ft. Lauderdale's new premiere high schools. Her father, a retired superintendent, had said, "Name your school and subject, just come back home." Something raw kept tugging at her heart and mind to stay. She had convinced six kids last year to continue school and not drop out. Three years ago, she had been instrumental in saving a child's life by convincing a young unwed sixteen-year-old to have her baby and give it up for adoption. She was five months pregnant and wanted to terminate the baby. Kathleen shook her head as she imagined a doctor performing such a task. The girl went on to graduate but unfortunately her life ended last summer by a drive by shooting in her neighborhood. The girl, Carol, had been sleeping in her bed when the incident happened. There were no arrest and no witnesses. All the talk around school was that it involved drugs—no surprise there.

"This is crazy! What am I doing? I'm driving around an area that is so bad, it's scary. Plus it's getting colder! Forget this, I'm turning around up ahead."

A voice said, "Left turn ahead, Wilson Street."

Listening to her GPS, she turned.

The voice said, "You have reached your destination."

Kathleen took a deep breath to calm her nerves and then put the Tahoe in park. She tapped along the steering wheel as she debated whether or not to get out. Thinking of Lisa and Mia, she turned off the engine and grabbed her sticky note and satchel. Placing them close to her body, she opened the door and got out. She only took one look back as she locked up her Tahoe.

CHAPTER 3

The wind was blowing harder now, and Kathleen felt chilled to the bone as she walked toward the Benedict Housing Complex. With this weather, Kathleen was surprised to see a small cluster of girls and guys hanging outside the building entrance. They appeared to be aged somewhere between twelve and eighteen years old. All were wearing hoods or hats, and they were laughing and carrying on some funny conversation. Most had their hands in their pockets, but some did not as they were smoking their cigarettes. When they spotted her, all chatter stopped.

One girl, Monique, who she recognized from school, called out "Hey, Ms. What you doing here?"

Kathleen just nodded and said, "Checking up on one of my sick students."

She didn't look back and kept walking. She could hear Monique tell the others, "Leave her alone man. She is cool."

"For once it is nice to be the cool teacher," she thought as she continued up the last two steps and was finally inside the building. With the door closed behind her it instantly felt warmer. She looked around for some kind of board that would display the layout of the building but found none. She did notice, however, an older woman curled up in the corner of the staircase sleeping—or at least she hoped she was sleeping. Fearing that she would get stuck in the elevator, she decided to take the stairs to the third floor despite the sleeping woman at her feet. So far, nothing scared her enough to make her decide to turn around. Rounding up to the second floor, the door to the hallway stood open, and she could hear a young woman with a baby on her hip screaming at another young girl about running low on diapers. The other girl had rollers in her hair and appeared to be about ten years old. She suddenly realized that she might have assumed wrong about the floor.

Timidly she asked, "Is unit three twenty-three on the third floor?"

Both girls stopped chattering and looked at Kathleen. The older one looked her up and down and was about to reply when Eddie appeared coming down the staircase.

"Ms. Bishop? What you doing here?"

Stammering, she finally got the right words out and replied, "I came to see you. I was worried when you didn't show up at school today. Why don't we head up to your room, and we can talk. Is your mom at home?"

Passing by Kathleen, he answered, "Sure, this way."

The girl with rollers started laughing and holding her stomach, "You crazy fool. You are on the second floor. You live above us, Eddie."

Looking around with his eyes glazed over, he then passed by Kathleen and began to stumble back into the staircase. Realizing he was stoned, Kathleen decided it was best and safe just to leave.

"Hey, Eddie, wait. Maybe you should just go on up and get a good night sleep, and I will see you in the morning."

Eddie grabbed hold of her arm and started whispering very slowly. She could only make out bits and pieces of what he was saying. Just as she was about to ask him to repeat what he said, the sound of footsteps approaching from above drew her attention.

Two white men dressed in black appeared. The larger man had a grim look on his face, and there was something unsettling about his movements. He was dressed in a tight black, short-sleeve T-shirt, dark jeans, and cowboy boots. Her mind told her right away something was not right.

"Why is he wearing short sleeves in this weather?" she asked herself. She continued to stare at his bare arms and then noticed a tattoo. As she followed the design around his right arm she saw it and froze. A shiny blade was protruding from his lower back. Instinct began to take over, and she broke away from Eddie and ran down the staircase. Rounding the first floor, she heard a grotesque gurgling sound from above. Assuming it was Eddie, she jumped the final three stairs in her high heels forgetting about the sleeping woman until it was too late.

Kathleen screamed, "Help me!" as she tripped over the woman, slamming hard into the side of the doorframe as she tried to catch herself from hitting the floor.

No one came to her rescue and the sleeping woman moaned, "Hey, what the hell?"

Not caring about the woman she had just ploughed into, she picked her satchel off the floor and searched for the entrance. Finding it she stumbled toward it and pushed opened the door as hard as she could. When the door flew open, the wind nearly knocked her back down. Holding tight to her satchel, she fumbled around for her keys as she ran to her Tahoe as fast as she could. Everything around her began to appear in slow motion. The chatter from the group of kids sounded distant and far away. She found her keys and then struggled to fit the right one in to unlock the door. Finally the door opened, and she jumped inside, locking the door behind her. Time began to speed up again as she jammed the key into the ignition and started the engine. Thankful the Tahoe started up, she threw it into reverse and pushed down hard on the gas pedal. Making a quick right turn, she put it in first gear and quickly peeled out of the lot with tires screaming; she never looked back.

CHAPTER 4

Detective Butch McNeil was sitting in his dimly lit office at the Chicago Police Department, which was just a few blocks away from Bellview High School. McNeil had served as one of Chicago's finest for twenty-six years and eighteen of those years as lead detective. During his twenty-six years on the job, he has been shot at twice, stabbed once, lost two marriages, and continued to struggle to raise his now sixteen-year-old daughter. While rubbing away at the tension that had built up in his neck throughout the day, McNeill was debating whether to call it a day. He glanced up at the clock, and it showed 4:50 P.M. It turned out to be a very cold Wednesday for mid-November. Deciding that he had seen enough and heard enough for one day, he slowly rose from his chair, twisting the soreness out of his back. The gunshot that he had taken back in February of last year still gave his upper back fits when he sat longer than two hours. Mandy, his daughter, had informed him that morning that she was trying out a new recipe and would like to eat before ten. That was Mandy's sarcastic way of saying he had been late too many times in the last couple of days. Walking out the door this morning, he had promised he would do everything possible to be home by 7:00. Wouldn't it be a nice surprise to show up at 5:30 and help cook?

He remembered reading somewhere that spending ten minutes engaged in a happy conversation with a teenager could lead to an hour of tension-free normalcy. Well, tonight was a good night to try out that theory. Reaching behind the door for his jacket, he glanced through the glass window and saw his partner, Detective Paula Williams, rounding the corner with a scowl on her face.

Leaning into his office, she fired away, "McNeil, we have a live one— let's go!"

Pulling his jacket on and grabbing his holster from the rack he looked at Williams and spoke, "You're on your own tonight. I've got plans."

She chuckled, "Good one, Butch! If I'm breaking my date tonight, so are you."

Detective Paula Williams was the most exotic female partner McNeil had ever had. Standing barefoot, she reached five feet ten inches with all the bells and whistles expected of a swimsuit supermodel. He often wondered but only asked once, why she had chosen this profession. After a tough punch in the side that was suppose to seem somewhat friendly and somewhat mean, he had left the subject at peace. Paula has been on the force now for fifteen years. With her wits and strong insight, she had been able to land a detective role in just under nine years. Paula was good, damn good at her job and had the records to back it up. She didn't like to be questioned about her abilities and was highly offended that people misjudged her based on her looks. When Butch returned from leave of absence after his last gunshot wound, he was placed with Paula as his new partner. His last partner, Detective Ricky Rodd, was killed on that cold February day as he lay beside him bleeding from his own gunshot wound. He often thought back to that moment and wondered why his partner entered the building first. If it had been the other way around, Ricky would be standing here looking at Paula.

Slowly over the last year and half, he has come to trust Paula's instincts and appreciate her judgment in some very hairy situations. Whether using a gun or her sweet angelic voice, she had saved his sorry ass on more than one occasion. Most of all, he had learned that when it came to working and reporting to the D.A., it was best to allow her to do the talking and leave the heavy lifting to him. They fit well together. If she wasn't twelve years his junior and thought of him as a father she'd never had, maybe he could try marriage number three.

Concentrating on the task at hand and blocking out the disappointment he can hear in his daughter's voice, he asked for the details that was sure to ruin his evening.

"We got four DOAs at the Benedict Housing Complex on Wilson."

Shit, not only was he going to miss his hour of normalcy with Mandy, but also he was going to miss the entire evening and night.

They made their way out the building and into the cold freezing wind. Paula was ahead of him, and she went straight for the driver side of their black sedan. With Paula, he never was sure who was going to drive. He generally let her lead the way, and then he took his place beside her. Tonight, she must have wanted to drive.

Driving toward Wilson Street, Paula asked, "So Butch, what is so important about tonight?"

"I was just trying to be a better dad, that's all."

He had shared a lot with his partner over the last several months. Paula had listened and given really good advice when it came to Mandy. They had met several times, and Mandy enjoyed her company and eventually invited her over for dinner. Dinner went so well that Mandy made a routine out of cooking for all three of them once a week—usually Sunday nights. Butch thought it was healthy having a woman around for her to talk to.

Paula reached over and tapped his hand. "Go ahead and make the call. No, she will not be happy, but she will understand. Just let her blow off some steam and take it like a man."

"Yeah, I know."

Frowning, he punched in speed dial to Mandy's phone and delivered the news. As expected, Mandy didn't take the news lightly. Holding the phone away from his ear, he cringed when he spoke, "I love you baby. I got to go." He closed the phone.

Taking Paula's phone off the seat, he held it out and said "Your next, princess."

It was her turn to frown now. She said, "Dial eight and hit send."

"Wow, he is already on speed dial, who is this guy?"

Taking the phone she began her quick regrets and ended the call.

"I got lucky," she said, "voice mail."

"And...who is this guy?"

Pulling onto Wilson Street, she said, "Too bad we're out of time. We're here."

CHAPTER 5

Butch peered out his window and found the Benedict Housing Complex lit up like a circus.

He mumbled, "Great, just what we need!"

Helicopters, flying overhead with searchlights shining down, were filming the parade that lay before them. He noticed lots of parked cars, mostly cops, ambulances, fire trucks, and SWAT.

"Look, McNeil, your favorite gal is here."

Butch scanned the parked cars again until he spotted the district attorney's dark blue Lexus. He then looked toward his right at the fine group of people employed by the city. There she stood talking to a group of officers. When she spotted their car she stopped talking and started walking toward them.

Paula said, "This is going to be fun!"

Butch gave her a look that could kill and then opened the door and stepped out into the cold night.

District Attorney Aileene Bell was walking swiftly toward Williams and McNeil. Dressed in her usual kick-ass dark navy suit with three-inch heels, she politely ignored all shouts from the media. Her blond hair was wrapped in a tight French knot except for the one long curl that flowed softly along her face. She was another gift to mankind with beauty and brains. Unfortunately, Butch had been on her shit list since their affair ended three weeks ago. In her eyes, it was Butch's fault and his fault alone. Butch, however, had a completely different opinion that didn't really matter in the grand scheme of affairs' gone bad. It was over, probably for the best, and neither of them wanted to try again; they only wanted to forget. So here they were again—forced to talk and work together like the last six months didn't exist.

"Detectives Williams and McNeil looks like we have another mess on our hands. Let's try to keep a lid on this until we have some time to sit down and discuss what we got. None of us wants a duplicate of the last media frenzy that made us all look like morons!"

Trying to remain civil, Butch replied with a simple, "After you."

With an annoyed look on her face, Aileene Bell turned and headed into the sea of people clustered around the entrance. Residents wearing expressions of excitement, disappointment, and ill attitudes about being roped off from their residence were gathered around the building. It was cold—too cold to be standing around outside. The crowd was given blankets and most of them were wrapped up with only their whites of their eyes showing. Some unfriendly comments were thrown toward Aileene, but she continued on with her straight shoulders and back as she reached the entrance of the building. It reminded Butch how quickly she could tune everything out and focus on the matter at hand. That is why she made one hell of a lawyer and one of the reasons he was so impressed with her at the beginning. She knew when to keep her cool and he had never seen her crack under pressure.

Pushing his thoughts of Aileene aside, he entered the building behind her with Paula in tow. Once the door was shut behind them, they were handed the fashionable booties and gloves. All were reminded on more than one occasion not to touch anything. It always amazed Butch that at age forty-nine, with over twenty-six years of experience with a gun, and he was still reminded by the ME to not touch the crime scene. He took the comments like a grain of salt but not Aileene.

"Do you think I'm stupid, Fred?" The medical examiner thought better and decided to go with, "I'm just doing my job, Ms. Bell. I don't want anything to be ruined."

Deciding to diffuse the situation, Butch asked Fred Bair, the medical examiner for the last eighteen years, "What we got?"

"Brace yourself because it's horrific. We have four brutal homicides, one a newborn about two months old."

Butch said, "Jesus! Williams, Bell, let's go. Walk us through it Dr. Bair."

Swearing under her breath, Paula looked up the staircase with fire in her eyes. Butch had seen that look way too many times and imagined he had the same look. Many of the cops were walking around with dazed, grim expressions probably wondering again why they had chosen this cheery profession. They all looked at the bottom of the stairwell where the yellow crime scene tape began. They hurriedly put on their gloves and booties and carefully followed up the stairs behind the M.E.

CHAPTER 6

Slowly placing one foot in front of the other, Aileene, Paula, and Butch began to follow Dr. Bair into the maze. The ME was short and bald. He was the butt of many jokes around the office, but Butch liked how he was known for just giving the facts. It was important to him because he then could form his own opinion without being swayed by others.

Bair pointed at the stairs leading up from the first floor, "We have two sets of bloody prints that appear to be left by the killers. This one here is an eleven and a half print from a cowboy boot and another one on top of the stairs is a nine and a half tennis-shoe print."

Butch reached inside his jacket and took out his notepad and wrote Killer is cocky; left prints behind.

Once on top of the second floor we came across our first victim.

"The victim died from a knife wound to the chest. It appears something is lodged in the throat. I'll know what later when we get him back to the morgue. The vic's name is Eddie Jones, age seventeen. We found his wallet in his back pocket, which had a couple of dollars and ID. Police also have the same ID from a young girl who found the body."

Butch jotted down in his pad Killer wasn't looking for something small; left wallet behind.

Paula touched Butches' sleeve and asked, "Hey, isn't that the kid from Bellview High? You know the one that popped off to me about pretty blonds in cop uniforms."

Butch said, "What?"

Paula responded, "You know the seminar we gave about drugs."

Butch thought back to the lecture he and Paula gave last week, and he took a closer look and tried to picture the kid from the high school.

"Too hard to tell, someone really did a number on him. Maybe."

Aileene piped in, "What seminar? Do you know this kid? We might be able to use that in our PR to help with some of the backlash we will get from this case. The media will have a field day when they hear a two-month-old baby was killed."

Noticing Butch's body language, Paula immediately spoke up and answered for him.

"McNeil and I are heading up the crime stopper organization at Bellview High School. We gave the usual speech last week about staying in school, staying away from drugs, and reporting crime."

Looking sadly at the kid, Aileene replied, "Let me guess, he didn't join the crime stoppers' club?"

No one else said anything, and it got really quiet as all pondered their thoughts. They finally turned away from Eddie and followed Bair up the next flight of stairs toward the third floor. Down the hall there was more activity outside unit 323. Carefully making their way down the hallway, Bair began to rattle off more facts.

"Folks, brace yourselves—it's very ugly in there."

Butch rounded the corner first and was immediately hit with rage. His eyes scanned the room, and he saw the baby first. One end of a long brown belt was wrapped around the baby's ankle, and the other end was tied around a ceiling fan. The baby had turned a shade of blue and was dangling in midair. Cameras were still flashing as the tech guys were still getting every angle for their investigation.

Bair said, "The baby has no stab wounds and looks to have died from suffocation, age and ID are still being verified."

Pushing her emotions aside, Paula stated, "This is for show. We are not dealing with our average criminal."

"I agree. He is sending someone a message. Who that someone is, I don't know," said Butch.

Aileene made no comment. Butch could tell she was trying to absorb everything without getting emotional. Aileene had two beautiful girls at home, and there was no doubt in Butch's mind that she was thinking of them now. Who was he kidding? He wasn't immune to this display just because he was some tough guy. He was thinking of her girls and his own daughter. He shook the cobwebs out of his head and wondered if he could really stop the monsters in the world from some day bringing harm to them?

Bair pointed down, "Here along the floor is a trail of blood that will lead back into the bedroom. The body was obviously moved because of the amount of blood on the couch."

Everyone could see the trail that wrapped around the mismatched furniture and continued around behind the wall. Bair was stating the obvious, but no one made any comment to the effect.

Again walking carefully in their booties, they followed Bair through the living room and down the hallway that led to the bedrooms. Somehow as they walked Aileene had moved ahead of Butch and Paula. Butch realized she was being true to her personality and entered first, which he knew would be a mistake. Before, he could stop and warn her, Aileene screamed, turned, and practically mowed him down fighting to get out of unit 323.

Paula, who entered second, just froze without making a sound. Butch took a deep breath, gently placed a hand on Paula's shoulder, and carefully moved her to the side to get around.

Butch grumbled in a strange voice, "What the hell happened in here?"

CHAPTER 7

Patch pulled his black Lincoln Escapade into an alley off Baxter Street. Looking around, he spotted only two cars parked along the dumpsters. Both cars were dark in color with tinted windows. One was the boss man's new Jaguar. The other was a Lincoln Town Car driven by the boss man's brother. He glanced around to make sure they were alone. They were, and no one noticed as Patch, six feet two inches, and Billy Joe, five feet nine inches, exited their vehicle and walked toward the back door of Evangelina's Restaurant. Working their way through the kitchen, the two men dodged the chef and staff who were busy cooking and preparing the night's dishes. The staff had grown accustomed to the men and learned early on through example not to ask questions. Along the wall that held the plates and platters was a staircase that led to Emilio Fernandez's office, the boss man. Billy Joe took the stairs first, and Patch followed. When they reached the top stair, Wally the pit bull greeted them. Wally was black, standing six feet five inches with bulging muscles and carried a loaded machine gun beneath his dark gray suit. No one was getting inside the office unless he approved first. Billy Joe gave the day's code, and Wally grunted a little, then stepped to the side, and allowed the men inside.

The office was bigger than the impression it gave from downstairs. One would think it was just a storage room with maybe room enough for a desk and two chairs. But once you stepped inside, it was every man's dream office. On one wall, it was lined with movie posters from the 1950s, '60s, and '70s. If Patch had to guess, he would say the one with Natalie Wood had a video camera hidden discreetly within. Along the other walls, sports memorabilia was proudly displayed from the brothers' two favorite teams, the Bulls and the Bears. Various jerseys and balls had been signed by noted players and coaches, and were placed behind elegant glass boxes. In the corner stood a well-stocked minibar set up with leather bar stools that matched the cherry wood pool table. Emilio's very large, cherry wood desk was placed in front of the windows. The furniture surrounding his desk was dark leather with thick wooden claw feet. Everything in this room screamed money, and Patch was sure the boss man's wife, the famed decorator, had arranged the décor.

In the center of the room, Emilio was sitting in an oversized chair watching the six o'clock news. Patch's eyes found the screen and began watching as the events unfolded at the Benedict Housing Complex. The camera had rolled over Aileene Bell, the stunning district attorney who had provided no details. Gathered around Bell were two detectives and Chicago's chief medical examiner. The camera continued to roll as the group entered the Benedict Housing Complex. The camera turned back to the lady holding the microphone who wore a sad and displeased look on her face. She had promised to deliver more, as the night was still young.

Swiveling around in his chair, Emilio spoke, "Please tell me you have my goods and money."

Billy Joe looked down and stepped side to side as Patch faced Emilio head on and replied, "No."

Emilio gave a nod and gestured toward Billy Joe, and a man stepped out from behind them and placed a gun to his back and pulled the trigger. No sound was made except for Billy Joe hitting the floor.

Emilio spoke, "I really appreciate your direct approach Patch, and I truly don't want to replace you. With that being said, please tell me you have some viable information that is going to spare your life. You are the only link between my family and that circus floating around on TV."

Patch met his gaze with his cold green eyes, "Eddie picked up the goods Monday morning from Billy Joe at the warehouse. On Tuesday, he met the new client and took one hundred thousand dollars as a deposit. Eddie was to return Wednesday morning at eight o'clock to hand over the goods and get four hundred thousand dollars from the customer. At ten this morning, Billy Joe gets a call from the customer that Eddie failed to show. At noon, Billy Joe and I arrange to meet the customer and things got out of hand. The customer pulled a gun, and I was forced to take him out."

Emilio waved a hand to interrupt, "Had the customer met you before?"

Feeling the sweat trickling down his back, he replied, "No, the only contacts were Billy Joe and Eddie."

For the first time, the man in the shadow spoke. "Eddie, and anyone close to Eddie, customer, and gesturing down to the floor, Billy Joe are all dead. We are missing half a million dollars worth of coke, and you, Patch, are the only witness seen at the crime. If you don't have any clues to lead us to the coke, why should you be standing here alive?"

Most everyone who works for the Fernandez family is scared of Emilio, but everyone has nightmares about his brother, Victor. At age thirty-five,

Victor is five years younger than Emilio. It is Victor who kills and never blinks an eye. He is a mastermind at playing people for fools. He can equally meet his brother's intelligence, but most never realize they have been out smarted until it is too late. Emilio gets the credit for building the Fernandez Empire into the largest and most profitable drug cartel in Chicago. Very few realize the real mastermind behind the business is Victor, and once they have figured that out, they are dead.

Both Emilio and Victor were born in Madrid, Spain. They came to America in their teens with their grandfather who was on the run from dealings just like the ones that occurred today. Except in their story, grandfather had been the one who stole the money and ran, instead of the customer who had been taken for a fool. Both brothers are charmers and have the great looks to go with it. Women give more than a second glance. Emilio is married with three young boys, and shockingly, he is faithful to his wife of fifteen years.

Victor continues the life of a Spanish playboy who travels around Europe and America frequently on business and pleasure. The Fernandez brothers have a strong legitimate steel company named Chicago Steel. For ten years now, the company has been so successful that it has done an incredible job of hiding the illegal drug trafficking business. The steel company has allowed Victor to travel to and from Europe under a disguise while he transports and distributes drug dealings with none the wiser.

Patch, slightly trembling, pulls out a pink sticky note from his right pocket in his jeans. "Eddie was talking to a young woman who doesn't belong at Benedict. She was carrying this note with Eddie's address and a large satchel. The woman appeared to be a teacher."

Victor walked over and took the note and replied, "You have twenty-four hours to find her."

Patch nodded his head to acknowledge and then glanced down toward Billy Joe lying on the floor in a pool of blood. A strange thought jumped in his mind, "What would Vivian think if she saw the mess on her stylish Italian rug?"

CHAPTER 8

Before pulling into a twenty-four-hour truck stop, Kathleen had been driving around in circles for what seemed like hours. Taking down her GPS, she typed in home. She was stunned to see she was seventy-eight miles away. She looked at the clock and it read 5:55 P.M. She would not be home till after 7:00 if she headed back right now. Placing her GPS in her lap, she laid her head back, and closed her eyes. Where had the time gone? Thinking back, she remembered traffic sitting still and taking a turn left and then, maybe five more turns until the traffic opened up, and she found herself on the interstate. "I'm so confused. Where am I?" she had asked herself.

She opened her eyes again and sat up. She looked around for any sign that might reveal her location but found none. Nothing looked familiar either. She had to look back at her GPS to find what interstate she was on. Thinking aloud, "Why didn't I just go home? Really—the Benedict Housing Complex? I really went inside!"

Just then, a man slammed a car door beside her Tahoe and she almost jumped out of her skin. The man stared at her with a curious look and then continued into the truck stop but glanced back once more to look at her again. Freaked out, she placed her GPS on the dash holder, started her engine, pulled out of the parking spot, and headed toward home. Getting back onto the interstate, she allowed her mind to go back and revisit what had happened at Eddie's place. She couldn't be sure if Eddie was hurt, but she was 100 percent certain she remembered the knife the man was holding. He was with someone else, but she couldn't get the taller man's face out of her mind.

"What if Eddie was hurt, and she could identify the man on the stairwell?"

He looked evil, and she still could feel the sensation along her neck that something is bad wrong. "Am I safe? Can I go home?" she wondered.

The man could not possibly know who she was. She had not identified herself to anyone, not even the young girls in the hallway. She remembered running to her car, but no one was chasing her. For now, she was safe, but for how long?

She continued on for several miles tossing around the pros and cons of going home. Finally she convinced herself that she was safe and continued on toward home. From home she could turn on the news and see if anything bad had happened at Benedict. Oh, how she wished her Tahoe radio hadn't died on Monday. She had planned on taking the Tahoe in this weekend and having the radio replaced. Tapping the dash, she said to herself, "Well, that was the old plan. I am replacing you tomorrow!"

When she was about fifteen miles from home, Kathleen had to swerve to the side of the road to let three police cars go by. It was at that moment that Monique's face appeared in Kathleen's mind and she parked her car along the highway.

"Oh my God, Monique saw me and recognized me!"

"What if the man asked around, and Monique gave my name? Poor Monique would not realize what she was saying or that the facts would hurt me. What if he tried to hurt Monique if she looked guilty when she denied knowing me to some stranger?"

Realizing others could be in serious danger, she was forced to call the police and report—what? "Oh yeah, I think I saw an evil man, or better yet, I think my student Eddie was making a horrific gurgling sound? What choice do I have?" She glanced at the clock, and it read 6:35 P.M. Almost three hours had passed. "Surely if something sinister had happened, others would know by now."

Still parked along the side of the road, she decided to make the call. She pulled her satchel up from the floorboard and began to look inside for her cell phone. Finding it, she also noticed her folder of business cards. Detective McNeil's face flashed before her eyes. "I have his card from the crime stopper club. The detective and his partner, the blond, were so nice to me." Fumbling through her cards, she found his and punched in the numbers to make the call. "Surely he would make sense out of all this and understand if I was completely misguided by the facts."

The call went straight to voice mail, so she decided to leave a message. She closed her phone and placed it on her lap. She rested her head back and closed her eyes. A few minutes passed and then she glanced out her Tahoe window. It was dark, windy, and cold outside and as Kathleen pulled back onto the highway, she had never felt more alone.

CHAPTER 9

Paula heard Butch's phone and told him, "Let's step outside. I need a break, and you should check your phone."

Butch was thinking of his daughter and suspected Paula was thinking the same. The girl inside the unit was Mandy's age and had lost her life to some psycho that decided to put her bloody corpse on display for all to see. He agreed, and they made their way back through the living room and into the 300's hallway of the Benedict. Paula stepped away and made her own personal call. This was common, to want to talk to someone who loved and cared about you after witnessing such a horrible crime scene. It was a way to block out the ugliness and step back into a safe dream world, if only for a short time. He could hear Paula chatting with her guy when his second voice mail sounded. It wasn't Mandy; it was another young lady that desperately needed his help.

"Paula, we got something. We got to roll!" Butch stuck his head back into 323, and announced, "Bair, gotta go. I will be in touch soon."

Paula ended her call, and they quickly and carefully made their way down the three flights of stairs. Butch pushed open the entrance doors, and they were both hit with the cold, punishing winds from outside. It was a good feeling for Butch as the coldness jarred the numbness in his head and allowed him to think more clearly again. Making their way toward their vehicle, they ignored the questions fired away by the media. Paula knew to take the passenger side since she had no idea what was going on. Butch jumped in behind the wheel and turned on his siren, not caring what it might look like to the media or anyone else watching. As he drove out of the packed parking lot, Aileene gave him a quizzical look, but he kept driving.

Once on the highway, Butch handed his cell phone to Paula. "Listen to my second voice mail. It is Eddie's teacher from Bellview High."

Paula took his phone and typed in the code Butch gave her and listened.

"Hi, Detective McNeil, this is Kathleen Bishop from Bellview High. Um, we met at crime stoppers club last week, and you gave me your card. I, um, well, I went to visit one of my students after school at the Benedict Housing Complex, and well, I think I might have heard something. I, um, did see someone who I think could be bad who had a knife. I am not at home. I am going to drive around some more until you call. My number is nine three five-four eight eight-zero nine six four. Please give me a call as soon as possible."

Paula said, "Shit! You keep driving, and I will call her back."

Kathleen Bishop was at a red light on Prince Boulevard when her cell phone began to ring in her lap. She fumbled a little but finally got it opened and said, "Hello?"

"Ms. Bishop, this is Detective Paula Williams, McNeil's partner, we met last week at the high school."

"Yes, I remember you. Thank you so much for returning my call. I feel sort of foolish and—"

Cutting Ms. Bishop off, Paula broke in as subtle as possible, "Kathleen, you are in real danger, and we need to get to you as soon as possible. Where are you?"

Instantly Kathleen's hand began to sweat as she held onto the phone. "I'm on Prince, Prince Boulevard. I don't understand. Does this mean something happened to Eddie?"

Leaning over to Butch, Paula whispered, "She is on Prince Boulevard."

Knowing the area well, Butch grabbed the phone away and said, "Kathleen, there is a Super Green Mart at the intersection of Third Street and Prince. Do you know where that is?"

Tears were beginning to slowly slide down Kathleen's face as she answered, "Yes."

"Good, park on the lawn and garden side. What are you driving?"

With a slight hiccup, she answered, "A dark green Tahoe."

"Okay, Ms. Bishop. Get there and stay put. We should be there in about fifteen minutes."

Butch closed his phone and placed it back into his jacket pocket.

Paula stated, "She has no idea the danger she is in. We have got to get to her first, or we are going to be looking at body number five tonight."

"Yeah, you are right. What the hell was she doing at the Benedict Housing Complex anyway?"

Paula twisted her lips in deep thought, and then finally said, "When we met her last week, she really seemed genuinely interested in her students. I don't think she is the type to be involved in drugs."

"No, I don't either. For whatever reason, she seemed to be in the wrong place at the wrong time."

Paula said, "Yeah, classic."

It took twenty-three minutes for the detectives to arrive. By that time, Kathleen already had a good hard cry and was slowly starting to pull herself together. The police car had sirens on when it entered the parking lot but they were turned off as the detectives spotted her Tahoe. As soon as they got out of their car, time began to pick up again. Opening the door, Kathleen quickly got out and started asking questions. "Please tell me what happened, I've been driving around for hours with no radio and—"

Without answering any questions, Butch guided Kathleen back into the car.

Calmly Butch said, "Ms. Bishop, I know you are scared right now and have lots of questions, but we need to move now to get you somewhere safe. Do you mind if I drive?"

She shook her head no and then slid over to the passenger side and allowed Butch to climb in behind the wheel. He fired up the engine and then swiftly pulled out of the parking lot with Detective Williams following closely behind.

CHAPTER 10

Patch entered his apartment on the second floor of an old warehouse that had been redesigned to house tenants. The apartment had four floors with two tenants to each floor. The rent was over the top, but the layout and the design for privacy was key to his job. The landlord had never seen Patch and never would. All contact went through a real estate agency owned by Chicago Steel. His rent was paid monthly, and the lease was always renewed yearly. If Patch didn't reside here, someone else employed by the Fernandez family would. There is a trail of false paperwork tied to this apartment, and no one would ever trace Patch or this apartment back to Emilio Fernandez.

Glancing at the other door on the second floor, he saw no one coming or going. He really didn't expect to. A wealthy businessman from San Francisco who occasionally visited when he had business downtown rented the other apartment. Taking his keys out of his pocket, he found the correct one and unlocked the deadbolt. Opening his door he swept the room with his eyes and noticed all looked good.

His apartment was moderately furnished but he could care less. All he needed was a desk with a computer, a couch, a nice TV, and a good comfortable queen-size bed. He would never entertain here because the family did not allow it. If Patch wanted to get away, cut loose, and have some fun, he went to Mexico. He generally booked a room at an all-inclusive resort and would drink and party himself silly. There he was sure to have some privacy from the family or at least he thought so anyway.

Walking into the kitchen, he placed his keys on the counter and then opened up the pantry door and grabbed a garbage bag. Next, he walked straight over to his desk with computer. There, he opened up his laptop and hit the power switch. With the garbage bag still in his hand, he headed toward his bedroom. Patch then began to strip down for a shower while waiting on the computer to fire up. Once naked, he gathered up his clothes and threw them in the garbage bag to be tossed. Ten minutes later, he was showered and emerged wearing old comfortable faded jeans and a dark navy T-shirt.

Settling down at his computer, Patch began to go to work on the witness. Looking at the clock, it read 7:15 P.M. According to Victor, he had about twenty-three hours left to find her. He shook his hands and popped his fingers and tried to block out the sense of urgency. He reminded himself that he was good, and he had been in tougher situations before and had come out a winner.

Typing a couple of keys, his first hit was an instant success. At the Bellview High School Web page, there was a list of the faculty along with pictures. Smiling to himself he thought, "This is too easy!"

Next, he hacked into the county database system used by government employees. He clicked on a few icons and then found the motor vehicle transportation department. He typed in the name given by the Bellview High Web site and waited for a response. For Bishop, there were four hits with various first and middle names for Kathleen, but only one with the right age group. He checked the box for Kathleen Erin Bishop, age twenty-six, and hit enter. The computer flashed another smaller screen with her address and vehicle registration information. He then enlarged the box and began to read. There had been no notes or links associated with her file. No arrest or warrants, not even a traffic ticket. He picked his cell phone up off the desk and dialed the boss man's number.

The only words spoken were "thirteen hundred Grigor Street, unit twelve," and he hung up.

With the address and vehicle information memorized, he logged out and shut down his computer. Heading back toward his bedroom, he made his way over to his closet. Looking at his choices, he finally decided on a windbreaker and running pants. He then pulled down his common everyday black backpack and began to fill it with his weapons of choice. Looking at himself in the mirror, he was satisfied with the man he had become—a jogger.

Walking back into the kitchen, he grabbed a protein shake from the fridge and the garbage bag filled with today's clothing, and headed out the door. Stepping into the hallway, he looked around and found no one again, and then locked his apartment. He made his way outside and felt the wind. Looking around he smiled at the night's conditions. Windy, cold, and dark with no moon, just the way he liked to work.

CHAPTER 11

Detectives Williams and McNeil safely escorted Kathleen into the Chicago Police Department. On the ride over here, Butch McNeil didn't talk. So she tried to allow herself to relax and concentrate on the past events. Now they had arrived, and she was following Paula Williams down a white hallway to a conference room set up just for her. Once inside, she was offered a dark leather chair and a cup of coffee. Settling in, she noticed the bare walls surrounding her as well as a video camera mounted in the top corner of the room.

Looking around, Kathleen counted five other people in the room with her. Butch introduced everyone but she really didn't listen or absorb the names. She zeroed in on the young guy who was a police artist. He had his sketchbook open with a few different pencils sharpened and ready to go. He noticed her looking, and he smiled back.

Paula closed the door behind Kathleen and then walked over to the large table and sat down with a tape recorder. She pressed a few buttons and then said, "Okay, all is ready."

Detective McNeil spoke next, "The date is Wednesday, November the seventeenth, and the time, seven thirty-five P.M."

He looked at Kathleen and then said, "This is Detective Butch McNeil, and I will now begin to interview a potential witness, one female, age twenty-six, named Kathleen Bishop, about the crimes that took place at the Benedict Housing Complex earlier today."

There was a brief pause as Butch took a sip of his coffee and then he continued rattling off the names of the other officers present. When he finished, he looked back at Kathleen and said, "Ms. Bishop, please describe slowly the events of the day as you witnessed them."

Kathleen faced Butch with her dark green emerald eyes and began to tell her story. She started with the conversation she had with Lisa. No one interrupted as she talked until she got to the part about deciding to go visit Eddie.

Paula asked, "Have you been to the Benedict Housing Complex before today?"

"No, I had only driven by it once but didn't stop and go inside."

Butch asked, "Why would you drive by the Benedict Housing Complex when you live on the other side of town?"

Kathleen didn't get defensive. She realized it was a valid question, and one she had asked herself before. Finally she said, "I have a lot of students that live there. One Saturday when I was bored, I decided to drive to that side of town just to get a feel of where my students lived."

No one said anything and she continued, "I just thought it would make me a better teacher if I had an idea of what their neighborhood looked liked. Before, I only had stories, and I just wanted to see it for myself."

"How long ago was that?" asked Paula.

Kathleen paused to think, "About five years ago, it was sometime in the course of my first year of teaching at Bellview High."

Butch asked, "Okay, when you finally arrived at the Benedict what did you see?"

Kathleen closed her eyes and took a deep breath.

Paula said, "Take your time."

"By the time I arrived, I had almost talked myself out of going. It was getting dark, and it was so cold. But, my concerns were for Lisa more so than Eddie."

"How so?"

"If Eddie dropped out of school, Lisa might too. I knew she had a baby, and I wanted her to stay in school. If she graduates high school, she has a better chance finding a good paying job to help support her baby."

"I see. What do you remember seeing outside when you arrived?"

"A group of kids hanging out and talking. I really don't understand why they would be outside in this weather? Anyway, I did recognize one student from our school, Monique."

"Did she recognize you?"

"Yeah, she told the others to leave me alone, and I kept walking and never stopped until I got inside the building."

"Do you remember seeing any cars in the parking lot that maybe stood out or looked like they didn't belong?" asked Butch.

Kathleen didn't answer right away and began to ponder the question. She finally shook her head no.

"All right, continue."

"Once inside, I decided to take the stairs even though they were partially blocked by a sleeping woman. I felt that would be safer than potentially getting stuck in an elevator."

"When you stepped over the sleeping lady, did she stir or ask you a question?"

Kathleen said, "No, she never moved. I hoped that she was asleep and not dead. Later, she cried out when I tripped over her on the way down. Anyway, I continued up the stairs but decided to stop at the second floor since the door was open, and two girls were standing there talking. I asked them if unit three hundred and twenty-three was on the third floor."

"Describe them."

"One was younger, maybe ten with rollers in her hair, black. The other girl looked to be a teenager, and she was carrying a baby. She was Hispanic."

Paula reached over and stopped the tape. She and another officer walked over to the side of the room and began to talk about the two girls. A few more minutes passed and the officer left the room. Settling back down in her chair, Paula hit the on button again.

Butch said, "What happened next?"

"Eddie appeared in the stairwell."

Paula asked, "Do you know from which floor?"

Kathleen paused a moment and tried to remember back, "I can not be positive, but I think it was from the floor above. Where I was standing, I think I would have noticed if he came up from behind me."

"That's good, what happened next?"

"This is where it all gets sort of fuzzy."

"Just do the best you can."

"Eddie was stoned, and I said something about coming back another day. He scared me a little."

"How so?" asked Butch.

"His eyes were red, and he was stumbling. He pulled me into the stairwell and then pulled me close and started talking very quietly. He was mumbling, and I couldn't understand what he was saying."

Butch leaned forward toward the table and asked, "Anything, any words or phrases at all?"

Kathleen frowned and just shook her head. "I was going to ask him to repeat what he said when I saw the man appear at the top of the stairs."

The police artist began to pick up one of his pencils, and he spoke for the first time, "Ms. Bishop, I need for you to describe the man as best as you can. Even if you think it is insignificant."

After fifteen minutes of more questions and answers, Kathleen looked distraught and shaken. Her shoes that she had bought last weekend were scratched from the fall in the stairwell. Her auburn hair was tangled as it flowed down her suit jacket. Her green silk shirt was stained from the spilled coffee that Paula had given her earlier. Her face had smudges of mascara from her crying binge in the parking lot while waiting on the detectives to arrive. She was a mess but alive. After arriving at the police station, she began to slowly pick up on the chatter around her. Eddie was not okay; he was dead, along with Lisa, her aunt, and baby Mia. Tears began to flow again at the thought of an innocent baby being caught in the wrong place at the wrong time. Who were these men who could kill an innocent child? She remembered the cold stare of death as she spotted the man in the stairwell. He had killed them all, and now she is next on the list.

"Kathleen?" Paula gently prodded her to continue, "You were describing the tattoo."

"Right...it was dark in color, and it wrapped around his arm. I think it was the right arm. It was like a vine, but I can't recall any specific design or pictures. All I remember is seeing the tattoo and then the knife. Something inside my head told me to run, and I did."

Paula walked around to the sketch artist and began to shake her head as she glanced at the picture. All was quiet for a few more minutes as the artist continued working. Finally, the artist held up his sketch and turned it around for all to view.

Kathleen turned a shade lighter and said, "It's him!"

"Is he the killer of baby Mia and all the others?" Kathleen wondered and shivered as she felt a cold chill down her spine and her hands began to sweat all at the same time. The sketch gave the appearance that he was staring her down, and he was coming after her next. She jumped up, too quickly, and her chair fell back behind her. She felt herself shaking, and her knees were going to fold at any moment so she walked over to the far corner and turned around with her back to the sketch.

Butch gave Paula the look, and she quickly got up and walked over and placed a hand on Kathleen's shoulder. She said, "You did well, Kathleen, and we are going to do everything possible to find him."

Turning back around, Kathleen asked, "What now?"

Paula replied, "For now, you have done all you can do at this point. We will take this sketch along with the description of the other man and pass it out to all policemen and media. You never can tell who will see this and recognize these men."

"I'm so frustrated. I wish I could remember more about the other man. Also, I know Eddie was trying to tell me something when he mumbled to me. I just can't remember what he said."

Butch answered, "Stress has a way of blocking out information sometimes. Hopefully once you have a chance to sleep and rest your body, you will remember more."

Looking up at the clock, she was shocked to see it was 9:30 P.M. Had she really been in here for two hours? She rubbed her face and began to run her hands through her tangled hair. She asked next, "When can I go home? I have things to do before school tomorrow, and I have a six forty-five a.m. faculty meeting."

Catching the look that Butch gave Paula, she knew before she even answered, her life had just drastically changed.

"Ms. Bishop, we think it is in your best interest to take a few days off of work and stay in protective custody for a while until we have a better handle on the situation."

Staring back at Detective Paula Williams, she began to protest. "My job isn't a job you can just walk away from for a couple of days. There are papers to grade, lessons to write, and deadlines for grades to be entered. There are over one hundred and twenty students that depend on me daily and—"

Butch interrupted, "You're right! You can't be replaced, but if you walk back into that building, whoever is out there looking for you, could possibly put the entire school in danger."

She looked back at Butch, glanced over to Paula, and finally her eyes rested on the sketch. She knew he was right. She slowly walked back to her chair and sat down. She reached down into her satchel and pulled out some papers to begin making notes for a substitute. Butch and Paula didn't say anything else and decided to leave the room with the sketch and give her some time and space to work.

After several minutes passed, Butch and Paula entered the room again without the sketch. Kathleen set down her pen and asked, "What do I tell my principal and students?"

It didn't take long for Paula to come up with a plan. "You know next week is the last full week before Thanksgiving. We can explain that you had a family emergency and had to leave immediately. You will miss two days this week and all of next week. Hopefully by the end of the Thanksgiving break, we will know more, and you can go back to work. If we tell anyone the truth, unfortunately it will only put that person's life in danger."

Knowing she was right, Kathleen agreed but spent the next five minutes trying to convince them she had to go home first. "There are documents on my computer that I need to send to my colleagues, I don't want to inconvenience them anymore than I have to. There are also detailed lesson plans that I can forward to the substitute. Please?"

With a heavy sigh of defeat, Butch finally agreed and the three of them picked up their coats and a few papers and headed out the door.

CHAPTER 12

Cruising by in his Lincoln Escapade, Patch easily spotted the two undercover policemen staked out in front of 1300 Grigor Street. His SUV continued on at an average speed for about three more blocks. He then slowed down and began to cruise the area looking for a shopping strip that would house some stores that would be open for twenty-four hours. He had to go another two blocks before he found what he was looking for. About five blocks away from Bishop's apartment was a Wal-Mart that was open twenty-four hours a day.

He circled the parking lot until he found the perfect spot to park his Escapade. Shutting off the engine he grabbed his backpack and locked up. Glancing around, all he noticed was a young couple heading toward their car. They were carrying fast food and chatting to one another, neither giving him a second look. He walked toward the Wal-Mart but didn't go in. Instead, he took the sidewalk that wrapped around the entrance and followed it toward the street he was previously driving on. As he made his way to the intersection he then began to stretch his legs while waiting on the light to change. Anyone passing by would only see him as a runner, nothing more.

The light changed, and he hit the pavement running toward Grigor Street. He continued running at a steady pace until he was one street away.

There he stopped and stretched out his legs again and then started walking. He quickly spotted a back alley that would lead up to the back of Bishop's apartment building and headed that way. He came to a sudden stop and placed both arms above his head as many runners do after a long hard run. What he was really doing though was mapping out in his head which windows and door was unit twelve.

It didn't take him long to figure out which was unit twelve. This apartment building was the same style and structure that you would find in many areas that rent to young working adults. He followed her back door up and then eyed each window. On the second level, there appeared to be a faint piece of material blowing in the wind. Smiling again, he muttered, "This is too easy."

He pulled his backpack from his back and opened it up and found the right gadgets needed for this job. Looking around once more and finding no one, he scaled up the apartment wall. Once along the side of her window, it appeared that Ms. Bishop had apparently left open her bathroom window for airing out some running shoes placed by the windowsill. He gently set the shoes aside and climbed inside to begin his work.

Patch carefully went to each of the five rooms in the apartment searching for any sign of life. Once assured that he was alone, he began quietly searching for any clues. After twenty minutes of going through drawers, clothing, cushions, cabinets, he realized the place was clean. No money and no drugs. There were a few photos of what appeared to be family and some close girlfriends. One drawer had a few photos of a guy with Bishop; apparently he was an ex since he was not on display with the other photos.

He decided to take one of the photos of the unknown ex-boyfriend and a few more that had family and some friends.

Next, he made his way over to her computer desk and rifled through her bills, jotting down credit card numbers and other key information that might be useful. In the file drawer he found birth certificate, passport, and social security card. He quickly wrote down all numbers. Along the wall held her college degree stating the University of Florida with her teaching degree. Alongside her diploma was a framed picture of Bishop with what appeared to be her parents taken outside a home on some beautiful coastal waterway.

Glancing down at his watch, he realized his time was up, and he made one more sweep of the apartment before heading back out the same way he entered. He had been in the apartment for less than thirty-five minutes and even though he found no money or goods, he found a wealth of information that was going to allow him to find Bishop and hopefully keep him alive.

Once outside, Patch began jogging again. When he was two blocks away from his car, he decided to turn back. He had a different plan now and it was one that was definitely going to send a message.

CHAPTER 13

Turning down Grigor Street, Detective Butch McNeil found the two policemen on watch and pulled in beside them. Detective Paula Williams, driving the Tahoe with Kathleen in the passenger seat, pulled in beside Butch and got out of the SUV to talk to the others. About three minutes later, Paula got back in with Kathleen and explained that the others were going to clear the apartment. Waiting patiently in the car for about another five minutes, the apartment was cleared and they were given the signal to come on in.

Once outside, Kathleen felt the wind strike against her face. As she looked around, she never realized how dark and eerie things appeared around her apartment complex. There were times when she would run at night and felt safe. Now she watched as the wind moved all the bushes along the side of her apartment and the big oak limbs were shaking along the parked cars in the street. She decided that after today, she would never run again alone at night. Kathleen walked behind Williams and made it safely across the street and began to climb her staircase that led to her door. With each step she could feel the hairs along her neck begin to stand up once more. As she reached the top, Butch grabbed her elbow and guided her in the apartment. He then asked, "Did you leave your bathroom window open?"

She nodded, "Yes, to air out my tennis shoes from my morning run. They got damp when it started to drizzle the last two blocks from home."

Satisfied, the other two officers stepped around Kathleen and went back outside to keep guard.

"Sorry the place is a mess, I have been busy getting projects graded this week. Thank goodness I finished, the grades are due on Friday. I just need about fifteen minutes to get the grades entered in my computer."

Nodding his approval, Butch made his way toward the kitchen and announced he would tidy up and take the trash out.

Paula stated, "I am going to start packing some clothes for you."

She didn't stand around for a response and took off to find the bedroom. Kathleen made her way over to the computer desk and quickly logged on. It didn't take long for her grade book to open, and she began to type in the grades. Every now and then, Kathleen would pause as she heard drawers opening and closing from her bedroom. It was hard for her to stay focused; she was not used to others in her apartment and certainly not to someone going through her personal belongings.

A few moments later, Paula emerged from the bedroom and asked, "Your shoes are still slightly wet. Do you still want me to pack them?"

"Yes, and make sure you grab me some workout clothing as well, please."

Paula turned back around and headed toward her room again. Finishing up her grades, she opened her documents and clicked on the week's lesson plans. She made a few changes and then she forwarded them to her colleagues. With all that accomplished, she began to feel a little better about leaving work.

As she shut down her computer, Butch came out of the kitchen and announced, "Everything looks good. I put all your meat in the freezer and took out anything else that might spoil. Also, I placed all your fresh fruits along with some drinks in a bag to take with us."

Kathleen nodded in approval and opened up the top drawer of her desk to file some papers. When the drawer was fully extended, she noticed a paper was sticking up from a file. Moving her hands over the file, she opened it up and noticed it was her credit card statement. The date was from a couple of weeks ago. "I shouldn't have touched that lately," she said to herself. Trying to remember back when she filed papers last, Paula emerged from her bedroom with two pieces of luggage and announced, "We need to go."

Kathleen glanced around and noticed everything else looked in place, so she shut the drawer, grabbed her satchel, and stood up to leave. "Wait! Paula, where were my tennis shoes?"

Placing her hand on her revolver, she answered, "On the lid of the toilet, why?"

Time started to slow down again and Kathleen turned back around toward her computer desk.

"Kathleen?"

In a quivering voice, Kathleen replied, "I left them on the window sill."

As soon as she got the words out of her mouth, both detectives dropped everything in their hands and pulled their guns. Kathleen saw two oranges roll across the floor as Butch rushed around the sofa and grabbed her. He gently as possible guided Kathleen to the front door. With his gun raised, he slowly opened the door and found the staircase that led to the sidewalk empty. Motioning to Paula to call her radio, he quickly closed the door and bolted it.

Detective Paula Williams was speaking into thin air, because no voice came back on the radio.

Turning toward Kathleen, Butch said, "I need you to go into the hall closet, shut the door, and sit down. I want you to remain as quiet as you can."

Kathleen didn't say a word and sprinted toward the closet as directed.

CHAPTER 14

It was just after ten on Wednesday night when two FBI agents walked into the Chicago Police Department and flashed their badges to the lady officer behind the counter.

"Good evening officer, my name is Bass Floyd, and this is Bethany Kay-Loviett. We would like to see the detectives in charge of the murder of Eddie Jones."

Officer Matilda Rose awkwardly smiled and picked up the phone and dialed Detective McNeil's office. Officer Matthews answered on the second ring, "McNeil's office, this is Officer Matthews."

"Yes, this is Officer Rose, is McNeil in?"

"No, he and Detective Williams left fifteen minutes ago."

"Are you assisting in the Eddie Jones case?"

"I am. Do you have something?"

"I sure do. Two FBI agents are headed back to see you," she said, smiling as she hung up the phone.

Matilda finished copying down their ID information and pointed, "Go down the hall and take the first left, room one fifteen."

Agent Kay-Loviett had just been assigned to the Chicago FBI office three months ago. Before, she worked out of the Washington, DC, field office. For seven long years she sat behind a desk researching, answering phones, and completing countless cross-references. Finally, she had been rewarded for her latest eye-opening discovery that landed her this job in the field. In the course of her desk work, she had discovered some facts and numbers that didn't add up with the great and mighty Chicago Steel Company. After hours of research and some phone calls, she put together a portfolio and took it to her boss, Agent Gary Fields. After her one-hour presentation, her boss was very quiet for several long minutes. Anyone that worked with Fields knew to be quiet while he was pondering. He eventually stood up and walked her to the door and asked her to wait outside as he made some calls. Several minutes later, his secretary gave Kay-Loviett the permission to enter his office again. Once inside, she was asked to shut the door and have a seat.

He finally said the words that Bethany had longed to hear for seven years.

"Great work, Agent Kay-Loviett. I am very impressed with your research and insight that you have given on this matter. How would you like to go to Chicago and head up a team that will take a closer look at this Chicago Steel Company?"

Bethany had been overjoyed to hear his words. Holding back the urge to get up and dance around the room, she got herself under control, stood up, walked over, and shook Agent Fields's hand. Twenty-four hours later, she had bags packed and was heading toward Chicago on a jet compliments of the FBI. Agent Bass Floyd, who was assigned to work with her on the case, met her at the airport.

Agent Floyd was very fit for forty-eight. He stood six feet one inch and was well toned from years of cycling. His hair was the only thing that hinted at his age. He had let nature take its course, and it had long ago turned gray and was thinning around the top. He brought to the table twenty years of field experience in Chicago, and he knew the ins and outs of all Chicago's major players. Combining his street knowledge and her research abilities, you had one hell of a team.

Over the last couple of months, Kay-Loviett and Floyd had spent countless hours watching and monitoring Emilio Fernandez. It didn't take them long to discover the drug operation that was supplying a good amount of cocaine to inner city kids in Chicago. From there, they were able to track his worldwide trade operation. Finally, after working several days and nights, they put together a plan that would bring down the Fernandez family. Unfortunately, something had gone terribly wrong. The undercover agent, who was supposed to meet Eddie Jones, had gone missing, along with five hundred thousand dollars of the FBI's money.

CHAPTER 15

Kathleen was hunched down in her closet clutching a white fluffy teddy bear. The teddy bear had been purchased last weekend when she was out shopping for shoes. She had come across the bear on her way out of the mall. Thinking her one and only niece, Maddie, would love the bear, she made her first Christmas gift purchase. She had forgotten all about the bear until she came across it when she was feeling her way around the bottom of the small closet. It was such a relief to find the teddy bear instead of some boots of a killer who had been lurking in the closet the whole time they were in the apartment. So for the last thirty minutes, Kathleen has been holding on tight to the bear and thinking about her family.

"Will I ever get to see my sister Ashton again? What about Mom, Dad, and Maddie?" She pictured her dad shaking his head and saying, "Why did she stay in Chicago?" Her mom would ask, "Was it us? Did she not want to live and teach near us?"

Horrible thoughts were tormenting Kathleen's mind as she desperately listened to any sounds being made on the other side of the closet door. Every now and then she would hear a bit of a whispered comment from Detectives Williams or McNeil. Sometimes she heard soft footprints walking back and forth between the door and what she thought was the window.

Holding the teddy bear tight, she began to silently cry. "There are so many things I haven't done yet. I want children, a husband. I want to see my mom's smile again and be held by my dad."

Bang, Bang, Bang!

"Detective McNeil, its Officer Lee Matthews, ID one-four-zero-seven-six, acknowledge."

"Officer Butch McNeil, ID one-seven-eight-zero-nine. I'm opening the door."

The door was gently opened and officer Matthews entered the apartment. Realizing it was safe, Paula walked over to the closet door and opened it up to find Kathleen clutching a teddy bear and crying. Gently kneeling down, Paula placed her hand on Kathleen's shoulder and helped her up and over to the couch. Butch pulled out an orange juice from the bag of fruit and told Kathleen to drink. Taking the juice in shaking hands, Kathleen began to drink.

"What happened? Why did it take the officers so long to answer?"

Paula's eyes shifted toward Officer Matthews who spoke, "All that matters now is that you are safe, and we are going to move you to a safe house. Detectives, if you would follow me outside please."

Placing a hand on top of hers, Paula promised to be right back and instructed Kathleen to try and drink some more and relax. And then with a smile, she said, "You are going to have to tell me the bear's name when I get back."

Stepping outside, Butch and Paula were introduced to the two FBI agents. Paula stood head to head with Agent Bethany Kay-Loviett who was also tall, but unlike Paula's blond hair, Kay-Loviett had jet-black, curly hair. Paula noticed right away how self-confident the agent appeared as she introduced herself as the head of a FBI team investigating a family suspected of running a drug cartel. She was dressed in jeans and wearing a navy jacket with matching navy gloves. As she produced her badge from under her jacket, Paula could see the intense weapons she was carrying.

Soon Agent Kay-Loviett began to explain the scene around them. "Detectives, we have two dead police officers sitting in their patrol car. It appears they were attacked somewhere around the stairs and dragged back to their vehicle. Apparently both men were taken out without any sound or commotion being heard by anyone. Whoever did this is a professional. Along with this, the FBI has an undercover agent who is missing, and my informant with whom we have been dealing has been murdered along with his baby girl and girlfriend. Now, I think our two cases are connected, and we need to start working together and sharing as much information as we can, as quickly as we can."

Butch raked his hands through his hair. It was a lot to take in. The two officers whom he had spoken to earlier were now dead. "What the hell is going on?" he thought. He turned his attention back to Kathleen and glanced back toward the apartment. He could see her through the window still sitting on the couch and clutching a teddy bear. This was not the woman he met a week ago at the high school. He took a deep breath and realized it was in Kathleen's best interest to put all political bullshit aside to keep her alive. He turned back toward Agent Kay-Loviett, "What can we do to help?"

And just like that, Butch had decided to share all evidence and information about the Benedict murder scene with the FBI. The task force back at the police station was not going to be too thrilled to see him again.

Quickly accepting their help, Kay-Loviett held out her hand to shake on it. "We have a plane on standby ready to escort the witness to a safe house. We can all board the plane and debrief each other en route to an unknown location. Once a location has been determined, only the four of us will know the destination. Is she ready to go?"

CHAPTER 16

Emilio and Victor were sitting in a twelve thousand dollar leather lounge suite in Emilio's home. Emilio lived on five very private acres in a gated community on the north side of Chicago. Even though the neighborhood had a gate with a guard, Emilio had his own security. A stone wall standing ten feet bordered his property, and there was an electronic gate at the entrance. The gate was controlled by one of the three full-time guards at the guardhouse. Several monitors had been placed in many strategic locations all over his property and were monitored twenty-four/seven. The guards, as well as the security system, were top of the line and the best that money could buy.

The Fernandez estate included a tennis court, pool, gardens, basketball court, and a house that was approximately nine thousand four hundred and eighty-two square feet. The grounds surrounding the house were made up of an intricate pattern of red, pink, yellow, and white flowers. The resort-style swimming pool surrounded by plush lounge chairs and tables was the center of the estate playground. To keep everything running properly, the estate required five full time staff. The staff arrived at 5:00 A.M. and left at 7:00 P.M. each day.

The house was designed by Vivian, Emilio's wife, who was an architect and gifted interior decorator. She had personally designed each room with its own style and purpose. Even the smallest of rooms contained beautiful and unique pieces of art from all around the world. Each of the three sons was given his own suite with sitting area, bathroom, and game room. At the end of the boys' wing was a larger game room with a bowling alley. On the opposite side of the house from the boys was the master bedroom wing. The master suite contained his and her sitting rooms, bathrooms, and closets. Also included on the wing were his and her gyms and a large study. It was in this study, on this quiet cold night, that plans were made to destroy one Kathleen Bishop.

It was after 7:00 P.M. when Emilio received the first call from Patch. Vivian and the kids were away at a school basketball game leaving Emilio alone with his brother Victor. Together they talked and argued until a plan was finally hashed out between them. Around 9:30 P.M., Vivian and the kids came home, and the kids were quickly whisked away to their prospective rooms. Vivian greeted her husband with a kiss, looked up at Victor with a smile, and said, "I am surprised to see you still here so late. What, no date tonight?"

"Tonight, business comes first," replied Victor.

"Well in that case, I will leave you two. I have some plans to review myself."

Victor watched as Vivian swayed gracefully out the study in her three-inch heels and designer jeans. Following his gaze, Emilio was about to give Victor a lecture when another call came in from Patch.

Patch would never set foot on the Fernandez estate, which explained why they received a second call. The phone that Patch used was an untraceable phone that did not exist. Emilio's phone was registered to none other than John Doe. This conversation would never be recorded and played later in a court of law. Emilio listened to a short message and hung up the phone.

"Patch is waiting nearby to take Bishop when she returns to her apartment. He is sending an e-mail of all her personal information, and he will call when he has her."

Victor took a swig from his glass of vodka and replied, "Did he tell you where he plans on taking her?"

Logging into a bogus e-mail account he replied, "No."

"Good. The less we know, the better," replied Victor as he walked around the couch to the computer desk.

On a computer screen, the personal details of Kathleen Bishop's life were displayed in front of the Fernandez brothers. Notes were made and more plans were discussed as they waited for the next call to come in from Patch.

CHAPTER 17

Another hour had passed and Emilio and Victor were still waiting to hear from Patch when Vivian waltzed back into the study and poured her a nightcap from the stocked bar. Looking at both brothers she said frowning, "Is something wrong?"

Walking toward her, Emilio smiled and gave his wife a hug and a quick kiss on her lips. "No, my dear, we have some buyers with questions that happen to live on the other side of the world. We should not be too much longer, just waiting on a few more calls."

Vivian was sixteen and working as a model in Rio when she met Emilio. Both of the brothers were together on business and had decided to head down to the beach after dinner. There on the beach were four young swimsuit models frolicking in the water with the sunset behind them. The photographer was shouting out commands as the girls continued playing with all smiles on their faces. Victor still remembers to this day the words spoken by his brother, "I want the one in the middle. Did the camera man call her Viv?"

Staring at Vivian, Victor was amazed at the woman she had become over the last twenty years. Emilio had charmed her that day and convinced her to meet him later that evening after her photo shoot. Over the next few years he courted her and then put her through college before finally marrying her. She now had a successful business with three very athletic strong-willed boys that kept her equally busy. Victor smiled; she was completely clueless of Emilio's side business.

Vivian seemed satisfied with her husband's answer and then went on to talk about the basketball game and what plans she was working on for tomorrow. While Vivian was carrying on about some cottage that she was designing for the McGuire family's lake property, the call finally came in.

Raising her hand up, Vivian said, "I will shut the door on my way out," and left the room.

Chuckling, Victor spoke, "You sure do have her trained Emilio."

Frowning, Emilio answered the phone on the fourth ring.

Moments passed and Emilio finally spoke, "Patch has failed to capture Ms. Bishop and has killed two policemen."

Placing his glass of vodka down hard on the table, Victor spoke angrily "Damn, does he know where she is now?"

"No, it appears more cops showed up with the FBI and they were able to escort Ms. Bishop out of her apartment to some unknown destination."

Victor replied, "What does he know?"

"Not much of anything."

After a few moments of silence, Victor announces, "It's time to make the call."

With a pained expression, Emilio picked his phone back up and dialed a number.

CHAPTER 18

The call came in around 11:00 P.M. to the Chicago Police Department. Words were spoken and information was exchanged. Someone was going to leave their night sift a lot richer than when they arrived.

At 11:45 P.M., Kathleen arrived by car at a private airport that she didn't know existed until now. Kathleen was nestled in the backseat of a sedan between Detective Paula Williams on her right and Detective Butch McNeil on her left. In the front seat were two FBI agents, the one driving was the female agent named Bethany Kay-Loviett. The other older agent was Bass Floyd. Both agents had introduced themselves to Kathleen once she was settled in the backseat. They made only one stop in route to the airport—the police station. Here, they transferred her bags to another vehicle, and they were off again. Not another word had been spoken since they left her apartment. Glancing around at the airport, Kathleen commented, "This is not exactly how I envisioned being swept off my feet and taken on a jet to a remote location somewhere." No one said a word, so she continued, "I thought I would be with a hot young sexy guy instead of two old men with guns."

Paula coughed, smiled, and then said, "I am glad you haven't lost your sense of humor."

Agent Floyd chimed in, "Yes, I second that. Are you ready to roll?"

Agent Kay-Loviett turned around and stated, "Once you step on that plane, you do everything we tell you from here on out. This is for your protection, as well as for the safety of all agents and officers involved. The moment you decide to do something on your own, someone can end up dead. Do you understand?"

And just like that, all the horror of the day's events came flooding back. Kathleen took a deep breath and glanced back at Butch, "I am sorry about your men. I wish I could go back and change the choices I made this afternoon after school. If I remember anything about Eddie's comments, you will be the first to know."

Butch replied, "You will remember. Your body just needs rest, and it will come to you."

Turning back toward Kay-Loviett, she stated, "I understand."

"Good, now let's board the plane," stated Kay-Loviett.

It only took a few moments for all to board the small jet and get buckled in before quickly taking off to the unknown. Once airborne, Paula got out of her seat and made her way over toward Kathleen. "Follow me," she said.

Kathleen followed Detective Williams to the back of the plane where she opened up a door to a sleeping cabin and bathroom. "Your bags are in that closet over there, I suggest you take a shower and try to get some sleep. We will wake you when we are about to land."

Before she could reply, Paula had left, closing the door behind her. Kathleen continued to stare at the closed door for a few more moments debating whether or not to stay. She finally decided that she might as well stay; it wasn't like they were going to share information about this case with her anyway. She turned around and walked over to the closet and pulled out both of her bags. In the first bag, she found sweats to sleep in, and her toothbrush and toothpaste. She zipped up the bag and then carried both back to the closet. Next, she made her way over to the bathroom and was surprised at how well stocked it was. Toothpaste, shampoo, conditioner, and lotions were all supplied. She locked the door and then stripped down and stepped into the shower.

As the warm water washed over Kathleen's face and down her body she began to wonder at the expense that was being made on her account. Exactly what had she witnessed and heard back at Eddie's place. Something was not adding up. Two officers had been killed guarding her apartment, and now she's in an expensive jet flying off to God knows where. What exactly had she gotten into?

Stepping out of the shower, she quickly dried off and pulled on her comfy Chicago Bears sweats. Once she was done in the bathroom she made her way toward the bed. She stumbled once before pulling down the covers and climbing in. She had thought sleep would be hard, but she was wrong. Once she settled in and pulled the covers tightly around her body she thought her mind would race with more questions and not enough answers. She closed her eyes and instantly sleep began to tug at her brain until she was pulled under.

Detective Paula Williams cracked the door to the cabin and peered inside. Satisfied, she closed the door, and returned to the others. "She is sound asleep. Whatever you slipped in her drink worked. I just hope the FBI has some special permission to do that to a witness."

Agent Floyd responded, "We sometimes make decisions that are in the best interest of our witnesses. The less stress the witness is under, the better it is for them to heal and remember things their mind is trying to work out."

Paula shrugged her shoulders and sat down. She was tired, her body ached, and she was ready for bed, unfortunately a long night awaited her. Motioning over to Butch with her arm, "Did you get a chance to call Mandy at the station?"

With a scowl written across his face he answered, "Yes, that didn't go over well. I called my sister Darlene, and she is going to stay with Mandy until I get back. She doesn't like Darlene and doesn't like being watched at age sixteen."

Smiling back, Paula placed her hand over his and squeezed.

"What about yourself? Did you get in touch with...What was his name?"

Half laughing, she stated, "I never gave you his name."

"Oh right, I remember now."

A few moments passed as Butch continued to gaze into Paula's eyes. Was he seeing something there between them that weren't there? He had definitely read his first two wives wrong as well as his latest screw up with Aileene Bell.

Butch suddenly sat up and pulled his hand away, "Oh shit! I forgot to call the district attorney back. She had called while I was at the station, and I let it go to voice mail."

Paula answered, "Just listen to your voice mail; it is too late to call now anyway. On second thought, call and wake her up. I'm not getting any sleep tonight, why should she?"

Smiling, Butch took out his phone and listened to his voice mail.

Aileene Bell was on the other end wailing away, "Butch, what the hell is going on? We now have two dead cops supposedly killed by some kind of professional. Next, I hear the FBI is involved. Call me ASAP!"

Agent Kay-Loviett spoke up, "If you are trying to make a call it will not go through. All calls are only made through that secure phone hanging on the wall. Plus from here on out, I approve all calls until witness is safely stashed."

Quickly Paula broke in and stated, "We will continue to lend you our support on this case, but I think the time has come for you to start talking and explain to us what the hell we have all gotten ourselves into!"

Butch was silently agreeing but either way, his decision to call Aileene back had just been made for him.

CHAPTER 19

The staircase was dark. The wooden steps were slick beneath my heels. There was a dripping noise coming from above. I slowly made my way up the stairs holding tightly to the railing. After a few more steps, I felt wetness along the rail and quickly jerked my hand away. I was now climbing more steps balancing each step with nothing to hold on to. As I rounded the corner of the last step, I saw a faint light glowing up ahead to the next floor. Rounding the platform, I began to climb more steps toward the light. With a few more steps the dripping noise became louder and a smell swept over my senses that made me want to vomit. I continued on up the stairs toward the light. Once at the top of the staircase there was a door cracked opened about an inch. I touched the door handle and immediately pulled my hand back. The door handle was burning hot. I slowly unwrapped the woolen scarf from my neck and placed it around my hand. With the scarf, I slowly tugged the door opened and gasped as I saw Eddie lying on the floor. He was bleeding and cradling something in his hands. I carefully kneeled down beside Eddie and opened up his arms to see what he was holding. As I lifted his bloody arm, I found baby Mia staring up at me. She began to talk, "Why are you here? What have you done to my mommy and daddy?" Looking down in shock, realizing she was too young to talk, I stepped back quickly. At that moment Eddie's hand jerked and grabbed my arm and pulled me into his face. He pulled me so close that his blood touched my cheek. He was whispering in my ear, "Take Mia and go!" Trying to pull away, I responded, "Where Eddie, go where?" He dropped my hand and a scream was let loose behind him. I looked up, and it was Lisa. She was racing toward me screaming while her entire body erupted in flames. With a few more steps, she slowly fell to the floor. My eyes looked back up the hallway and saw a form emerging forward. He slowly moved each foot down the hallway as flames began to form around the walls. Just as the fire made its way to the ceiling, his face appeared before me. He was smiling with his cold eyes and then he raised his arm above his head. I saw his tattoo with the vine of aces wrapped around his bulky arms. The knife appeared in his other hand, and I began to scream. I tried to move, but Mia was holding my scarf and pulling me down. I was slowly falling on top of Eddie, and I couldn't stop Mia. The smell of death was all around me and was drowning my senses. This time it was stronger as Lisa's body was continuing to burn.

I screamed again and finally wrestled away from Mia. Eyes opening wide, Eddie began to scream, "Go and get Mia!"

Seeing the man with the knife, I screamed louder "I can't!"

"Kathleen! Kathleen! It is just a dream, honey."

Her eyes quickly adjusted to the light, and she soon realized she was sitting up in a bed and hitting Detective Butch McNeil. Embarrassed, she quickly fell into Butch's arms and mumbled, "I, I was running. I was so scared, I saw the man. He burned Lisa."

Butch gently rubbed her shoulders and back, and stayed with Kathleen till her breathing eased back to normal. Slowly she let go and then lay back down on the bed with her head resting on her pillow.

It didn't take long for Kathleen to fall back to sleep with the influence of the drug. Butch got up and then resituated the blanket to tuck her in. Looking down at her sleeping, he felt horrible. He knew if he didn't resolve this case soon, there would be more nightmares to follow. He waited another minute or so before finally satisfied she would continue to sleep peacefully. He carefully left her and closed the door and then made his way back to the main cabin to join the others.

Once outside the cabin Butch asked, "What the hell did you give her? She was knocked out again after two minutes."

Kay-Loviett answered, "Don't worry it won't hurt her. Hopefully she will be able to tell us about her dream when she wakes up. Maybe she can shed some more light on the events that took place at the Benedict today."

Settling back down in his chair, Butch began to go back over the files on the Fernandez family.

Paula spoke, "What we have here is a dangerous family that has unlimited funds. They would never have built this empire behind a well-respected international company if they weren't brilliant. I give them forty-eight hours tops to figure out that it was an undercover FBI agent trying to buy coke."

Agent Floyd looked up and agreed with Paula, "I think you are right."

Kay-Loviett began to speak, "Then we need to work fast."

Butch began to make a list, "This is what we know.

One—an undercover agent approached Eddie for major sale.

Two—Eddie talked to a man name Billy Joe about the sale.

Three—Eddie introduced the agent to Billy Joe.

Four—A price and amount are discussed and agreed on.

Five—On Tuesday, a location was set up. Eddie delivered some coke, and the agent paid a deposit of a hundred thousand.

Six—Agent was to finish the drop and receive the goods from Eddie on Wednesday morning at eight.

Seven—Eddie was a no show.

Eight—Agent called Billy Joe and set up a meeting at ten A.M. Agent was reassured the sale would continue with or without Eddie.

Nine—At ten oh five A.M. all contact with agent was lost.

Ten—Sometime after school, around three twenty P.M., Lisa and her family are murdered.

Eleven—Kathleen Bishop arrived at the Benedict House sometime around three forty-five.

Twelve—Kathleen found Eddie, talked to him in stairwell, and then saw two men—the killers.

Thirteen—At seven P.M. we met up with Kathleen.

Fourteen—Sometime around ten P.M., two police officers were murdered outside Kathleen's apartment

"What if the agent had tipped off Eddie somehow, and Eddie decided not to show until he could figure out more?" asked Kay-Loviett.

Paula answered, "If that was true, Eddie would take the fall when the Fernandez brothers caught on they were being set up."

Floyd jumped in and commented, "So Eddie took one hundred thousand dollars and all the goods and ran? I think he would be more afraid of the Fernandez wrath when they found their money and goods were missing."

Butch replied, "I think all of you are correct. Kathleen stated that Eddie appeared high. What if he took the goods and just decided to chill until he could figure out his next move. Eddie doesn't appear to be the brightest light on a Christmas tree. Maybe he thought he had more time to figure it out."

All chatter stopped when Kathleen entered the room and spoke, "The tattoo was a vine of aces like in a deck of cards."

CHAPTER 20

Patch was back at his apartment packing some luggage for what seemed to be an all-expense-paid trip to the unknown. Not sure of what to pack, he threw a little of everything in a bag and zipped it up. Walking over to his computer, he stared at the names given to him: Detectives Butch McNeil and Paula Williams, and FBI agents Bass Floyd and Bethany Kay-Loviett. His job was to track down as much personal information as he could about the four people and report to a private airport on the outside of town by no later than 12:15 A.M. While searching for information, Patch's mind began to wander, "Was now the time to get out?"

Over the last few years, he had managed to stash a little over two hundred and fifty thousand dollars in a safe deposit box at a local bank along the Texas-Mexico border. Surely with that much cash he could find a spot along the coast and live out the rest of his life without the demands of the Fernandez family. Of course he would have to change his identity, which would not be hard considering he already had a passport and credit card in a different name. His new identity was already locked up safely with the cash. He would just have to get there before he got killed. Looking at the list, he kept pondering *FBI*.

If the FBI were involved, then the Fernandez family had finally screwed up, and their world as they know it could come crashing down. On the other hand, how was Emilio able to get him the names of those detectives, as well as the FBI so quickly? Patch really didn't know how far the family's pocketbook had reached or could reach.

Patch was starting to get more paranoid. "Could they already know about my safety deposit box? Have they been secretly following me from time to time? What about all those trips to Mexico—was someone watching?"

Patch was only coming up with more questions and no real answers. The clock read 11:45 P.M. He only had ten more minutes before he needed to leave. Turning his thoughts back toward the computer he hit a few more buttons. His last search had yielded the most interesting hit; Agent Bass Floyd's checking account reflected serious financial problems. He had a wife of ten years, Libby, and seven-year-old twin daughters, Emily and Michelle. It appeared that Libby didn't bring in any income. The only pay was from the United States government, with a few other small cash deposits. The account showed a lot of withdraws for cash, as well as the usual bills, and credit card and mortgage payments.

"What are you buying with cash, Agent Floyd?" Patch wondered aloud. "Are you gambling or do you have something as simple as a mistress that you are keeping in a fine apartment somewhere?" He smiled, "Either way, I will find out when I have more time."

He quickly logged off and shut down his computer. Getting up, he took another quick scan of the apartment, grabbed his bags and computer, and headed out the door.

Traffic was light so Patch arrived at the private airport before his deadline. He quickly parked his vehicle and stepped out, grabbing his bags from the passenger seat. A man he had never seen before walked briskly up and introduced himself as Zane Black. Standing eye to eye with Patch, he extended his hand. Even though he was the same height, he had about five years on him. Mr. Black had the appearance of a California surfer, complete with wavy blond hair and a deep tan. His dress was casual—shorts, T-shirt, and flip-flops; Considering that the temperature was forty-two degrees outside.

"All that was missing was the waves and surfboard," Patch thought. He started to ask Zane if he was sure he was at the right airport and hanger when a black Lincoln town car driven by no other than Victor Fernandez himself rounded the corner.

"Good thing we made it here before the boss man," said Zane. "I don't know what you think, but I think something big is going down."

Again Patch gave Zane the once over, completely blown away that this bozo was employed by the family. Things were definitely out of sync, and he sure hoped he made the right choice by coming instead of fleeing to Mexico.

Kathleen settled down in a seat beside Paula and asked if she would give her some insight as to what was going on.

"Things just don't add up? Why is the FBI involved in Eddie's murder? I just think there is more going on than you are telling me."

Paula looked back at Kathleen with tired eyes and hair that had been pulled back into a ponytail. She was wearing no makeup, but still gave the appearance of a supermodel that was just finishing a photo shoot and was tired. Flashing her winning smile, Paula spoke frankly, "Yes, there is more, but you are not going to be told."

Kathleen was about to protest when Kay-Loviett walked over and took a seat across from her.

"She is right. We will not tell you anymore for your own safety. I know it is hard, but you are going to have to place your trust and your life in our hands."

Butch leaned in over Paula and offered, "In about forty minutes, we are going to land in Miami. Once we land, we will be greeted by another FBI agent and board another plane to an island in the Caribbean."

Kathleen stood up. "Miami? My family lives in Ft. Lauderdale. Can I see them or at least call them?"

"No. That's out of the question," said Floyd. "Anyway it is too early in the morning. If you call, you will definitely alarm them that something is not right."

"Besides, there won't be time. We will quickly introduce you to the agent, and he will then take you away on another plane," replied Kay-Loviett.

Kathleen settled back down in her chair. She looked lost and defeated.

"When you reach your final destination, a plan will be in effect, and you will be able to talk to your family. Just try to be patient. Remember we all have your best interests in mind and will make decisions based on sound facts at the appropriate time," said Paula quietly.

Just then the pilot interrupted over the loud speaker and asked for all to take their seats and buckle up for their descent into Miami.

Buckling up, Kathleen tried to focus on the next few minutes and what possibly lay ahead. An island in the Caribbean? The only place she had ever been was the Bahamas. She had not visited any of the other dozen or so islands before. As the plane touched down, she wondered quietly, "Which one am I going to?"

CHAPTER 21

Patch boarded the small jet followed by Zane and Victor. There were no other passengers. It didn't take long for the jet to be cleared and soon they were jetting down the runway. When the pilot turned off the lighted seatbelt sign, Patch handed over his information on the detectives and FBI agents to Victor.

"Get some sleep, Patch," said Victor in a polite tone.

Patch didn't need to be told twice to leave, so he grabbed a Corona from the minibar and walked to the back of the plane and found a nice comfortable chair that would recline to a bed. There he settled in, finished his beer and quickly fell asleep.

Patch slept through the entire flight. He was slowly coming around from his deep and dreamless sleep, when he heard the pilot.

"We will soon land in Miami. Please return your seat to an upright position and buckle your seatbelt for the remainder of the flight."

Patch quickly got up and used the facilities. He had just sat down when he noticed the time. It was 5:15 A.M. Thursday morning—over twelve hours had passed since he'd killed Eddie. Thinking back to his encounters with Eddie, he always knew the kid would screw up somehow. Eddie just couldn't keep his nose clean. He always figured Eddie would end up killed, but somehow he always pictured Victor committing the deed, not him.

Patch began to think about Eddie's movements the last two days. "Did I miss something?" he wondered. "Where did Eddie hide the money and coke? Do the brothers really think they are going to recover their lost property?" It would not surprise Patch if some of Eddie's friends were halfway around the world now with the cash and goods. It was the Fernandez family's fault for allowing Eddie to hold onto such a valuable amount of goods. Billy Joe had spoke on Eddie's behalf and praised his efforts and connections. Patch shook his head, "Look where that got you, Billy Joe."

Patch brought his thoughts back to the present and readjusted his chair. He then leaned over in the aisle to see what Victor and Zane had been up to for the last several hours. He could faintly hear Victor talking, but he could only see the back of his head. Hitting a few more buttons and finally getting his seat in the upright position, Patch was able to see Victor talking to a man dressed in a black suit. The man's face was obstructed by another chair. He could make out Zane's voice, but who was this person in the suit?

"Did I miss something earlier? Was there another passenger that maybe was with the pilot up front?"

He was about to get up and walk over to see what was going on when he felt the plane begin to tilt downward toward the landing strip. Over the jet engines and brakes, Patch tried vainly to make out the conversation in the front of the plane. Unfortunately, over all the noise, he only could catch the words "island of Barbados."

As soon as the jet rolled to a stop, the pilot announced, "Welcome to Miami, where it is currently seventy-two degrees. I hope you had a pleasant flight, and we look forward to serving you again some day. It is now safe to move around the cabin."

Unbuckling his seatbelt, Patch stood up and was shocked when he realized that man in the black suit was Zane Black. Zane's hair had been trimmed, and he was sporting a pair of Ray-Bans. Over the last couple of hours, Zane had been transformed from a surfer dude to a professional Mr. Black.

Patch murmured quietly beneath his breath, "Nothing surprises me with this family."

Part Two

CHAPTER 22

Thursday, 2:00 P.M.

Surprised, Kathleen actually seemed rested when she stepped out of a taxicab in front of the Grand Barbados Resort and Spa. It was afternoon now and a lot had transpired over the last twenty-four hours. Even though she felt better, her memory was very foggy from the plane ride. She couldn't understand why she had a hard time remembering all the events and the time frame once she left Chicago. She did remember landing in Miami and being introduced to two new agents who would watch over her along with Detectives Butch McNeil and Paula Williams. It seemed strange for Kathleen to say good-bye to FBI agents Kay-Loviett and Floyd. Somehow she assumed they were going with her and the detectives to Barbados, but she was wrong.

The agents were leaving her in the hands of Paula and Butch, who were to be a couple on their honeymoon. Kay- Loviett had informed Kathleen to appear on holiday from work as a receptionist. It was at that time, agent Floyd handed Kathleen a secure phone and a new ID. Kathleen was now Trisha Lee Abbot.

The story was kept simple. While at work at her office in Nashville, Tennessee, Trisha had dialed into a local radio station hoping to win a trip to Barbados. Luckily she was the ninety-ninth caller and won a ticket to the International Wine Tasting Festival that was being held at the Grand Barbados Resort and Spa. The trip included their finest ocean view suite, $1,500 in cash, and all meals, including wine.

At the airport, Kathleen was shocked to actually receive the cash and her resort voucher.

"When you step off this plane there will be no more contact between you and the detectives," said Kay-Loviett. "Once you land in Barbados, take the first cab to the resort and present your voucher to the front desk. Here is another hundred to take care of the taxi."

"Paula and I will be right behind you in the next cab. We will accidently bump into you at the reception area and introduce ourselves to you," said Butch.

"You have an extra bag with your luggage. The other agents took the liberty of getting you a swimsuit and a few other island outfits. Hope you don't mind that I glanced at your sizes when I packed your clothes. Just leave the tags on the items that don't fit," said Paula smiling.

"You are playing a new character in a fantasy vacation opportunity," Kay-Loviett said. "Go with it and try to enjoy yourself."

"Easier said than done," Kathleen thought.

A man opened the taxi door for Kathleen and said, "Welcome to the lovely Grand Barbados Resort and Spa."

Kathleen took his offered hand and replied, "Thank you, I am so excited to be here!"

After giving her new name, Trisha Abbot, to the concierge, she was handed a welcome glass of champagne and was led up the stairs with her luggage to the reception office. There were quite a few people checking in, so Kathleen took the opportunity to glance around at her surroundings.

The resort was indeed grand. The floor was made of wood that appeared to have been just polished. The counter was made of stone into which beautiful mosaics had been inlaid. There were bright magnificent flowers in varies pots of colors placed around the entrance and the reception room. Along the right wall of the counter was a ten-foot high waterfall that allowed water to run down into a manmade stream that led away from the reception toward the interior of the building.

Observing the people, she noticed there were mostly couples checking in. All were wearing island wear and sporting big grins. Looking over her clothes, she realized she looked out of place. She was wearing jeans with a long sleeve white T-shirt. She had removed her thick jacket at the airport and managed somehow to make room for it in one of her three bags. Maybe she should have peeped into her new luggage piece and changed into one of the new outfits on the plane. Just then, she jumped as she heard a women cry out and then start laughing. A young man around his midthirties had come up from behind her and grabbed her around the waist. Now she was turned toward him and kissing him passionately in front of everyone.

"Great, too bad Kay-Loviett couldn't have provided me with a good-looking husband for this trip. That would have definitely helped me blend in."

Looking around some more, there was no sign of Butch or Paula, now known as Bob and Mary Jacobs. She was not too concerned because she was given a cell phone with their numbers on speed dial. The phone had given her some comfort if that was possible under the circumstances. Floyd had even told her that she would be able to call her parents Saturday morning using the phone. Now that gave her real comfort.

"May I help you?"

Kathleen spun back around to find a lovely young lady standing behind the reception desk. She was wearing a pink linen dress with the resort logo on it; her hair pulled back, and there was a yellow flower tucked at her ear. She was truly stunning and projected self-confidence. Instantly, Kathleen was put at ease. She handed the lady her voucher and said, "Hello, my name is Trisha Abbot, and I am here to check in."

Returning her smile the woman said, "Excellent. We are so glad to have you with us, Ms. Abbot. Are you expecting anyone else or are you alone on holiday?"

Kathleen bit her lower lip as she tried to figure out what to say. Finally the right words came to her, "No, it is just me. I'm looking forward to a nice long break from a dead-end job."

Kathleen thought that wasn't too bad a response. "Maybe they were right, and I can just pretend and actually try to enjoy this trip," she thought.

The receptionist handed Kathleen her key and said, "Very well, you are in one of our finest ocean view suites located in villa ten. Your room number is ten twenty."

Next she waved her hands toward someone to her side and continued, "Raphael, the young gentlemen behind you, will help you with your bags. Please enjoy your stay and let us know if there is anything that we can do to make your stay as enjoyable as possible."

"Thank you, I plan to hit the beach immediately. I can't wait to feel this beautiful sunshine on my body!"

Turning around to find Raphael, she spotted Butch and Paula coming up to the counter right behind her. Paula said, "I just love your shoes! They are just precious!"

"Thank you, I bought them in a store in Nashville."

Paula broke out in a smile, "We are from Atlanta, Georgia, not too far from your state."

Butch asked, "Is this your first time here?"

Kathleen replied, "Yes, I actually won this trip at a local radio show."

Paula stuck her hand out, "My name is Mary, and this is my new husband Bob Jacobs."

Extending her hand, "I am Trisha Abbot. Nice to meet you."

Butch glanced at the young lady at the counter and replied, "Well, we are next. We hope to see you around, have a nice trip."

"Thank you."

Just like that, Kathleen had already met up with the Jacobs. Raphael was patiently standing by with her bags and then once she was done talking, he asked for her key and that she follow him. He led her down a hall that followed the stream of water and opened up to a large covered courtyard surrounded by tables and a bar made of mahogany wood. Each table was covered with white linen and had a small vase of pink and yellow flowers placed in the center. The chairs were wrought iron and had pink and white striped cushions that were secured to the chairs with ties. There were a few couples sitting around having various cocktails of many different colors. Most ladies were wearing swimsuits with sarongs or a cover-up dress with sandals.

"I wonder what my clothes are going to look like. I can just imagine Paula calling into some unknown person with all my details: five foot three, auburn hair, size four, shoes size six, and average shape," she thought.

"We are just going to follow this sidewalk all the way to the end to get to villa ten. We have provided a map in your room that shows all the pools, restaurants and bars and all other amenities," said Raphael.

Following along behind him there were a few more villas that had pool and garden views. With each step Kathleen could hear the sound of the ocean getting louder and her excitement began to grow. The sidewalk came to an end at villa ten, just like he promised. They then climbed one flight of stairs to the top floor and found room 1020. Villa ten had two rooms on the first floor and only one room on the top floor—her room. Opening the door for her, Raphael stepped aside and allowed Kathleen to enter first. She was speechless. The room was very large and decorated with exquisite furnishings. There was a sitting room to the left with a bar and TV. The lounge suite was made of cane and the cushions were covered with a blue and white floral design fabric. The cane coffee table held a vase of fresh flowers along with a welcome basket from the hotel. Toward the end of the room stood the king-size master bed and a dresser made of cherry. The bed had a white comforter with blue and white pillows to match the lounge suite. To the side of the bed was another room that opened up to the master bath. The bathroom had a large tub with walk in shower beside it, all made of natural stone. Along the countertop was a dark wicker basket that held all the amenities that she could possible want.

When she thought it couldn't get any nicer, Kathleen was blown away when she stepped out onto her balcony. The balcony opened up with sliding doors to reveal a large timber deck with two lounge chairs, table and chairs for four, and a hot tub off to the far corner overlooking the water. Turning around toward Raphael, she said, "It is perfect, thank you very much!"

Smiling back, Raphael gestured toward the map on the table and said, "The bar is also stocked. Enjoy your stay. I will see myself out."

She offered a tip, and he politely explained tipping was not necessary at the resort and left.

Kathleen watched as he left and pulled the door closed behind him. She then walked over to her luggage and immediately grabbed the new bag. She laid it on the bed and opened it to find two swimsuits, a sarong and cover up, two pair of shorts, a razorback tank top, a floral top, two pair of shoes, a pair of sandals, and a tan straw beach bag. Inspecting all the pieces and sizes, she was impressed. Deciding on the two-piece yellow and red bikini with the matching red sarong, she headed toward the bathroom. Trying it on, she smiled at how she looked in the full-length mirror. Cutting the tags off with some clippers, she then tried on the sandals and then walked back into the bedroom to get her beach bag.

The final thing needed before leaving for the beach was to pack her beach bag. So she made her way back into the bathroom to load up on suntan lotions and a towel. Taking one last look she was then satisfied she got everything needed for an afternoon on the beach. When she rounded the corner of her bathroom, she heard a noise that made her freeze dead in her tracks.

CHAPTER 23

Kathleen stopped all movement and then carefully set her beach bag down on the tile floor. Scanning the room for anything she could use as a weapon, she spotted a heavy wooden candlestick. Quickly she removed the candle and placed it on the counter. Raising her arm high with the candlestick, she eased around the corner.

At that moment she was surprised that she didn't find the killer staring back at her with his cold eyes, laughing. Instead of a deranged killer holding a knife, she found a magazine lying on the floor by the coffee table. The ocean breeze off the balcony had caught the pages and sent it sailing to the floor. The pages were still flapping when she walked over and picked it up off the floor.

Placing the magazine back on the coffee table, she set down the candlestick and then walked over to the front door to make sure it was locked. It was. Next, she stepped out onto the balcony to make sure she was alone. Seeing no one there, she took a deep breath. Her imagination was beginning to get the best of her. Walking closer to the edge, she could see the water below and happy couples walking all around. Deciding to go and join them, she quickly turned around and ran straight into Paula.

"Shit! What are you doing here?"

With a frown Paula responded, "I wanted to see how easy it was to break into your room without you noticing."

Kathleen pushed by her and walked back into the bedroom. Falling down on the bed she mumbled, "Great, I guess I failed."

Paula walked past her and made her way over to the stocked minibar. She grabbed a bottle of water, walked over to the bed, and sat beside Kathleen. "Here, drink some water."

Without looking up, Kathleen said, "Thanks."

"Well at least you heard something, and I didn't walk straight into the bathroom and scream, boo!"

Kathleen looked up to meet Paula's eyes and said, "You're right. I feel much better now."

Paula didn't push the issue anymore. She felt bad enough so she looked over at all the clothing displayed on the bed.

"Hey, not bad, I think they gave you the better stuff."

For the first time Kathleen noticed what Paula was wearing, a black one-piece swimsuit with a sheer white cover up. She looked amazing.

"I don't know. Your suit is nice. Is that a Donna Karan?" Kathleen asked.

Paula responded, "Yeah, but it is still not as nice as yours. The swimsuit looks like it was designed just for you."

A small smile escaped, "Yeah, I was surprised at how well it fit. It makes me feel like all those early-morning runs in the freezing cold finally paid off."

"Absolutely! So, it looks like you were headed down toward the beach before I broke in?"

"Yes, I was just packing a bag. Did you see all the things in the bathroom?"

"Sweetie, my room is nothing like yours. We are located below you though. We are in room ten ten."

"So do you have to share a room with "Bob"?" Kathleen asked.

Paula threw a beach towel at Kathleen and laughed, "Very funny! Now I am going back to my husband, and we are going to hit the beach as well. Butch already scoped out the place and found several open chairs around the north side of the beach. We will sit there, try to sit somewhere within eyesight, okay?"

With a sigh, Kathleen responded, "Okay."

Sensing something wrong, Paula sat back down on the bed beside Kathleen and asked, "What's wrong? I'm really sorry if I scared you earlier."

Looking around and pointing at the room, "I just feel a little guilty. Here I am at an incredible resort in one of their finest rooms, and I got here because Eddie, Lisa, and Mia are dead."

Paula stood up and placed her hands on Kathleen's hand and pulled her off the bed into a standing position. She then remarked, "Yes, it sucks!" Kathleen didn't respond so Paula continued. "Nothing will change the facts, and you are here at a beautiful resort, ALIVE! Celebrate your life. You could have easily been lying beside Eddie yesterday and not standing here today."

Letting go of her hand, Kathleen knew she was right. She could not go back and bring her students back to life. She had to continue on. "It is just hard, that's all."

Paula nodded and said, "Yeah, I know."

Kathleen turned back around and walked over to the clothing on the bed. She picked up her other swimsuit and replied, "I think I did get the better stuff."

Realizing that she was going to make it and not have an emotional breakdown, Paula headed out the door and said over her shoulder, "See you at the beach."

Kathleen pushed the bad memories away, put her towel and bottled water in her beach bag, and tossed in the magazine and room key from the coffee table. Looking around once more, she decided that was all she needed; she headed out the door. Once outside, she turned around and pushed at the doorknob to make sure it was closed and locked. It was. She then turned back around and made her way down the flight of stairs. Reaching the bottom step, she glanced around until she found room 1010, Butch and Paula's room. Estimating how many steps it was from her room, she felt a little safer.

Soon, Kathleen made her way around the villa to a pathway lined with pink azaleas that led to the beach. Following the pathway, she headed toward what she hoped was a comfy lounge chair where she could get some much needed rest and relaxation.

From a balcony on villa nine, a man watched each step Kathleen made. Walking over to his dresser, he pulled out a pair of swim trunks and immediately changed. Walking into the bathroom and finding the same amenities, he grabbed some lotion and a towel and headed out the door.

CHAPTER 24

Kathleen was walking along the beach when she spotted Butch and Paula on lounge chairs in the shade of a tiki hut; they were drinking blue drinks that were adorned with little umbrellas. They were laughing and holding hands. Butch was stroking Paula's long blond hair with his other hand. From all appearances, they looked like a couple in love having a good time. Kathleen decided to sit close to the bar, so she stopped about four huts away from "Bob and Mary" and settled in on one of the lounge chairs. Since she didn't have a special someone, she placed her beach bag in the other chair provided. She had just unpacked her lotions when a waiter approached her.

"Good afternoon, my lady. May I bring you something to drink or eat?"

"That would be lovely." Kathleen took the drink list he offered and began to scan the names of each drink provided. She worked her finger down the menu as she read and stopped when she found the drink she was looking for. "I will have a chocolate mudslide please, and I would love a chicken salad as well."

"Very good, may I please have your room number?"

"Yes, I am in villa ten, room ten twenty."

"Fantastic, I will be back soon with your order. My name is Dennis, and I will be your waiter till five o'clock. Just let me know if you need anything else."

"Thank you, Dennis. My name is Trisha."

He smiled back and then turned and walked toward the bar to place her order. It was at this bar when Kathleen first noticed him.

A gentleman was standing talking to a young brunette wearing a tiny hot pink swimsuit. He had dark hair and stood over six feet tall. He was beautiful. He had one hand on the bar holding a beer and the other holding a towel. His gold and turquoise swim trunks highlighted his dark creamy tan, and his white T-shirt showed a body that worked out often. His shirt was not too tight; it was just right.

The waiter at the bar approached the young hottie and gave her two drinks. Taking her drinks, she smiled and waved good-bye to the handsome man as she made her way back toward the beach. Two huts down, waiting on the brunette was a man stretched out in a lounge chair reading a book. He never glanced up as she approached; he only lifted his hand. The lady took one glance back to the bar and then sat down beside her man on the other lounge chair. The man at the bar never glanced back toward the hottie; instead he was carrying on a conversation with her waiter, Dennis.

Laughter rung out over the water and Kathleen turned away from the bar and looked out to sea. There splashing around in the water were Bob and Mary. Kathleen smiled. To her it looked a little comical seeing a supermodel with an aged guy like Butch. She looked around to see if others were watching. Some couples were, and there were a few smiles on their faces as well.

"They don't exactly fit together do they?"

Startled, Kathleen turned to her right and there stood the beautiful man from the bar holding a mudslide.

"I hope you don't mind, but I asked the waiter if I could bring you your drink."

To make sure, Kathleen looked toward the bar and saw Dennis smiling and gesturing with his hands toward the man and her drink.

A little caught off guard, she took the drink from his outstretched hand and replied, "Thank you."

The man spoke, "With love anything is possible, don't you agree?"

Noticing the confused look on Kathleen's face, he pointed out over the water toward Butch and Paula. At that moment, Butch had Paula in his arms and was turning her around in the water as Paula lay on her back with her arms stretched out beside her. She was smiling, and Butch was kissing her neck.

"Yes, at least I hope so."

"My name is Michael, Michael Brunson"

Kathleen placed her hand in his and said, "I'm Ka...Trisha Abbot"

Smiling, he spoke, "What was that, did you just decide to give me your real name or fake name?"

Kathleen felt herself turn red and stated, "It's a long story."

"Well, Trisha, I hope it is one I get to hear sometime. Are you here for the wine tasting celebration?"

Amazingly she answered in a very calm voice, "Yes, I just arrived today. I plan to attend later tonight after I catch my breath and unwind a bit."

Kathleen placed her lips on the straw and began to tug at her cold refreshing drink. She was telling her mind to calm down and what had Paula told her? Oh yeah, to celebrate life.

She asked, "So are you here for the wine festival or just vacation?"

Without asking, Michael bent over and picked up her bag and sat it on the sand and took the seat by Kathleen. He then replied, "Both. I make wine, so I am technically on business, but I definitely need the vacation."

Kathleen began to put together in her mind what he said about his name, Brunson. "Are you the same Brunson as Brunson Wine?"

Smiling back, "Yes, that is my family. We have been in the wine business now for three generations."

At that moment his cell phone began to ring, and he said, "I'm sorry, but I must take this."

He gracefully got out of the chair and walked a few steps away to answer his phone.

Kathleen continued to stare at his back not wanting to take her eyes off of him. After about a minute, Michael looked back over his shoulder and replied, "I have to work now, but I hope to see you tonight, Trisha."

Kathleen nodded her head yes and finally got the right words out she was thinking, "I'm sure we will run into each other again."

With that he smiled and turned around and walked off.

Kathleen thought, "Wow, did that just happen?" Looking around to see if anyone noticed the happiness of a love struck fool, she noticed Butch and Paula working their way out of the water. They were holding hands and talking to one another. They looked so natural that Kathleen began to think they really were a couple.

Paula sat down close to Butch and said, "I feel like all eyes are on me."

Glancing around Butch said, "They are! You are the hottest thing on the beach, and I get to prance around like a little puppy that just got a new toy."

Striking his chest with her hand, "Did you have to kiss my neck and chest like that?"

To anyone the gesture looked playful, but Butch realized he might have crossed over a line in the ocean. "Sorry, I was just really getting into character. If you want to get me back, I'll lay on my stomach, and you can rub my back." Turning over in his chair, Butch laid face down.

Dumbstruck, Paula began to lean over and rub his back.

Rubbing deep into his lower back, Paula asked, "How long do you think we will be here?"

Moaning, he answered, "I think the feds are going to move fast on this. I wouldn't be surprised if we were done with all of this in one week's time. Get my upper shoulder, the one with the ugly bullet scar."

Removing her hands and sitting back down she said, "I feel a little guilty for using her as bait."

Turning back over he frowned, "Me, too. Just remember what we saw hanging from the ceiling in that apartment. That will keep you focused and in character, luvie."

Paula felt the gaze again and turned around toward the villa behind them. She caught a glimpse of a man that she thought she recognized but wasn't sure.

Butch sat up and said he was going to go to the bar and order a sandwich and asked if she wanted one.

"Yes, Just ham, cheese, and avocado on wheat. While you order, I am going to go for a little stroll and check the perimeter."

They both got up, and Butch reached out and kissed Paula on the lips and whispered, "Be careful love."

Slinging her bag over her shoulder and patting her weapon, she said, "Always."

Paula left the beach and found the footpath that would take her back toward the villas and began to follow it. The man was sitting at one of the tables on the well-manicured lawn. As she made her way up the pathway, he began to get up out of his chair and move toward villa nine. Staying several feet behind, Paula began to follow him. The pathway led to the front of the villa just like the one from villa ten. There she rounded the corner and saw a shadow go around the staircase and then heard footsteps go up the stairs. Listening for the sound of a door opening and closing, she then began to climb the stairs. Halfway up, she glanced behind her to make sure she was alone. Reassured that she was not being followed, she continued up the stairs. Once at the top she saw the door to room 920. The door was standing slightly open. Placing one hand in her bag and the other hand on the door, she began to carefully push the door inward. The door made the smallest of squeaks but opened up to what appeared to be an empty room. Just as Paula decided to check behind her, a hand covered her mouth and another hand wrapped around her body. In one quick moment, Paula was lifted forward and the door was slammed behind her.

CHAPTER 25

Paula couldn't get to her gun, and she could not scream. A strong man had outsmarted her and was dragging her toward the bed. Paula's eyes were bulging wide open, and she was finding it hard to catch her breath. The man was partially covering her nose as well as her mouth making it difficult to breathe. She was able to get one leg at an angle and kick at the man behind her. He was stronger, and he didn't even budge as she struck once more with her leg. Paula saw that she was getting closer to the bed, and she was terrified of what he might do to her. She knew this job could be dangerous. She thought, "Oh why did I leave Butch on the beach and come up here all alone? Why didn't I tell him I thought I'd recognized someone?"

Paula had few options; she was wearing only her swimsuit and very sheer cover-up and her weapon was in the bag on the floor by the front door, several steps away. She tried another move that she was taught in one of her latest self-defense workshops, but somehow he knew the move was coming. The stranger blocked her leg kick with his knee and then twisted her around to face him and then he let go of her as she fell hard onto the bed. A scream was beginning to emerge when she stopped short, sat up on the bed, and slapped the man hard across the face.

"George! You bastard! What the hell? What are you doing here?"

Placing his lips to hers, he fell into her and began to kiss her madly. Wrapping her arms around his neck, she kissed him back. For a long passionate moment, they lay entwined, kissing wildly. Slowly, Paula began to wrap one leg around George and with her right hand she quickly grabbed his shoulder and flipped him off the bed. Rolling off and landing hard on the floor, George lifted his hands in surrender. "I'm sorry, babe. I thought you would be surprised and glad to see me."

Standing over him, Paula gazed back with fire in her eyes, "I could have killed you. I had my hand on my weapon."

Laughing, he gasped, "Was this before or after I had you lying on the bed?"

Paula placed her foot on his chest and sat on the edge of the bed. "I'm serious! You could blow this case for me. I am protecting a witness who is in a shitload of trouble."

"Yeah, I thought that is what you were doing out in the ocean with McNeil."

Placing her hand through her hair, she screamed, "Come on, you are jealous of McNeil—seriously?"

"Well, I didn't think I had to be until I saw him place his mouth all over your chest!"

Frowning she spoke, "We are working as a couple on their honeymoon, okay?"

"Well, I sure fell for it, and so did everyone else gazing out at the ocean."

Standing up and lifting her foot off his chest, she walked back to the front door and grabbed her bag. Turning back toward him she said, "You have to go home, George and tell no one where I am."

Smiling back with his winning smile that she fell in love with, "Too late, babe. I am one of the FBI guys working the same case. We are all on the same team now."

Paula looked shocked and asked, "What?"

"Remember when McNeil made a pact with Kay-Loviett? Well, Bart and I just happened to be at the office last night when Kay-Loviett made the call."

Walking toward Paula he wrapped his arms around her waist and said, "Too bad you don't get to stay in my room tonight, it is much better than yours on the bottom floor. Did you see the stuff in the bathroom?"

Knocking his hands away, "I have to go back to the beach now. My husband is going to start missing me. Don't you worry though—he will be thrilled to hear that there are two more FBI men watching over us."

"No, the other two that escorted you guys to the island have left. It is just Bart and me."

Paula tilted her head, "Why?"

He answered, "I don't know. A lot of changes have been going on—sorry, all classified stuff. If I told you, I would have to marry you."

Paula said nothing and turned toward the door.

George asked, "Are you going to tell him about us?"

Looking back over her shoulder Paula said, "No," and she walked out, closing the door behind her.

George shook his head and just smiled.

CHAPTER 26

Paula quickly fled down the stairs from villa nine and found the pathway toward the beach. She was able to spot Butch right away. He was sitting on a stool at the beach bar talking with Kathleen. Walking over toward them, Butch called out, "Hey, Mary, do you remember Trisha from checking in this morning? Her room is right above ours."

Leaning in to kiss Paula, he whispered, "Where have you been? Don't do that again. I thought something bad had happened."

Pulling away and greeting Kathleen, she spoke, "Honey, I met two new acquaintances of our friend Kay from Georgia. I am sure we will bump into each other tonight at the wine festival." Looking at Butch and then over to Kathleen, "Are you going tonight, dear?"

Kathleen said, "Yes, did you know that the Brunson family is here representing the Brunson Winery?"

Butch replied, "Oh sweetie, I don't know nothing about wine, but I'm sure my wife has heard of them."

Paula gave him a friendly peck on the check and motioned over to his beer, "His favorite drink is beer; however I did get him to try something new today."

"Yes you did sugar cakes, but I still like my beer."

Paula smiled, "Well, I have heard of Brunson wine. They make a fantastic chardonnay. Did you meet them?"

"I don't know how many family members are here, but I did meet Michael Brunson down on the beach earlier," replied Kathleen.

"Great, there really is no telling who we will see tonight, so just keep your eyes open."

Kathleen only partly smiled and then grabbed her drink from the bar and replied, "I'm going to see if I can catch a few more rays of sun, but maybe I will see you tonight though."

Butch said, "Yep, see you later."

Kathleen turned away from the happy couple as Paula winked at her, and she headed back toward her two empty lounge chairs.

Dennis the waiter called out an order number, and Butch raised his hand. Taking both plates of sandwiches, he motioned Paula toward one of the empty tables set up with no one else around. Sliding his chair toward her, and putting his arm around her, he stated, "I was serious, earlier. You had me very worried. I approached Kathleen because I thought something had happened to you."

Paula's expression was a little grim. "Well I thought I was in trouble, too, until he identified himself as FBI. There are two of them. The one I met is George Brown. He has a partner named Bart. I did not get a chance to meet him, but I'm sure we will see them tonight."

"So now there are four agents here?"

She answered, "That was the same question I asked, but no. The two we met earlier at the airport did not make it out here. Kay-Loviett sent these two guys instead."

"Feds! I wish Kay-Loviett would have told us or at least warned us of a change. Wait, did he show you an ID?"

Paula thought back to her kiss with George. She had been dating him for some time now but had not gone public about their relationship. She still had not found the right words to tell Butch or anyone else down at the station that she was dating FBI. When she first saw George, he had been working out at her gym on a Saturday morning. Paula watched him on and off for a good thirty minutes before getting up the nerve to go and talk to him. When she finally came up with a plan, she got a call from Butch that made her leave on some urgent assignment before she had a chance.

The next time she saw him was the following Friday night. That time she didn't have to think of a reason because he was the one hitting on her. After a light workout, they left that night together for one of the wildest weekends of her life. Work really never came into the picture until two days later when they both came up for air. It was only then when he revealed what he did for a living. In her mind's eye, Paula could still see the first time she saw George strap on his gun; she finally stated, "Yes, a badge was presented, and I'm positive he is FBI."

Relaxing a little and removing his arm, Butch began to eat his sandwich. "So, does he look like FBI or is he trying to blend in like us?"

"Let's just say they have a better room. George is staying in the same setup as Kathleen in villa nine. I don't know where Bart is staying. Surely they aren't splurging for two luxury suites along with Kathleen's."

Putting his sandwich down, Butch said, "It would not surprise me. They seem to have unlimited funds unlike the Chicago PD."

"We will see them tonight and set up something. I agree with you, we need to be better informed about changes."

Butch nodded, and they both continued eating and staring out toward the beach at Kathleen.

Kathleen was lying in her lounge chair, sipping her second mudslide, and reading the magazine she brought with her from the room. The magazine had all kinds of information about Barbados. There were so many things to see and do. According to the map, they were across the street from the local shopping market. Kathleen thought, "Maybe I have time to go hit a few shops before dinner. Of all the clothes that were packed, there wasn't anything for evening. I have to find something to wear tonight."

Finishing her drink, she placed it on the table nearby and began to pack up from the beach. She stood up and threw her lotions and magazine in her bag and gathered up her towel. Wrapping her sarong around her waist and sliding her feet into her sandals, she headed back up the pathway toward room 1020.

CHAPTER 27

Chicago

It was Thursday afternoon and District Attorney Aileene Bell was sitting at her desk and talking on the phone in her downtown office. Her office was located on the third floor of the Dunbar Building on Chestnut Lane. It was a great location because it was only two blocks away from the county courthouse. Today, Aileene was dressed in a chic khaki wool pantsuit priced at six hundred dollars. As she talked away on the phone, she crossed her legs and her three-hundred-dollar Italian leather shoes came into view. Aileene liked clothes, and she was always seen wearing the latest styles in or out of the courtroom or office. Aileene began to twirl a piece of her long blond hair as it worked around down the side of her face. The rest of her hair was carefully and perfectly pulled back.

Aileene Bell came from money; her father was a retired judge. It was expected that Aileene would attend Harvard, graduate with a law degree, and work her way toward becoming a judge like her father. So far she had not disappointed anyone. A few more years as DA and some good publicity with the right case, and she would run for county judge. The only thing currently missing was a husband. Aileene had two daughters aged eight and six. A drunk driver killed her husband, Don Bell, four years ago. There still was a lot of public sympathy toward Aileene and her two adorable children, and that would only help her chances at winning the judgeship. If it were up to her, she would give it all up just to have Don back in her life.

Hanging up her phone, Aileene glanced at her last family portrait that was taken two months before the accident. The girls, ages four and two, were sitting on a blanket with Don and Aileene stretched out behind them. The picture was taken by a local photographer at the city park on a nice autumn afternoon. She missed Don; he was her right-arm man and had supported her career early on. They had met at Harvard Law School and knew right away they were meant to marry. They both were ambitious and set very high goals. In the eight years that they were married, Don was able to establish one of the most successful law firms in Chicago. Aileene was thirty-six and Don was only thirty-eight when he was killed that dreadful night. Looking away from the portrait, Aileene wiped away a little moisture under her eye. Gazing to the left at another picture on her shelf, she smiled back at her two daughters in ballet outfits. The girls have been enrolled in ballet now for two years.

It was at the ballet studio that Aileene had met Detective Butch McNeil. On a cold rainy evening about a year ago, Butch had shared an umbrella with Aileene as they climbed the steps up to the studio to pick up their daughters. From that day on, she had used his daughter Mandy as a babysitter for her girls, and somehow over the course of about a month, she began to date Butch. Now, things were a little awkward since the breakup. The girls often asked for Butch and would ask Mandy when her dad was coming back over.

Glancing back over more photos of the girls, she noticed it was 1:00 P.M. Since arriving at the office, she had answered about a dozen calls from sources within the media. All were asking about last night's tragic events at the Benedict Housing complex and the two dead cops found inside their patrol car on Grigor Street. Ms. Bell tried to answer questions without giving away the fact that she was completely out of the loop on last night's situation. She herself had more questions than answers. "Why was the FBI involved in a case that probably involved money and drugs?"

Although, she did think these murders were vicious and over the top, it still was not uncommon when drugs were involved. Most murderers wanted to send a message to others not to double-cross them. Her mind wandered back to the horrific scene at the Benedict. She shuddered at the thought of the two mutilated bodies that were left for them in the back room.

Just then her secretary knocked on the door and her mind came back to the present. She stated, "The FBI are here."

If she wasn't so pressed for information, Aileene would have kept them waiting like they kept her waiting the last hour. The appointment was made for 12:00, and Aileene had decided to wait and eat lunch after their visit. Now she was hungry, and they finally show an hour late. Deciding not to play games, she stated, "Thank you, Misty. Please, let them in."

Standing up and walking around her desk, Aileene stretched out her hand and met FBI agents Bethany Kay-Loviett and Bass Floyd. Gesturing for both of them to have a seat in her matching leather chairs, Aileene walked back around and sat at her desk. Making her move first, Aileene stated, "First of all, I don't like to wait on someone when an appointment is set. Second, I like to know the facts of a crime scene from my lead detectives before the FBI is brought in. Last, would either of you care to explain why my two best detectives are unavailable and unreachable by cell phone?"

With a look of annoyance, Kay Loviett said, "With all due respect, District Attorney, the FBI has fully taken over the murder case at Benedict Housing and the two dead policemen. And before you protest, Detective Butch McNeil gave us the green light and has been working with us for the last twenty-four hours."

Picking up a pen, Aileene asked, "How can I get in touch with Detective McNeil?"

Floyd answered, "Unfortunately you can't. Detective McNeil, along with Williams, are watching and protecting a witness from the Benedict Housing Complex. We have all of them tucked away with two other FBI agents in an unknown location for everyone's safety."

Aileene Bell put her pen down, sat back in her chair to think, and asked, "Is the witness being used to draw out the suspects?"

Kay-Loviett was surprised by the question. Aileene Bell was not one to be underestimated. Maybe it was time to explain the real reason for their visit. "District Attorney, are you afraid to take down Emilio Fernandez, founder of the Chicago Steel Company?"

Barbados

Patch was among the palms along the walkway as Kathleen was making her way back to villa ten. She was walking directly toward him and had no idea the plans he had made just for her. When she was within two feet, he was ready to make his move but was stopped instantly when another couple approached from the opposite direction. Patch mumbled to himself, "Damn, but soon, very soon Kathleen."

As the couple neared Kathleen, she spoke, "Hello, how are you?"

No one had stopped walking as the couple responded briefly. Patch continued to watch as Kathleen finally made it around the corner to her villa. When she was at the base of the stairs, she stopped and turned around to look behind her. She looked right at Patch, but never saw him. She continued to look around and then satisfied somehow, she turned back around and climbed the stairs to her room and entered quickly.

Once in her room, Kathleen locked her front door and then walked toward her balcony to open the back door. Feeling a little silly, she stepped out onto the balcony, looked around, and then walked over and peeked down below. Patch could still see her, and he smiled when he realized she was being cautious.

With a sense of security, Kathleen left the balcony and locked the door behind her. She then walked into her bathroom and looked around. Still no one was lurking about. Saying aloud, "Better check under the bed just in case."

Kathleen made her way over to the bed and then bent over and lifted the skirt and smiled when she saw that it too was clear. She stood back up and then dug around in her beach bag until she found her phone. She hit one, for Butch's number.

On the second ring, Paula answered, "Hello?"

"Hi, Paula, it's Kathleen. I don't have anything to wear tonight to the wine tasting festival. The clothes they packed are for day not evening. Do you have the same problem?"

Paula replied, "Yes, I need some more clothes as well, but I was planning on just picking something up at the resort gift shop and charging it to the room."

Kathleen continued, "Well if it is safe, I want to go across the street to the market to buy some clothes. Do you think that would be okay?"

Paula said, "That should be fine, we have two FBI agents looking over your shoulders as well. If you give us about fifteen minutes, we will contact them and tell them you are on the move. Butch and I are going to check on some things at the festival. Be safe, we will catch up with you tonight around six."

"Good, I will see you tonight."

Kathleen hung up the phone and went into the master bath and turned on the shower. She then began removing her sarong and swimsuit. Grabbing a razor and washcloth from the basket, she walked in the roomy shower and placed her body directly under the warm water.

Patch was waiting on the outside balcony. When he heard the water running, he carefully and quietly entered the master bedroom. Without making a sound, he slowly made his way toward the master bath. He could see Kathleen pushing the lever on the shampoo dispenser mounted on the wall. Her perfectly sculpted body was completely wet and ready for the shower. With the desired amount of shampoo in her hands, she began to run her hands and fingers through her long auburn hair. Her muscles in her arms and upper back began to flex as she washed out the sand and grit from the beach. Never once turning around, Kathleen stuck her head under the showerhead and rinsed out the shampoo. Next Kathleen pushed the lever from the conditioner dispenser and started the process all over again. At this point, she completely turned around to grab the soap. Never opening her eyes, she began rub her hands on the bar of soap and then began washing her arms, then neck, and last, chest before turning back around. Picking up the bar of soap again off the stand, she bent over slightly and began to rub her legs. Sensing his time was up, Patch stepped away from the bathroom and walked back out onto the balcony.

The cool breeze was definitely what Patch needed to knock the cobwebs out of his head. With cold sweaty hands, he picked up his phone and hit speed dial to make the call. "She is showering and then plans to go to the market in search for some clothes for tonight," he reported into the phone. Patch hung up the phone and then made his way down the balcony wall.

CHAPTER 28

After hours of sorting through paperwork that Agents Kay- Loviett and Floyd presented, Aileene Bell stood up and walked over to the window of her office to peer outside at the city below. It was 4:00 P.M., and she was tired. She had missed her 3:00 appointment with a lawyer who was a public defender and now had to reschedule in her already overbooked calendar. The case that was just laid out in front of her concerning Emilio Fernandez was now going to make November and December a nightmare. Walking back over to her desk, she picked up the phone and summoned Misty to her office. Gazing at the agents she said, "I would be more confident going to the judge for a warrant if your undercover agent reappeared. With that being said, I think we still have enough with his finance records and the agent's logs of his undercover work."

Misty walked in the office holding pen and paper and said, "Yes, Ms. Bell?"

"Ah, Thank you Misty. Please see that Agents Kay-Loviett and Floyd have everything they need. I am going to the courthouse to have a word with the judge. Also, I need you to clear my schedule for tomorrow."

With a sour look on her face, Misty agreed. Aileene frowned back and replied, "I will also need you to call Mandy the babysitter and tell her that I will be late tonight. Order whatever the agents want to eat but make mine the usual." Aileene then finished packing her briefcase and headed out the door saying, "Wish me luck!"

With a smile on her face, Kay-Loviett said, "I think we will have a pizza, Misty."

Agent Floyd commented, "Yes, that sounds good. Thank you, Misty."

The traffic was backed up outside so the District Attorney decided to walk the few blocks to the courthouse. Judge Rebecca Minor had agreed to clear the last thirty minutes of the day for Aileene. Judge Minor was tough but good, and the last thing Aileene needed was to keep the Judge waiting. So bracing herself against the cold and the crowded sidewalk, she began to walk. Just when Aileene was about to cross the last major intersection, a white service van accelerated and ran the red light. Aileene only had a chance to turn her head at the noise as the van made its way toward her within inches. From out of nowhere, a man appeared beside her and threw her back toward the sidewalk. With tires squealing, the van swerved back onto the road and sped away down an empty alley. With a hard landing, Aileene slightly pushed herself up on her side to see what was going on.

The man wearing a long winter coat said, "Are you alright? My God! That van almost ran over you!"

In a shaky voice, Aileene responded, "Yes, I think I'm fine." Looking down at her pants she noticed a rip toward the bottom. She slowly got up and discovered dirt and grime along her backside. Shaking her pants off, she mumbled under her voice, "Just great!"

The Good Samaritan handed Aileene her briefcase and offered, "Let me help you across the street." Before Aileene could say no, the man grabbed her elbow and guided her across the street safely.

Once across Aileene said, "Thank you for all your help. Did you happen to see the license plate of the van?"

The man shook his head and said, "No, but I will be happy to stay with you and fill out a statement for the police."

Aileene said, "That is very kind, but I am headed now to the courthouse. You see I'm a lawyer, I'll know who to talk to, but thank you very much."

The man said his farewells and continued on down the busy sidewalk.

A few more steps and Aileene was finally at the courthouse. Feeling a little insecure, she entered the building and gave her purse and ID over to the guard. The guard took one look at Aileene and said, "Ms. District Attorney, what happened to you?"

Taking her purse back, Aileene looked at Officer Lewis and said, "I was almost run over by a white van that ran a red light."

The officer looked alert and asked, "What, just now? Was it an old or new van? Did you get the license?"

Feeling time slipping away, Aileene responded, "Yes, but it all happened too quickly. Right now, I am more concerned about standing up Judge Minor."

Officer Lewis placed a hand on Aileene's elbow and said, "I will walk up with you."

Aileene was about to decline when she realized she was shaking. Together they walked over to the elevator, and he pushed the button to go up. By the time the doors opened and she stepped into the elevator, a flood of emotions began to wash over her. Quickly and embarrassed, Aileene reached inside her briefcase and pulled out a tissue to wipe her face. Officer Lewis stepped back and gave her some room. Very few people had seen Aileene Bell cry. Announcing to the officer, "I'm sorry, I just was thinking of my girls. They already lost one parent to someone's recklessness."

Just then the door opened to the judge's floor. "No apology needed, Ms. Bell. Now you go on for your appointment, and I am going to go back downstairs and call in what happened."

Turning around, Aileene said kindly, "Thank you Officer Lewis" and quickly walked away toward the judge's chambers.

CHAPTER 29

Kathleen was having a good time walking around the markets and talking to the locals in their shops. She was wearing her new outfit of white shorts and a floral top, all compliments of the agents. The first item that Kathleen bought was a light brown straw hat. It was hard to choose because there were so many hats on display at a sidewalk stand. The vendor was helpful, and Kathleen had tried on at least a dozen before finally settling on a cowboy-style hat. Walking into the shop, she paid and then found another mirror and immediately pulled her long hair into a low ponytail. She then cut the tags with the offered scissors and wore the hat out of the store.

Patch was in a mischievous mood and decided to enter the same store as Kathleen. His disguise must have worked because she walked right past and never noticed him. He also purchased a hat from the saleslady and then continued out the store behind Kathleen.

Kathleen passed up about three stores before entering a small women's boutique shop. There was a long white skirt and a pink off-the-shoulder top displayed in the window that caught her eye. Once inside, she walked over to the window and felt the material and decided right away she would purchase it. The saleslady was very eager to get her size and a dressing room.

In about fifteen minutes, Kathleen had already been to two stores and spent one hundred and eighty dollars. She smiled to herself as she realized it was not her own money. Making her way down the sidewalk she came across a store that had several lovely dresses in the window. Deciding to go inside, she opened up the door and entered the small shop. A nice lady made her way over and asked, "Good afternoon, may I help you look for something in particular?"

Returning the lady's smile, Kathleen spoke, "I am trying to find a couple of dresses for the wine tasting festival. I have come across several I like, but I am not sure what other women will be wearing."

The local smiled even bigger and replied, "I have just what you are looking for, follow me."

Kathleen followed the lady over to the back wall and looked at a few dresses that the lady was pointing at. "These dresses are similar to the dress code expected at the festival. All the ladies like to get dressed up, and you will see a wide variety of long and short dresses."

Kathleen picked up a lime green dress and walked over to the mirror. She held the dress in front of her and then with her other hand took off her hat and removed her ponytail. Her hair tumbled over the small straps around the hanger, and she liked how her auburn hair and skin tone looked with the dress. She handed the dress to the lady to put in the dressing room and started going through more dresses. When she was done, she had eight dresses waiting on her in the dressing room. Turning back toward the saleslady, Kathleen said, "I think I'm ready to try them on."

The saleslady walked Kathleen over to the dressing room and untied the cloth and held it back for Kathleen to enter. Once inside, she tied the fabric closed and Kathleen began to undress. She decided to try on the lime green dress first. The size and fit were perfect. Mumbling to herself, "This is a first," she stepped outside to look at herself in the mirror.

Kathleen did a double take at herself. Wow, the dress did wonders for her appearance. Looking at her feet, she followed the split that climbed her right leg halfway up her thigh. The top of the dress had a draped neckline that plunged to her waist. Turning around to look, she saw the crisscross straps running along her bare back. The dress made her feel beautiful and sexy. Turning back around to face the front, she was stunned to see Michael Brunson in the mirror gazing at her with a grin on his face.

Michael Brunson was standing there staring back at her holding a pair of shiny strappy heals. Realizing she spotted him he said, "I think these were made to go with that dress."

At that moment the saleslady chimed in, "Did you say you wore size six? Let me grab your size."

Kathleen was speechless as they continued to chatter around her. Finally, Kathleen reached out and grabbed the shoes as the lady made her way toward her. Sitting on the small red leather ottoman, Kathleen placed the shoes on her feet and stood.

The saleslady asked, "How do they feel? Do they fit?"

Nodding her head yes, Kathleen looked over to Michael and said, "I'm surprised to see you in a lady's shop. Are you shopping for someone?"

Michael answered, "Yes, my mother has a birthday this month. I have gone to several shops now and nothing has really caught my eye yet. At least, not until now."

Blushing Kathleen looked down at her feet and then realizing she looked embarrassed, she looked back up at Michael. He was standing there smiling with his hands on his hips. He then walked closer and asked, "If you don't already have a date tonight, would you like to be my date?"

Kathleen could still feel the heat in her cheeks when she agreed. He winked back at her and then asked, "Is eight o'clock too late? I plan on taking a break from my wine display at that time."

"No, eight is just perfect. That will give me time to walk around and see all the displays."

Michael stated, "Great, I will book a table for two at the Melina Restaurant. It is located inside the hotel."

"Yes, I know the one. I will see you later then."

Michael smiled and walked out the front door of the shop. Kathleen looked over at the saleslady who was smiling back at Kathleen. "Looks like you have a nice evening planned—good for you."

Kathleen took one more look in the mirror and said, "I will take the dress and the shoes."

Kathleen left the shop forty minutes later with her arms full of several hanging bags and shopping bags. Around her left shoulder were smaller bags dangling down past her waist. With thoughts of getting her clothing back to the hotel without wrinkles, she never once looked around.

Kathleen made her way down the sidewalk, and walked right past both FBI agents and never blinked. She had never met George or Bart and was really not seeking them out anyway. Somehow with the shopping, she was able to block out the reasons why she was on the island. The only thing on her mind at the moment was Michael and how to fix her hair for tonight.

On the other corner of the street, Patch was sitting at a table with a newspaper. Patch's tattoo was covered by makeup and he was wearing his new hat with sunglasses. Patch gave the appearance of a tourist who was patiently waiting for his wife. He easily spotted both agents early on but didn't give them much thought. He was good and knew it. Seeing Kathleen walk out of the shop, he gently placed his newspaper down on the table and waited a few moments before getting up to follow her again.

CHAPTER 30

Judge Rebecca Minor was an African American woman in her midfifties. Over the last fifteen years, she had built a solid reputation for being fair and honest to all parties. She despised grandstanding in her courtroom just about as much as she loathed anyone who was tardy to court or appointments. She glanced at her clock; it was now 4:33. She liked Ms. Bell, and so far had never been disappointed by her. "Where are you Aileene? Something must be really important for you to have called and asked me to clear my schedule," she said to herself.

Two minutes later, Aileene stood outside the Judge's chamber door and knocked. Realizing that she was already late, she skipped the ladies room and was doing the best she could to fix her appearance. She was in the process of finding a rubber band for her hair when Judge Minor opened the door.

Judge Minor stepped to the side and motioned Aileene inside her chambers. She was all ready to fire away at the District Attorney until her eyes raked over Aileene, and she said instead, "What happened to you?"

"I was almost run over by a service van on the way over here."

"I am sorry, Aileene. Do we need to table this until tomorrow?"

"No, this is important, but thanks."

Judge Minor walked over to her fridge and pulled out an orange juice and handed it to Aileene.

"Aileene took a big swig and said, "Thanks."

"Let's go sit over there on the couch. It will be more comfortable."

Aileene followed her over and took a seat on the leather couch. Placing her juice on a coaster on a nearby table, she then opened her briefcase and pulled out the documents on Emilio Fernandez. Seeing the name on top, Judge Minor immediately picked up the papers without waiting for directions and said, "Oh, Ms. Bell, tell me you are not going after Chicago Steel?"

Aileene stated simply, "Yes, I am."

Settled back in her seat the Judge continued "Well, whatever you got, better be good enough because I'm not ready to retire just yet."

Aileene picked up the log from the missing undercover agent and began to read. The logs showed how Agent Dave Wittfield first met the deceased Eddie Jones and ended with his last report of a meeting with Billy Joe at 10:00 A.M. on Wednesday. After she was done, she picked up the financial records that Agent Kay-Loviett had put together, and began to explain the numbers and the mismatched bank accounts spread among three overseas banks. There were two accounts located in the Caymans that had numbers that did not reflect earnings reported to the IRS in 2009.

Aileene went on to explain that this was the first red flag that set the ball rolling for Agent Bethany Kay-Loviett. She then began to pull all accounts and began the tedious task of breaking them down and analyzing each one. When the agent was finally done for the year 2009, there were over two million dollars that was unaccounted for.

Aileene Bell finished her report with a summary of numbers from Evangelina, the restaurant on Baxter Street. Apparently the restaurant was placed in Vivian Fernandez's name instead of Emilio's. This set up gave an appearance that money was hidden under his wife's name. Lastly, Aileene said, "The numbers just don't add up."

Judge Minor never once interrupted as Aileene spilled out the case with all the facts and numbers. When Aileene was done, twenty minutes had passed without the judge saying one word. This was not uncommon; the judge had a reputation of listening and not speaking, until the very end. It was at that time, she would either rip your case to shreds and say "warrant denied" or ask questions that would hopefully move toward your warrant.

Finally the judge spoke, "This is all very interesting, but before we move on bringing down Chicago's leading steel company, I would like to have the body of Agent Dave Wittfield dead or alive."

It was hard, but Aileene sat quietly and waited for the judge to finish and not interrupt with comments or complaints.

Continuing, the judge said, "Now with that being said, I think we have more concrete evidence against the restaurant. For the time being, I am only willing to sign a warrant for the financial records at Evangelina's Restaurant. This will allow you to receive the financial books and build a stronger case with or without Agent Wittfield."

Aileene's mouth twisted as she thought about Judge Minor's decision.

"Off the record, Aileene, I think you have something really explosive here, and it could potentially make or break your career. I think moving on the restaurant first will allow you to see what track your investigation needs to take next. I feel this is the safest move for all parties at stake."

Aileene nodded her head yes and said, "Okay, I will move forward on the restaurant and see what turns up. Hopefully we won't find the remains of one dead agent in the freezer."

Judge Minor stood up and walked over to her desk and dialed her secretary. Ten minutes later, the secretary walked in with some paperwork. Judge Minor picked up her glasses and began to read over the document with a fine toothcomb. After another ten minutes, the judge finally signed, dated, and stamped the document.

Judge Minor handed Aileene the warrant and said, "Good luck, District Attorney."

Placing the warrant in her briefcase with all the other documents, Aileene stood and thanked the judge.

Before Aileene was out the door, the judge called back to her. In a concerned voice, the judge said, "Watch your back, Aileene. You don't know if the incident with the van earlier was an accident or not."

Aileene could feel a cold chill move up her spine as she spoke, "You might be right. I think I will take a cab back to the office."

"Wise choice. Keep me posted."

Aileene just nodded and then walked out pulling the door closed behind her.

It was 5:25 P.M. when Aileene stepped out of the elevator and once again was greeted by Officer Lewis.

"Ms. Bell, I filed the report and all patrolmen in the area have been alerted to keep a look out for the van."

"Thank you. I will be taking a cab back to my office."

The officer responded, "Stay here inside, and I will go out and get you one."

The officer headed out the door and never gave Aileene a chance to decline the offer. As she waited, she looked around and noticed a few people staring at her. She thought, "Is it my appearance or is someone following me?"

She tried to push all the thoughts away as she saw Officer Lewis coming back through the double doors and waving his hands for her to follow. As she walked toward him, she turned around just to see the faces of the people around her once more. She had a good memory and hoped she would not see any of them back at her Dunbar building.

CHAPTER 31

"Mary and Bob" were holding hands, talking and smiling as they made their way around the displays set up for the wine tasting event. They were sampling very little and even when they did receive a glass, they only took little sips. "This sucks, here I am decked out head to toe in a killer designer dress, and I can not fully enjoy all that is being offered. Talk about pressure!"

Butch squeezed her hand and said, "Well, you could be back home freezing your ass off and completing a mile high of paperwork from the Benedict House."

She smiled, "You're right. It was so nice to spend a day in warm weather without lifting a pen."

"Yeah, and how about that little shopping spree on the Feds' money?"

She laughed, "Now that was priceless!"

The FBI was charged for her $355 dress. She had not planned on spending that much, but it was hard to find one that fit her body and height. When she walked out of the bathroom all dolled up, Butch had looked like someone had just pistol-whipped him. Her red dress was fitted and strapless. Her chest looked squeezed in and ready to pop out of the size two dress, which was the only size that would fit the rest of her body.

She had decided to wear her blond hair down and roll the tips into spiral curls. Her makeup was perfect but not too over the top. Her shiny red two-inch heels made her about six feet. Butch did not look bad himself. He had gone down and bought him some black slacks and a nice linen dress shirt. Together they truly looked great and like a happy couple, exactly like the script they were set to play.

Paula looked around the room and finally found what she was looking for. She squeezed Butch's hand and said, "Follow me." Passing two more displays, she finally arrived at the Brunson Winery display.

Behind the white cloth table stood a man around six feet two inches with olive skin. The man's shirt was embroidered with the name Michael Brunson and a grape logo and the words Brunson Winery. The man was helping another couple, so Paula waited patiently and said to Butch quietly. "This is the man that met Kathleen on the beach today. I just wanted to make sure he was legit."

The man finished pouring a glass of wine for the couple and wished them well. He then turned toward the stunning couple and said, "What a beautiful dress for such a beautiful night."

Looking at Butch he asked, "May I pour the lovely lady a glass of my fine chardonnay?"

Butch's face turned a little pink with jealousy but replied, "Yes, that would be lovely, and make it two, please." He placed his arm tightly around Paula's waist.

Paula, sensing Butch's reaction, took her arm and wrapped it around his waist in return. Smiling back at Michael Brunson she asked, "So is this a family-owned business?"

Pouring the wine into both glasses, Michael answered, "Yes, I am the third generation to make wine for my family. Our company is based out of our vineyard in Sicily, Italy."

After taking a sip of the wine, Butch asked, "So do you come to this festival every year?"

Before Michael had a chance to answer, a young lady appeared from behind a cloth wall and said, "I think this is our eighth visit, isn't it Mr. Brunson?"

Seeing his young assistant, Maria, he answered, "Yes, I believe you are right, Maria. It is amazing how time quickly goes by."

Looking at the couple, Maria said, "Excuse me, I hate to interrupt, but Mr. Brunson, there is a couple that wish to speak to you about purchasing a couple of cases for their restaurant."

Michael glanced back at Butch and Paula and said, "Excuse me. Maria will help you with anything you like. Have a pleasant evening."

Mr. Brunson then walked around the cloth backing and left. Turning to face Butch, Paula said, "This is really good wine, we should buy a bottle."

Butch looked at Paula with that smile and couldn't say no. He took out his wallet and asked Maria, "How much for a bottle?"

Maria said with a smile, "You are sampling one of our finest bottled year and Chardonnay. This bottle is five hundred and eighty-five dollars."

Sticking his wallet back into his pocket, Butch replied, "Thank you. We will think about it."

Not giving up, Maria said, "I think I have something you would like that is just as nice and smooth as the one you are sampling." She reached behind and grabbed another bottle and pulled out the cork. "Try this. I think you will like it very much."

Taking the glasses offered, Butch and Paula both tried a sip and nodded their heads in agreement. Paula spoke, "This is very nice as well, what is the price?"

This time Maria smiled and gave a little laugh, "The bottle is sold for sixty-five dollars."

Butch still couldn't believe this was somehow a bargain, but felt that he had to take out his wallet and make the purchase. Paula was being no help at all with her teasing body language.

Paula finally said, "We can have some tonight in our hot tub. Wouldn't that be fun, Bob?"

Pinching her waist, Butch replied, "Anything for my sugar buns!"

Butch handed Maria a hundred, and Maria made change. A new bottle was removed from the shelf and wrapped in tissue and placed in a bag that probably cost ten dollars just to make. Spinning around and grabbing Paula's hand, Butch said under his breath, "A couple wanted to buy a couple of cases—no wonder he left and Maria took over."

Squeezing his hand and placing a light kiss on Butch's cheek, Paula said, "Don't worry, we will write it off on our expense account."

"You damn straight we will."

Paula and Butch had covered a few more displays when they ran into Kathleen. Paula spoke first. "Hello, Trisha. What a beautiful dress. You look stunning!"

Kathleen turned a little pink and fidgeted with her hands some but answered, "Thanks, Mary, you look very nice yourself."

Turning toward Butch, Kathleen stated, "You look quite handsome, Bob. Are y'all enjoying your evening?"

Butch held up his wine bag and said, "Yes, we made our first purchase from Brunson Winery."

Paula chimed in, "They make very good wine. We met the owner, Mr. Brunson. He seemed like a fine man."

Kathleen caught the wink in Paula's eye and understood that Michael was okay to talk to. Smiling back, Kathleen announced, "That is fantastic. I am having dinner tonight with Mr. Brunson at eight o'clock in the main dining hall restaurant."

Butch answered, "Well, we hope you have a nice dinner."

"Have both of you had dinner already?" Kathleen asked.

Paula said, "Yes, we ate around six at the Moon restaurant. The food was delicious."

"I am glad you two are having a nice evening," Kathleen said. "I am sure I will see you again soon." With a smile, Kathleen said her good-byes, turned around, and headed back in the direction of the Brunson Winery's display.

Paula commented, "I am glad she is having dinner with someone tonight. That will be much safer than dining alone."

Butch responded, "I am not surprised to hear she has a date, a young single beautiful woman wouldn't last long at this event."

"Yeah, you're right. She did look quite amazing in that green dress."

Butch and Paula continued on around the rest of the displays. After a few steps, Butch completely stopped dead in his tracks and said, "Do you see that man staring at you at three o'clock."

Paula glanced over to her right shoulder and found FBI agent George Brown staring a hole into her. Trying to sound lighthearted, "That is one of the FBI agents, George Brown."

"Well, I don't care if he is the director of the FBI. He has no right to be undressing you with his eyes."

Paula looked back at Butch and said, "Down boy, he is doing no such thing. Besides, how do you think you've been acting tonight? You've not exactly acted like a choirboy."

Butch tensed a little at her sting but stated, "It's my job to be your husband, remember?"

Kissing him on his lips, Paula said softly, "How could I possibly forget."

Afterward she glanced back at George, but he had walked away irritated at the scene 'Mary' had made in front of all to view.

CHAPTER 32

Around 7:30 P.M., Butch left Paula at a little boutique that was adjacent to the wine displays and had wandered over to meet up with George. He found George sitting at a table beside the patio bar having a glass of water and eating a steak. He casually walked over and asked, "How is the steak?"

George finished chewing and then grabbed his napkin and wiped his mouth. With the other arm he gestured for Butch to have a seat in the empty chair beside him. "The steak is great. I highly suggest it and have them cook it medium rare."

Butch casually picked up the menu and glanced around at the items listed. A beautiful waitress appeared and asked if she could get him something to eat or drink. Placing the menu aside, "Just a glass of water for now, thanks."

The waitress grabbed a jug of water off the bar and came to the table and poured a glass for Butch and refilled George's water. George said, "Thank you," and she walked away with a smile.

George looked to be in his midthirties, had a well-toned body, and wore his blond hair short; he had the typical look of all FBI agents. "So how long have you been with the agency?"

George looked around before answering and replied, "About twelve years now. How about you?"

Butch answered, "Too long. I have over twenty-five years on the force." Butch took another sip of his water and continued, "What is the latest information coming from Kay-Loviett?"

George leaned forward and placed his elbows on the table and whispered, "They found Lisa's finger lodged in Eddie's throat."

Butch replied, "Jesus! The ME had said something was lodged inside but wasn't able to identify it right away."

"Whomever we are dealing with is twisted."

"So what do you think about this plan," Butch asked. "Do you think they are going to show?"

"Well, actually Kay-Loviett said it looked like one person committed the crimes at Kathleen's apartment."

"But there were two sets of footprints at the Benedict House."

"Maybe someone else is also a target, and they split up," George said.

"Maybe. Has any other crime been reported that matches their profile?"

George rolled his glass of water between his hands and said, "No, but I think someone will show up here. There is too much money involved, and crime families don't like to leave witnesses around." George placed his glass back down and leaned back in his chair. He motioned for the cute waitress, and she came along quickly. "That cherry cheesecake over there looks delicious. Could you bring me a slice with some black coffee, please?"

The young waitress, wearing the resort's logo pink linen dress, turned toward Butch to see if he wanted anything. "No thanks, I will just stick to my water."

Butch looked at the young agent's toned body and felt really old and out of shape. "So what is your specialty within the agency?"

George answered, "I studied criminal science at the University of North Carolina and then specialized in criminal behavior of sociopaths."

"Did you get a chance to view the crime scene?"

George frowned and replied, "I viewed the crime photos." A moment passed and then George said, "His work was over the top. There was no need to mutilate the bodies like that after they were already dead. They assigned me this case because we are looking at a wicked and twisted individual, and I think he will show up here if he has not already."

The waitress reappeared and dropped off his cheesecake and coffee. George immediately devoured the cake in a matter of seconds. Butch heard his stomach growl, and he reminded his brain that he had just eaten about two hours ago.

George picked up his napkin and wiped his mouth and leaned back in his chair with his coffee. At that moment another gentlemen in his midthirties with short blond hair pulled out a seat and sat down. George said, "This is my partner, Agent Bart Simmons."

Butch thought, "Are all of these guys alike? Do they mold them at the Bureau?"

The man stuck out his hand, and Butch leaned forward to shake his hand. Agent Bart spoke, "Kathleen just walked into the ladies room, and I was about to go and do a perimeter check."

Butch stood and said, "I will go with you, and then I am going to head up to the room and try to get some sleep."

George stood as well and agreed to pick back up on surveillance. Taking his coffee, he walked off in search of the ladies room.

Paula walked out of the boutique carrying two small bags. From behind her she heard a voice, "Did you buy a special nightie? Your husband is on his way back up to the room."

Paula turned around and answered with a frown, "No, I bought an outfit for tomorrow."

Smiling and displaying his perfect teeth, George said, "Butch takes over my detail at ten thirty. Why don't I swing by your place or better yet, why don't you come over, and we can get in the awesome hot tub on the balcony?"

"Have you lost your mind? What if a situation arises—we show up half naked and wet?"

"I promise not to get your hair wet, just bring your clothes and gear" and with that he walked away without a care in the world.

Butch did a sweep of the wine displays as Bart took the outer area around the resort. Rounding the last corner he found Paula talking to Agent George. Paula looked annoyed, but George was smiling, and then he quickly walked away with a big grin. Butch walked up on Paula and lightly touched her arm, "That young agent harassing you?"

Turning to fully face Butch she replied, "No, not really. I'm just tired."

"We can head back up to our room now. We both need some sleep."

Paula grabbed Butch's hand and the two of them headed out the door and down the path that led to villa ten. Patch was there along the trail watching the two detectives. As they passed by, he followed them at a safe distance.

Butch and Paula got to their room without any hiccup. Once inside, Butch made a sweep of the area and announced to Paula, "All clear."

Paula bolted the front door and made her way into the bathroom to undress. Butch watched her close the door and then decided to call his daughter. On the second ring, Mandy answered her cell, "Hello?"

Butch said, "Hi, sweetie, how are things going?"

Mandy replied with a little huff in her voice, "I'm at Ms. Bell' house. I'm babysitting the girls, and gonna stay the night."

"I see. Ms. Bell is working late, huh?"

"Yes, she told me it involved the same case that you were on. Where are you, Dad? When are you coming home?"

Butch looked down at the tile floor and shook his head, "I don't know how long this is going to take. I am glad you're at Aileene's house with the girls though. I know you don't like staying at my sister Darlene's house."

"How very perceptive you have become, Dad!"

Not wanting to fight, Butch told her that he loved her, and he would do everything possible to get home as soon as possible. A few more tense exchanges followed before Butch hung up the phone. As he was setting his phone down, Paula stepped out of the bathroom wearing the standard hotel robe.

She immediately walked over to the bed, removed the covers and laid face down on the pillow. Paula spoke in a muffled voice, "You can sleep beside me. This bed is big enough for the two of us. Just don't wake me when you leave."

With that, not another word was spoken, and Paula fell asleep. Butch quietly walked over to the bathroom and used the facilities and stripped down to his boxers. He made his way back to the bed but placed his weapon on the nightstand before getting into the bed with Paula.

From the balcony, Patch watched the events unfold and then left the same way he had entered. He went in search for Ms. Bishop.

CHAPTER 33

Patch was sitting at a bar having a cocktail when he spotted Kathleen Bishop or should he say Trisha Abbot, browsing in one of the resort's boutiques. He quickly scanned the area and was able to pick out both agents easily within moments. One agent was sitting at a table and the other one was standing along the end of the bar. Both were dressed in slacks with island-wear tops but neither blended in like tourists to Patch. Looking around some more his eyes spotted Melanie, his date for the evening. He smiled and waved to her as she looked around for him. Finally spotting Patch, Melanie walked up and took the seat beside him.

"You look very nice, Melanie."

"Thank you, Jonathan."

Melanie was a local girl out for some fun when she came across Patch at the bar earlier today. She had talked sweet and batted her eyelashes and flirted with Patch for over an hour before he finally asked if she wanted to join him for dinner tonight at 8:00. Little did she know that he found her annoying, but she blended in well with the crowd and that is what finally got her a date, not the endless chatting and over-the-top flirting.

To her credit, Melanie was pretty cute with her wavy, brown shoulder-length hair. She was average height, and her striking blue dress showed off her excellent legs. Patch stood up and extended his hand to Melanie, "Shall we go to dinner now?"

Melanie placed her hand inside his and said, "Yes, Jonathan, that would be lovely."

Together they walked inside the restaurant, and Jonathan gave his name to the young hostess. She escorted them to a table for two. Choosing the chair he wanted for her, Patch pulled it out, and Melanie took a seat. He then walked back around, took the seat that gave the best view of the restaurant, and sat down.

The hostess handed them their menus and announced, "Someone will be around shortly, and I hope you enjoy the evening."

Patch took the menu and replied, "Thank you."

Melanie frowned a little at the hostess. Patch could tell right away she was insecure and didn't like to be in the presence of other beautiful women. Patch tried to appease her and said, "The blue dress brings out the color in your eyes. I like both very much."

Melanie's face instantly lit up, and she smiled showing her perfect white teeth.

Satisfied that Melanie was happy again, Patch looked around and noticed how the restaurant was decorated nicely with cool island colors and had several potted plants. The large pots and plants allowed the guest moderate privacy, which was also perfect for spying.

Patch's attention was brought back to the table when a young waiter arrived.

"Hello, my name is Vondie, and I will be your waiter this evening. Would you like to place a drink order while you have a look at the menu?"

Melanie agreed and ordered the house wine, and Patch settled on a Corona. They were assured their drinks would arrive shortly and then Vondie left them.

Melanie had picked back up on a conversation they were having earlier when Patch saw Michael Brunson and Kathleen Bishop walk by a few tables over on his right. Kathleen looked amazing in her green dress with her hair falling down in curls along her shoulders and bare back. His thoughts immediately went back to this afternoon when he saw her showering in her room. He must have formed some kind of expression because Melanie stopped talking and was staring at him. He returned Melanie's gaze and gave her a coy smile. "I'm sorry, darling, my mind wandered a bit. What looks good to you on the menu?"

Kathleen was holding on to Michael's arm as he led her around the dinner tables. They finally arrived at their table and noticed immediately that it was designed for privacy. The table was covered with white cloth and had a beautiful arrangement of orchids in the middle. Beside the table was a chilled bottle of Brunson wine in a silver canister on stilts. Michael pulled the chair back for Kathleen, and she tried to sit as gracefully as possible considering the thigh-high split in her dress. Feeling his eyes all over her legs, she looked up and said, "I don't think the designer intended anyone to actually sit in this dress."

Michael laughed out loud and said, "On the contrary, Trisha, I think the designer knew exactly what he was designing."

Kathleen felt the heat in her cheeks but looked up and met Michael's eyes and smiled back. She asked, "And how do you know the designer was a he?"

Michael winked at her and said, "Just a hunch."

Michael then pulled the other chair out and took a seat. The waiter appeared immediately and began to pour them a glass of chardonnay. Michael lifted his glass and said, "To a wonderful evening with some very good wine."

Kathleen smiled back at Michael and lifted her glass to touch his. After the clink of the glasses, she brought the glass to her lips, inhaled, took a slow sip, and savored all the many flavors before finally swallowing. "Michael, this is really good! What is the name and year?"

"I am glad you like it," said Michael, smiling. "The name is Brunson Blue, and the year is 1998. This bottle is typically not sold at restaurants. I brought it with me for us to have with dinner tonight."

Kathleen replied, "Well if you are out to impress me, it's working."

Michael stated simply, "Yes, I am out to impress you."

Feeling herself blush again, she picked up the menu the waiter had left and began to scan the options. Michael placed a hand over hers and with the other hand he gently touched below her chin and raised it up so he could see her eyes. "Are you blushing?"

Kathleen was speechless and could only just continue to stare into his dark green eyes. She was mesmerized with everything about tonight. Here she was sitting at dinner with a man she had just met who took her breath away. Everything about him was gorgeous. He had impeccable manners, a wonderful personality, a good, reliable job, and he was a very classy dresser. Of course it didn't hurt that he had a killer body and was heir to a fortune. Kathleen kept asking herself, "What is wrong with this picture? A guy like that doesn't just pick up a stranger who happens to be a teacher. No wait, he thinks I'm a receptionist."

She continued to gaze into his eyes hoping to see something that would give her answers to why she was here with him. Moments must have passed because the waiter appeared out of nowhere. Michael broke the stare first and released his hands from hers; he held the menu up and ordered a starter that she couldn't even pronounce. The waiter confirmed the order and disappeared again. Kathleen decided to keep the conversation light and asked, "Have you eaten here before? What do you suggest?"

"Yes, I have eaten here on many occasions, and everything is very good. If you like seafood, they have a really good broiled fish that is stuffed with shrimp and crab. The sauce they put over it is made with white wine and avocados. It is truly divine, and you must try it before you leave the resort."

Kathleen answered, "I love fish and especially shrimp, so I will give it a try tonight."

Michael smiled back pleased and motioned for the waiter. When the waiter appeared he said, "We will both have the fish with seafood stuffing."

The waiter left as quickly as he appeared and once again, Kathleen was left alone with Michael. She was struggling not to gawk at his beautiful face when Michael said, "What are you thinking? You look like a woman in deep thought?"

Kathleen slightly titled her head and just said it, "What are you doing here with me tonight?"

"Trisha, I don't understand?"

"I am a receptionist from Tennessee, and you live in Sicily and run a family vineyard. Out of all the beautiful women here, why did you choose to have dinner with me?"

Michael leaned forward in his chair and whispered, "Because you are genuine and real. I don't see that everyday with the people that surrounded me."

As if it was planned in a script somewhere, the band began to play, and Michael touched her hand and asked, "Please, dance with me?"

She couldn't get a sound out, so she just nodded yes. He quickly came around and pulled her chair out from under her and helped her stand. Together they walked to the center of the dance floor and began to dance with his body very close to hers. They danced around the room as if no one else existed. The music sounded very faint to Kathleen as she flowed from side to side. She could feel his tight muscles beneath his jacket as her arms and chest rubbed against him. When the song came to an end, neither noticed, and they still continued dancing slowly. Suddenly aware of his surroundings, Michael stopped and guided her back to their table. As soon as they both sat down, their first dish arrived.

Trying to concentrate on the plate of food, Kathleen picked up a slice of homemade bread and began to spread the spinach, artichoke, and cheese dip on it. Finished with the task, she placed her knife down and then took a bite. It was superb. She glanced over to Michael, and he had just started the same task, and she watched him slowly take a bite.

When she finished chewing her first bite, she asked, "Do you have to work tomorrow during the day?"

Michael grinned back and said, "I think you just read my mind."

Blushing slightly, Kathleen refused to look down this time and continued to hold his stare. Michael continued, "Spend the day with me tomorrow. Let me surprise you, just come dressed casually and bring a bag with your swimsuit."

Without thinking, Kathleen immediately nodded her head yes and said, "There is nothing I would rather do than spend the day with you."

Michael lifted his wine glass to hers and said, "Tomorrow it is."

The night continued to be so effortless for a first date. They talked and laughed and shared stories about their families and work. Of course it was hard for Kathleen at times to remember that she was Trisha Abbot. Other than a few awkward moments where she had to make some things up, it was a very lovely evening.

The main dish was served and as he promised, the fish was delicious. After dinner, they both decided to share the flan for dessert. It didn't take long for the waiter to bring the flan out on a platter with two spoons. At this point in the date, they were acting like school kids. They were taking turns feeding each other, and then they fought over who was getting the last piece. Kathleen thought, "This is perfect!"

The night finally was coming to an end when the waiter brought over the check and Michael settled up. Michael said, "This evening surpassed all my expectations. I hope you had as good a time as I did."

She reached over and grabbed his hand and squeezed it, "Tonight was amazing, and I am very excited about spending more time together tomorrow."

Michael helped her out of her seat, and then they began to make their way out of the restaurant. When Kathleen approached the door, she felt as if she was being watched. She stopped walking and quickly turned around to only see various couples sitting at tables enjoying their night out. She realized then that it was probably the agents looking after her, so she shrugged off the coldness on her neck and continued out the door behind Michael.

Patch had just finished paying his bill when he saw Kathleen turn around and glance over the restaurant. He thought, "You feel my presence, don't you, Kathleen?" And then he looked at Melanie and smiled.

CHAPTER 34

Kathleen had her arm draped around Michael's extended arm as they made their way through the resort and outside into the gardens and patio bar. Kathleen's heart was aching for this night to continue, but her mind knew better. Stepping away and removing her arm, she said to Michael, "Thank you for a wonderful evening. I look forward to seeing you tomorrow."

Michael pulled at Kathleen's arm, stepped toward her, and kissed her on the lips. The kiss was short, but her heart was doing flip-flops. Not being able to help herself, she raised her arms around his neck and kissed him back with a long passionate kiss. Feeling the heat and her blood rush through her body, she knew she must stop. Slowly she let go and took a step back, smiling. Michael put his hands in his pockets and grinned back, "I will meet you in the lobby at nine in the morning."

Kathleen nodded and slowly turned around and headed down the path that led to villa ten.

Patch escorted Melanie out of the restaurant and said, "Thanks for a great evening. I have an early appointment tomorrow, but maybe we can do this again sometime."

Melanie read his body language and realized that this date was over. She smiled back and said, "Sure." She walked away toward the bar at the resort lounge area. As she walked away, she was hoping he would call her back and ask for a number, but no luck there. Glancing at her watch, she saw that it was only 9:30; she figured that the night was still young and at least she got a fantastic meal out of the date.

Patch made his way out toward the patio bar and found Kathleen in Mr. Brunson's arms. Glancing around he only saw one agent standing along the pathway that led to villa seven. Patch decided to go ahead and walk down the pathway that led to villas eight to ten a few steps ahead of Kathleen. As he passed the happy couple, he was able to hear their good-byes and then her footsteps walking behind him. When Patch approached the split in the pathway he chose the path to villa eight without ever glancing back toward her.

Floating along the pathway on cloud nine, Kathleen somehow made her way back to her room. Her mind was racing with images and thoughts of the evening. She really liked this guy and he seemed to feel the same way about her. Who would have thought that in the course of forty-eight hours she would feel so many different mixes of emotions? With images of Eddie and Lisa filling her mind, she quickly got her head out of the clouds and looked around to make sure she was alone. Kathleen then reached inside her handbag and found her key and glancing around once more, she let herself in the room.

Once inside, she bolted the door and walked around checking behind all doors and even under the bed, again. Satisfied she was alone, she walked over to the balcony, unlocked the door, and walked out to get some fresh air. With the salt air and breeze filling her senses, sleepiness began to overwhelm her. Walking to the edge of the balcony she looked around over the railings and felt completely alone and safe. She returned inside her room and locked the balcony door behind her. Seeing the flimsy lock, she decided to push the large leather chair in front of the glass door. Thinking of baby Mia, she felt clever instead of foolish. Next, she sat on the bed and removed her strappy shoes. The effects of the last two days were really taking a toll on her body, and it was all she could do to get up and remove her dress before falling back into the comfy bed.

Victor was standing on the balcony of 1020 and peering into Kathleen's room. He could see her lying on the bed naked with her eyes closed. "Nice. I am going to take it very slow with this one and enjoy every minute," he said to himself. He continued staring, scanning her entire body from her red painted toes to her rich auburn hair. She looked at peace, and he could see her chest rising and falling with each breath she took. She really was quite striking with very unique features. It wasn't often you found a female with natural red hair and olive skin. And her hair was natural.

Reaching inside his jacket he removed his cell phone and dialed Patch. "I need you back in Chicago. I can finish up here. The plane is scheduled to leave at midnight."

Just like that he barked his command, and Patch would listen and follow without any questions asked.

Kathleen was fighting sleep because she needed to get back up and brush her teeth and remove her makeup. She felt the right side of her body jerk and instead of falling into a deeper sleep, she sat straight up. Suddenly she felt very exposed and grabbed the beach towel lying on the floor and wrapped up. Looking around the room and then toward the glass door she thought she saw a shadow move over a lounge chair. She quickly made it to her bathroom and threw on the white guest robe. Stepping back into the bedroom, she slowly walked toward the balcony but could only see tree limbs moving in the ocean breeze. She thought, "It was just the limbs creating shadows that danced around the balcony furniture and floor." Still feeling a little spooked, she reached to the side of the glass doors and began to pull the fabric across the entire length of the glass. The fabric was sheer but it gave her some comfort. Heading back toward the bathroom, she began her nightly ritual and then changed into her cotton tank top with matching shorts. Finally ready for bed, she made her way back into the bedroom never once spotting the malicious look on Victor's face as he peered through the tiny crack between the fabric and wall.

CHAPTER 35

Aileene was headed toward Baxter Street with her warrant when she got the call back from Agent Kay-Loviett. The agent had put a team together and was driving toward Evangelina's Restaurant as she spoke. From the looks of traffic, it appeared they would arrive about the same time. The clock on the dash read 5:32, but it would take another thirty minutes just to go another fifteen miles. With some luck on her side, she hoped to arrive around 6:00. It would help if she had a siren but really did not want to call attention to herself as she arrived at the restaurant. She wanted this search to go as smoothly as possible. Even the agents were arriving in unmarked cars. Hopefully with a team of about five, they would look as discrete as possible. The last thing Aileene needed was the media showing up and filming a chaotic scene only to find her with egg on her face after finding zilch in the restaurant. Realizing this would be her only opportunity to call the girls, she picked up the phone and hit speed dial.

Mandy answered on the third ring, "Hello?"

"Hi, Mandy, how is everything going there?"

"Hi, Ms. Bell. All is good. The girls just finished eating and are working on their homework while I clean up the kitchen. Do you have time to talk to them?"

"Yes, only a few minutes though. Hey, Mandy, make sure you lock all the doors okay?"

Mandy rolled her eyes and responded, "My dad is a cop, remember? That is a habit I formed at age two, but I will double-check now while you talk to the girls."

"Thank you, dear."

Mandy handed the phone to the youngest daughter, Feebe, and she heard a shrill voice, "Mommy, when you coming home?"

Mandy walked the entire bottom floor checking all eight doors. She also opened up the door to the garage and made sure the garage door was closed. Satisfied, Mandy returned to the kitchen where the girls were sitting at the table with their homework and began to finish up the dishes. When the oldest girl Shelly was finished talking, she took the phone and spoke to Aileene.

"Ms. Bell, I checked all the doors and garage doors, we are locked up tight so don't worry about us."

Aileene thought to herself, "Easier said than done." "Thanks, Mandy. I really appreciate you staying over tonight. I don't know how late I will be. Also, if the girls want to crash in my bed tonight, let them. Gotta go now, bye, Mandy."

"Good-bye," replied Mandy, and then she hung up the phone and picked up the last dish to dry.

Aileene had just hung up the phone when she heard a siren coming up behind her. Noticing it was a fire truck she pulled to the side as much as possible considering that she was on a three-lane highway. After about two minutes, she was back up to speed and was now only about five miles away from the restaurant. It was about two miles later that she began to see the smoke and traffic began to slow considerable. She said, "Oh come on, this is not what I need."

For the next five minutes she had only crept about a mile. Looking at her GPS, she realized that she was a little over a mile away and determined the fire must be somewhere close to where she was going. Another five minutes passed and she could now see what all the commotion was about. According to her GPS, her destination was engulfed in flames. "Oh my God! Surely that is not Evangelina on fire?"

She pulled her car to the curb, turned off the engine, and grabbed her briefcase and locked up the door. Immediately a policeman came running over toward her. "Ms. you are going to have to move your car."

Aileene pulled out her ID and said to the cop, "I have a warrant to enter the Evangelina Restaurant. Please tell me that is not it on fire?"

The officer did a double take and said, "I'm sorry Ms. Bell. I didn't realize it was you, and yes, that mess is the Evangelina Restaurant."

Aileene said, "Shit, shit, shit!"

The officer continued to stare as Aileene walked back and forth behind the police barricade in front of him. Pulling out her cell phone, she dialed Agent Kay-Loviett. As soon as she answered, Aileene said, "The damn restaurant is on fire!"

Kay-Loviett responded, "You have got to be joking?"

"I wish I was."

"We see the smoke up ahead. I am going to use the siren now, and we will be there in a minute."

Aileene couldn't believe what she was seeing. She walked back over to the officer and asked, "Do you have any idea how this started?"

The officer pointed to the fire chief that was a few steps away inside the barricade. "Chief Sharp should be able to help you. Let me escort you over there."

Aileene followed behind closely to the officer and was quickly introduced to Chief Sharp. "I have a search warrant for this restaurant, and I have a team of FBI agents about to show up. Do you have any idea how this fire happened?"

The Chief replied, "Unofficially, it appears to be a grease fire in the kitchen."

Aileene then asked, "Do you know if it was started intentionally?"

"I'm sorry, Ms. Bell, but it is too early to tell. However, you probably would be interested to know that they found a body inside."

Aileene turned around at the sound of Kay-Loviett's voice, and she could see the team of agents running toward her with badges flashing.

Kay-Loviett walked right up to the chief and asked the same questions and a few more about the fire. When she was done she walked over close to Aileene and then motioned her to step away for some privacy.

Aileene whispered, "What do you think happened?"

Kay-Loviett looked sharply at Aileene and said, "What we have here is a leak. They knew we were coming and torched the place. I just hope that is not Agent Dave Wittfield lying in the rubble."

CHAPTER 36

It was 10:45 P.M., when Paula rolled over in bed and made the decision to go see George. Looking around the room she could see she was alone. She must have been sleeping very deeply to have not heard Butch get up and leave. Slowly getting out of bed, she stretched and then made her way toward the closet. Opening up her luggage, she grabbed jeans and a T-shirt, and quickly put them on.

Walking back over to her nightstand, she picked up her piece, checked it for bullets, and shoved it in her waistband at her hip. She wasn't sure where Butch or Agent Bart Simmons were, so she eased the door open and looked out the small crack. Seeing no one standing around, she opened the door fully and made her way down the path toward villa nine.

Reaching the staircase that led up to room 920, Paula once again looked around to make sure she was not seen. Confident she hadn't been noticed, she climbed the stairs and then gently tapped on George's door. George opened the door with a big grin and yanked Paula inside. George bolted the door back and said, "I turned the hot tub on a while ago, so it should be nice and hot now."

Paula never turned around, instead she dropped one shoe at a time, and then she pulled her shirt over her head and threw it toward the bed.

Next, she reached inside her pocket, pulled out a clip, and with one swift motion she wrapped her long blond hair up on top of her head. George was gawking at her bare back and said, "Turn around. I want to see you."

Slowly Paula removed her gun and placed it on the table and then she unbuttoned her jeans and pulled them down. She finally turned around only wearing her underwear. Last, she twisted her fingers along the top of her lace thong and gently pulled them down and stepped out. She said, "You promised not to get my hair wet, remember?"

Chicago

It was 8:30 P.M. and Kay-Loviett and Aileene Bell were downtown at the Chicago Police Department sitting in a large conference room with Agent Bass Floyd and police officer Lee Matthews. They were putting a task force together to monitor the Fernandez family and Chicago Steel Company. Their biggest concern at the moment was to determine the source of the leak and to see if their witness was safe.

Floyd said, "This isn't good. We planned to have at least a good forty-eight hours before they found Ms. Bishop. If there is a leak, they already know where she is and very well could already have people on the island."

After an hour later and several lengthy discussions, Kay-Loviett said, "I'm pulling McNeil and Williams off the witness and bringing them back here" and with that she picked up her phone and dialed McNeil's number.

"They are two hours ahead of us right?"

Floyd answered, "Correct it should be around 11:30 there."

Butch was just finished checking around villa ten, when he felt his phone vibrate in his coat pocket. Looking around to see if he was still alone, he removed the phone and answered, "McNeil."

"It's Kay-Loviett. We have a situation here, and we need you and Williams back in Chicago."

Butch said, "What about Kathleen?"

"I want you to leave her with Agents Brown and Simmons. She will be covered, and they will be ready if anyone shows."

"Are you sending more agents?"

"Yes, I have two more leaving out in the morning. Look, I think the real threat now is back in Chicago. The Fernandez family knows we are coming after them, and we could really use your help."

McNeil asked, "How soon do we need to leave?"

"I have a plane waiting on you now at the airport. Agent Floyd is talking to our agents as we speak. The witness will be covered. Just get to the airport as soon as possible."

Butch agreed and quickly hung up the phone and started his way back around villa ten toward his room. When he rounded the corner, Paula appeared coming up the pathway from villa nine.

Butch took a double take and said, "I thought you were asleep?"

Paula shook her head no and said, "I woke up and couldn't go back to sleep, so I decided to take a look around. All looks good toward villa nine."

Butch was about to ask another question and then quickly remembered his pressing news, "We have to leave ASAP. There is a plane already waiting on us at the airport."

Paula looked surprised and asked, "What is wrong?"

"I'm not real sure. I only had a quick conversation with Kay-Loviett. It appears something big is happening and she didn't have the time or just didn't want to get into it over the phone."

Paula started to climb the stairs and said, "I will go and get Kathleen."

Butch grabbed Paula's arm and said, "No, we are to leave her here with the other agents to watch her."

Paula pursed her lips and said, "Okay, but I think we should tell her in person that we are leaving."

Butch said, "I don't know. I think we should let her sleep. She needs the sleep to help her remember what Eddie said."

Paula said, "Do you think it really will make a difference? I just don't want to leave her without saying good-bye."

"Me neither, but I think this is one decision we have to make in her best interest."

Going back down the two steps, Paula shook her head and said, "She is going to be so mad."

Butch opened their room door, and they walked in and quickly threw everything in a bag.

Ten minutes later they were out the door and walking along the pathway when they ran into Agent George.

Paula stopped walking and placed her bag on the ground and said, "We are headed out now. Take good care of her. I still think she is in danger."

George responded, "We will. Have a safe flight."

With that Butch picked up Paula's bag, and they continued down the path. A few steps later Paula glanced over to see George giving her a wink, and she smiled back.

CHAPTER 37

Aileene Bell finally pulled into her driveway at 10:30 P.M. While waiting on the garage door to open, she glanced around and saw no lights on except the fixture in the foyer. That was a good sign. Mandy was asleep instead of watching TV or playing on the computer in the study. All the girls had school tomorrow, and Butch would be pleased to know that Mandy was not still up.

Aileene pulled into the garage and immediately hit the garage door to close. Glancing in her back mirror and looking around, she felt safe to now exit her car. This was a routine that she had followed since practicing as a prosecuting attorney. You never knew when a person would want revenge from a past conviction. Now that she was district attorney, the risk was even greater that harm could come her way. Putting the bad thoughts out of her mind, she opened her car door, then turned toward the seat, and grabbed her briefcase that was resting on the passenger seat. Aileene got out and then made her way inside the house.

Immediately after opening and closing the door, she entered her code in the alarm system. Turning around, she headed for the study. Once she made her way inside, she turned on the study light and walked over to her desk. Setting her briefcase down on the floor, she noticed that Mandy had only left two phone messages. Picking up each message she quickly read over each one and decided that nothing was too important that couldn't wait until tomorrow.

Aileene sat down and removed her high heels. She then stood back up and carried her shoes out of the study with her; she turned out the light and headed toward the kitchen. Once in the kitchen, she flipped the light switch and walked over to the fridge and found a leftover salad and a bottle of wine. Pulling them both out, she set them on the counter and then removed a wine glass from a cabinet and a fork from a drawer. With her items she made her way around the island and sat on her cushioned barstool.

With one hand she poured the bottle of wine and with the other she punched the fork into the salad. After a few bites she had had enough of the day-old salad. The lettuce was just a little too soggy. Standing up with her wineglass, she walked over to the trash canister and threw away the plastic container holding the salad. Taking her shoes off the counter, she left the kitchen with her wine glass and turned off the light. Walking toward the foyer light she made her way to the spiral staircase and then began to climb the stairs to the second floor.

With each step, she could feel her body aching. The hard fall she took earlier today outside the courthouse was now showing its ugly face. She was sure to see a nice big bruise on her ass in the morning. After everything that had happened over the last two days, she was exhausted. When she finally reached the second floor, she noticed immediately that something was not right. The door to the guest room was standing wide open, and the bed was still made up.

She quickly walked over to the girls' rooms and found the same: doors open and beds made. Turning toward the opposite side of the hallway, she quickly walked to the master bedroom and opened the door slowly. The room was dark, but with the streetlight shining through the window, she could make out Mandy, Shelly, and Feebe all asleep in her bed.

A rush of emotions washed over Aileene as she remembered telling Mandy that the girls could sleep in her bed. It was unusual to find Mandy here though. She always slept in the guest room. As she made her way over to the bed she could see Mandy was in the middle and the youngest was curled up next to her with her head resting on Mandy's shoulder. Smiling and thinking quietly, "If Butch could be here to see this!"

Looking at her nightstand the time read 10:45, Butch should be in the air by now and headed home from God knows where. Kay-Loviett had not shared the witness's location, and she didn't ask. From listening to their conversations, she had concluded he was on an island with a two-hour time difference. Staring back at the three girls she noticed how they all looked like little angels as they slept. Not a sound was made just peace and quiet as their chest rose and fell with each breath. Satisfied that all were sleeping well, she turned back to the master bedroom door and shut it. As another precaution she locked the door.

Quietly she walked into the master bath, closed the door, and then turned on the light. She took another sip of her wine and then set the wineglass on the counter. Walking over to the shower, she leaned in, pulled the handle out, and adjusted the temperature. Turning back around, she removed her dirty clothing and then held them up for a closer inspection. Frowning, she threw her designer pantsuit in the laundry basket and walked into the doorless shower and under the warm water. The water felt fantastic, but she decided to make it a little hotter hoping that would ease some of the soreness out from the fall. Finally after about five minutes of standing under the hot water, she began to wash her hair and body.

Fifteen minutes later, Aileene stepped out of the shower with one towel wrapped around her hair and another around her body. Walking over to the mirror and vanity, she pulled out a brush from the drawer and unwrapped the towel from her head. Quickly, she began to brush out her wet hair. Next, she picked up the blow dryer from the bottom drawer and began to dry her hair. After about five minutes, she felt that would be enough for now, and turned off the dryer and placed it back in the drawer below. Unwrapping her towel from her body she turned around to see if there were any signs of bruising. There was—on her right cheek a large bruise was beginning to form. Frowning, she wrapped the towel back around her body, and then made her way to the master closet.

She opened the door and immediately the light came on triggered by the opening door. She removed her towel and walked over to her wall of drawers to pull out her pink cotton sleepwear set. Finding them on top, she bent over and began to step into the bottoms. When she stood up, she pulled the top over her head and turned around toward the mirror and froze. She opened her mouth but not a sound came out as she read the message written on the glass.

This is a warning District Attorney! You are not as safe as you think. Back off now and the girls will live.

Walking over to the mirror, she could see that the message had been written using red lipstick. She timidly placed a shaking finger on one of the letters and found that it was still wet. She immediately began screaming for the girls and ran out of her closet and opened the bathroom doors to find Mandy sitting up startled from all the noise.

Glancing and seeing the girls still beside Mandy she made it over to the bedroom door and found that it was unlocked. Panicking now, she locked the door and ran over to her family portrait hanging on the wall. She quickly threw it off the nail and began to open her wall safe with shaking hands. With the safe door finally opened, she removed her pistol, turned the safety off, and turned back around to a screaming Mandy.

"What is going on Ms. Bell? You are frightening me?" Mandy cried.

Aileene whispered, "Keep the girls in the bed and try to stay calm. Someone is in the house."

Mandy wrapped both girls in her arms and held them tight. Seeing their mom holding a gun and checking the bedroom and bath the girls began to squirm and whimper. Feebe asked, "Mom, what are you doing?"

After looking under the bed, Aileene finally put the gun on the nightstand and sat down on the bed and held her girls tightly. After a few moments of silence, Aileene released all the girls and said, "Everything is going to be fine now. Mommy is just going to make a phone call and have someone come over and check the house."

Aileene was trying to reassure herself just as much as the girls. Mandy finally spoke. "It is really late. Why don't you girls lay back down with me and try to go back to sleep."

Shelly was having none of this and got out of bed and walked around to the other side where Aileene was sitting in a chair on the other side of the nightstand. With the house phone clutched in her hand, Aileene held out her free hand for Shelly to climb into her lap as she began to dial the number. After one ring, the phone was answered on the other end. Aileene spoke slowly and clearly, "It's District Attorney Aileene Bell, I need someone at my house, forty-eight Birch Street, now!"

The officer on the other end asked, "What is the situation, District Attorney?"

"Someone has been in my house and possibly still is."

Noticing Shelly's body tensing, she squeezed her tighter and said, "For now my family is safe, and we are armed and locked inside the master bedroom located on the second floor."

The officer responded, "Stay there, Ms. Bell, and remain on the line. We should have an officer there in less than seven minutes."

With his response, Aileene was able to smile at Shelly and then nudge her in the direction of the bed. Carrying her phone with her, Aileene got out of the chair and got in the bed with all the girls. Aileene was on the end of the bed with her loaded pistol within arm's reach sitting right beside her on the nightstand. She would not hesitate to use the gun if necessary. She thought, "This is my house damn it, and no one is going to lay a finger on my girls!

For the next several minutes nobody said a word as Aileene stroked Shelly's hair with her free hand. Feebe had already gone back to sleep in Mandy's arms—the joy of being six. She thought, "They are so young and innocent at that age." Obviously she had never been fully awakened to notice what was going on, unlike Shelly who was just two years older. Shelly's body was still very tense, and Aileene squeezed her arm around her a little harder.

Finally a voice on the other end of the line spoke. "Ms. Bell, this is officer Lee Matthews. We have five officers in the house now, and they will radio back to me when it is safe for you to go to your bedroom door and open it. Don't be alarmed when you hear some noise. They are thoroughly checking each room."

Aileene replied with a quivering voice, "Thank you."

Ten more minutes passed before Officer Matthews reported, "Ms. Bell, there is an officer outside of your bedroom door now. Please put down any weapon you have and open the door."

Aileene released Shelly and said, "It is okay now. There is an officer outside the door. I am going to go over and open the door now. You stay here on the bed with Mandy, all right?"

Shelly nodded yes, and Aileene got out of the bed, put the safety back on the gun, walked over to the door, and unlocked it. Turning once more back to her girls, she then turned on the light and opened the door. Aileene was finally able to let out a deep breath when she saw the officer. Opening the door wider, she motioned for him to come in.

"Ms. Bell, I am Officer Jennings. The house is secure, but I would feel better after we have a chance to walk through this room."

Aileene spoke, "There is a message in the closet."

Officer Jennings motioned for the others to come in and Aileene went back and sat on the bed with the girls. Glancing over at the clock, it read 11:35 P.M., and Shelly was still awake.

"Mandy, I would like for you to take the girls back to Shelly's room and sleep there tonight."

As Aileene picked up Feebe, Shelly was starting to protest, but Mandy quickly took over and said, "It will be fun to all sleep in your bed for a change. Come on."

Reluctantly Shelly grabbed Mandy's outstretched hand and an officer followed the group out the door and into Shelly's room down the hall. Satisfied that they were safe, Aileene shut the door and asked the officer to stay close. At that time, Aileene made her way back into her master suite and into the closet. Once inside, she reached around an officer, pulled a housecoat from a hanger, and pulled it on over her sleepwear.

She spoke in a much calmer voice now, "I touched it, and it was still wet. That was when I realized someone was here while I was in the shower. I immediately called out to the girls and made my way into the bedroom. They had woken up to my screaming and were confused. I then ran to the bedroom door and checked to make sure it was still locked."

Officer Jennings asked, "And was it?"

Aileene said with a frown, "No."

Another hour had passed as Aileene did a walk through the house with the officers and gave her statement of events. They were now seated in the study and going back over the events of the day. She had just finished describing her run in with the white service van when Agents Kay-Loviett and Floyd arrived.

Just like her previous conversations with the agents, she was able to give the street name but no other detail about the van other than it was white. Next, the tech guys entered and the taller one said, "All finished up in her closet and master bedroom. We found the red lipstick. The intruder put the tube back into her makeup drawer in the bathroom. We bagged it for prints, but we don't anticipate finding any since he left it behind for us."

Kay-Loviett said, "He is taunting us. Does this jerk really expect us to just turn our back on this case now just because he threatened her family?"

Aileene gave Kay-Loviett a look that could kill but said nothing. Deep down she knew she was right. None of them were going to back down, especially now that today's events had proven they were on the right track. Aileene stood up and walked over toward her desk and sat down in her leather chair. Lifting her briefcase off the floor, she noticed it seemed heavier or was she just that tired. Aileene spoke, "I should check this to make sure all the paperwork is still in here. If he took this he would know exactly what evidence we had to build a case against him as well as Chicago Steel."

Placing the briefcase down on top of her desk, she undid the latches and popped the case open. Suddenly Aileene stood up, walked backward with a face white as a ghost, and then fell to the floor knocking her leather chair over. Everyone in the room jumped to attention and went over to Aileene and the briefcase.

Looking into the briefcase they all could clearly see what had made Aileene faint. After looking, Kay-Loviett wished she had stayed put. Agent Floyd reached down and picked Aileene off the floor and carried her out of the study. Kay-Loviett finally found her words and spoke to the officers, "It appears the Fernandez family discovered our undercover agent."

Kay-Loviett quickly closed the briefcase that contained Agent Dave Wittfield's hand with his wristwatch and wedding ring. The hand was really the only identifiable body part; the rest were just parts and pieces of his body.

CHAPTER 38

A flight attendant woke Detectives Butch McNeil and Paula Williams twenty minutes before landing in Chicago. Butch looked at his watch, and it read 6:30 Barbados time. Calculating in his head the time difference, he removed his watch and rolled the dial to read 4:30. Paula slowly rolled her head around to face Butch. With a yawn she asked, "What time is it?"

Butch yawned back and said, "Early—four thirty Chicago time."

Paula moaned and closed her eyes. "Is someone meeting us with a car?"

Butch replied, "Yes, at least I think that is what she said."

Paula stared back at Butch and smiled, "We need more sleep. Do you think they will just take us home and have us report tomorrow at eight?"

Butch frowned, "Babe, it is tomorrow."

The jet landed smoothly, and they taxied down the runway and finally stopped by a black sedan a couple of minutes later. The airport was not exactly busy this time of day. With the looks of things, it appeared the FBI had not forgotten them. Agents Kay-Loviett and Bass Floyd got out of their car and stood waiting as the jet cut its engines and began the process of unloading its passengers. Once the door was open, and the stairs were let down, Paula finally dragged herself off the seat and began to pull her luggage down from the overhead compartment.

Butch said, "Here, let me get that."

Paula stepped back and allowed Butch to help her. When Butch had her bag, he turned around to face Paula, and she said, "It was sorta nice having a husband to wait on me, even if it was only just one day in paradise."

Butch grinned back and playfully said, "Can you imagine what would have happened if we stayed a full week?"

Paula laughed out loud and grabbed her bag from Butch and led the way off the jet.

Below, Butch could see Kay-Loviett pacing back in forth in front of the sedan. Walking over with his bag, he finally approached the agents and said, "Good morning. I am surprised to see you two here. I thought you would have sent someone else to collect us."

Kay-Loviett walked around the back of the car and hit a button on her key ring and the trunk popped up. As Butch placed both pieces of their luggage in the back, he heard Kay-Loviett say, "Things have gotten more complicated."

Butch could see that Kay-Loviett was fidgeting some and that seem a little out of character for her. He was about to ask a question when Agent Floyd jumped into the conversation. "Last night we had an incident after we talked to you on the phone. First of all, no one is hurt and everyone involved is safe."

Paula spoke, "What happened—this almost sounds personal."

Agent Kay-Loviett answered, "It is. The Fernandez family sent a man to Aileene Bell's house last night with the intent to scare us off this case."

Immediately, Butch took a step toward Kay-Loviett and said, "Oh my God! My daughter was there to babysit. Are you sure everyone is okay?"

Agent Floyd answered, "Yes, Aileene is the most shaken up. Her oldest daughter was really frightened and asked a lot of questions. You would be very proud of your daughter, Mandy. She remained calm and in control, and did a lot to ease the little girls' minds about the situation."

Kay-Loviett placed a hand on Butch's shoulder and said, "Let's get out of here, and I will take you to them. I will tell you everything once we get in the car."

With that everyone piled into the sedan and sped away from the private airport.

CHAPTER 39

Kathleen rolled over in bed and looked around the room. She smiled really big and laughed out loud a little. "Am I really here in paradise? Truly, this is no dream!"

She glanced over at the bedside clock and saw that it was 7:00 A.M. She slowly got out of bed and yawned as she stood up and stretched. Kathleen calculated that she had slept almost ten hours, and boy, did she need it. Walking over toward her balcony door, she removed the furniture that she had placed in front of the door as a precaution and then opened it. She was immediately hit with the cool ocean breeze and the smell of saltwater. Smiling, she said, "A girl could get used to this!"

Walking out toward the edge of the balcony she could see the beach below and a few workers walking around setting cushions on the lounge chairs. It was going to be another gorgeous day without a cloud in the sky. The staff was already hard at work. She could see the same waiter from yesterday afternoon bringing a cup of coffee to a young lady stretched out under an umbrella reading the day's paper. Realizing she only had two hours before she met up with Michael, she hurried back inside in search of her workout clothes.

Opening up the closet she pulled out her clothing from one of her bags and frowned. "This is not exactly the right season for sweats."

She held on to the sports bra and threw the sweats back inside. Walking over to the dresser, she opened the top drawer and took out the swimsuit bottoms that she had not worn yet. Thinking this will have to work, she removed her nightclothes and quickly put the bottoms and bra on. She decided that she would run on the beach and left the tennis shoes in her bag. Opening the second drawer, she pulled out a beach cover-up and threw it over on top. Next, she walked into the bathroom and brushed her teeth and used the facilities. Walking over to the sink, she washed up and quickly pulled her long hair back into a ponytail. Looking in the large mirror she was pleased with the outcome. Grabbing the key and a towel she put her sandals on and headed out the door.

Walking down the pathway, Kathleen never once gave Butch or Paula a second thought nor the cell phone still charging in her room. She was only thinking about getting her run in and getting back to quickly change for an exciting day with Michael. Making her way toward the beach, she spotted a vacant chair and placed her towel, sandals, and cover-up on top. She decided to slip the key in her sports bra instead of putting it with the other items. Moving a few steps away from the chair, she began to lean over to one side and stretch. After about three minutes of stretching, she was off running along the coastline.

Kathleen never timed herself. She would just run until she felt herself getting tired, and then she would turn around and push herself all the way back. Probably thirty minutes had gone by before Kathleen realized just how far away she had gotten from the resort. Seeing no other resorts along the beach, she decided to turn around and head back. It was at this time that she began to feel isolated and alone. She felt a chill go down her sweaty spine as she realized she should have notified someone that she left. "Would someone have noticed me leaving? Is someone watching me at all times?" she asked herself.

Feeling a little uneasy she picked up her pace. She had not noticed that it was a little more difficult to run on sand versus pavement until now as her calves were beginning to ache a little. Without slowing her pace, she continued on. A few more minutes passed, and she could see a couple up ahead walking. She immediately felt a sense of relief and began to slow down. A few more steps later, an image of Michael began to fill her thoughts, and she could already picture him in only swim trunks and a grin. "I wonder where he is going to take me today?" she thought.

Without realizing it she had picked up the pace and never once thought about her aching calves all the way back.

Chicago

It took forty-five minutes to reach the ranch that was located well beyond Chicago's city limits. By that time, Agents Kay-Loviett and Bass Floyd had completely briefed Butch and Paula on all the details of the events from the day before. Taking a winding road off a rural highway, the sedan made its way down a paved road lined with white fences. With each turn Butch could feel the anxiety building inside him. He wanted so desperately to see for himself that all his girls were safe. It was funny, even though Aileene and he had decided to call it quits, he still thought of her and her girls a part of his extended family. It was easy to love Shelly and Feebe. They were free-spirited and independent little girls, just like their mother. His thoughts wandered to Mandy, and he immediately smiled. "That was my girl! Only Mandy could take a horrific event and turn it into just a grain of salt."

After hearing stories from Floyd, Mandy had really stepped up and taken care of the girls. He was very proud of her and couldn't wait to tell her himself. Butch continued to stare out the window and counted nine horses and two stables with arenas before the sedan finally stopped outside what appeared to be the main house. The house looked to be about thirty-five hundred square feet and was built out of stone and cedar, and had a circular driveway in front. The ranch was truly beautiful with special quality of solitude.

Before he could open the door, he saw Aileene running out of the house to greet him. She was dressed in jeans and a Chicago Cubs sweatshirt with her hair loose and bouncing with each step. For once Aileene forgot about appearance and ran down the remaining steps and threw herself into Butch's arms. Butch embraced her and gently rubbed her back with one hand and with the other smoothed her blond hair. He was speechless at first, but then he quickly fell back into the routine as Aileene's protector and guardian.

He stated quietly for her to hear only, "Shh, now everything is going to be just fine. I'm home now and no one is going to mess with you or our girls."

Paula got out of the car and watched the events unfold without a word. She thought to herself, "He still loves her," and a smile crept across her face. She had always liked Aileene. She was tough, and she knew what she wanted out of life despite choosing a profession that was dominated by men. Somehow with a demanding job she was still able to be a great mom to her precious little darlings. Those were strong characteristics for any women to have and Paula had always secretly admired her.

Butch broke away first but reached down and grabbed Aileene's hands and placed them in his. "Let's go inside now. I want to see the girls, and you can tell me all about it."

Nodding, Aileene turned toward the house and led Butch up the stairs without even acknowledging the agents or Paula. Looking back, Butch saw the others and Paula getting everything out of the car. Paula had made a gesture with her hands to go on up with Aileene, so he did.

Once inside, the house was eerily quiet. Never letting go of her hand, he walked around to examine the house. It was very typical of a ranch house with its leather and wood furniture. The house gave off a strong masculine appearance, but at the same time, it was comfortable and warm. He walked across the rug made out of hide and found his way to the kitchen. There he could smell vanilla coffee brewing and saw a couple of muffins set out on the table. The girls were nowhere in sight. Looking back at Aileene, he asked, "Are the girls still sleeping?"

She answered, "Yes," and motioned for him to have a seat and then said, "I will make us some coffee."

Butch nodded his head but said, "I still want to check on the girls."

Aileene could fully understand and relate to the pressing need to just see them and make sure they were all safe. She pointed down a hallway and said, "Third door on your left. Be careful—the door squeaks."

Butch headed quietly toward the hallway, and then placed his hand on the correct doorknob. He slowly opened the door and slightly pulled up so it would not squeak, and wake the girls. The movement must have worked because the door never made a sound. Quietly, he walked over to the bed and found all three girls wrapped up tight in a denim comforter. Mandy was in the middle, and she had an arm wrapped around each girl. The girls were snuggled tight beneath Mandy's arms and were sleeping soundly. He resisted the urge to bend down and kiss all of them out of fear of waking them up.

Looking at the girls, it was easy to see they were not all related. Mandy had straight black hair and thick black eyebrows, while the other two girls had a head full of golden ringlets and light skin. Looking at their embrace one could easily see that they all cared for one another despite the fact that they were unrelated. At that moment, Butch was so relieved to see them and was so glad Mandy continued to care for the girls despite his past mistakes with Aileene. Satisfied they were safe and sound, Butch slowly turned around, made his way out of the bedroom, and quietly closed the door the same way he opened it.

He walked back to the kitchen and found Aileene surrounded by Paula, Kay-Loviett, and Floyd. They were talking about their next move when Butch entered the kitchen and took a mug of coffee from Aileene. Turning toward Butch, Aileene spoke with fire in her eyes, "Those girls are my life. But I refuse to live my life in fear and always looking over my shoulders. That is no life for them or me to have. We are going to continue this investigation, and I am going to make Emilio Fernandez wish he never set eyes on me or my family."

Butch set down his coffee mug and picked up Aileene's hand and kissed it gently. "We will bring him down. You can count on that!"

"I think it is wise for you to stay here with the girls for now, just until we can figure out our next move," said Paula.

"Yes," agreed Agent Floyd. "Plus we would have to use more men watching you when they could be out working with us to catch Emilio."

Aileene looked at all of them and finally said, "You are right, the more men we have to help build a case, the better. I want to be kept informed daily, so I will be ready to move forward when this case goes to trial."

All agreed and then they made their way over to the large kitchen table to plot a net to catch the Fernandez family.

CHAPTER 40

Kathleen had just stepped out of the shower when she heard her cell phone ring. A lump quickly formed in her throat as she quickly wrapped up in a towel and made her way to her nightstand. Picking up the phone on the fourth ring, she said, "Hello?"

No voice answered, and the call was quickly disconnected or lost. Kathleen checked her messages and did not find any. Pressing another button she found her missed call number and hit send. She did not recognize the number but was certain it was not the number Butch or Paula had used earlier to contact her. A male voice answered "Hello?" on the second ring.

Kathleen stated, "Hi, this is Trisha Abbott, I just missed a call from this number."

The man on the other end responded, "Yes, this is Agent Bart Simmons. You're a fast runner. Next time a heads up would be great so I can wear proper shoes. But nonetheless, I enjoyed the workout."

Kathleen's face turned a little pink and on instinct she turned around to look to make sure she was alone in her room. Finally after being a little embarrassed and spooked she said, "You were running with me the whole time?"

The agent answered, "Yes, you would have never spotted me though—I'm that good."

Kathleen didn't know what next to say so she just remained quiet.

The agent said, "Are you still there?"

Kathleen said, "Yes, um I hope it is all right, but, um, I sort of made plans today."

It was now Agent Simmons's turn to remain quiet. She continued, "The plans are with Michael Brunson. Um, Detective Paula Williams told me that he checked out and I could spend time with him."

The agent finally spoke and said, "Yes, he was the one you had dinner with, correct?"

"Yes, we had dinner last night, and he invited me to spend the day with him before he had to work tonight at the wine festival."

Agent Simmons said, "Yes, I was given the information about Mr. Brunson. Agent Brown and I will be on your detail today."

Kathleen interrupted, "Why not Butch or Paula? I mean, well, I just haven't met you, I don't know what you look like."

The agent responded, "That is a good thing that means I'm doing my job well. Also, plans have changed. The detectives were called back to Chicago last night and did not want to wake you since it was the middle of the night."

Kathleen was a little surprised and said, "Why? Is everything okay?"

"Nothing for you to worry about, they just needed more manpower on the case. So what time are you meeting Mr. Brunson?"

Kathleen was a little put off with the fact that she was left on the island with two agents that she had never met. There wasn't anything she could do about it now, but would have at least liked to have received a courtesy call. If not last night, sometime this morning when everyone was awake. She finally said aloud, "I am meeting him in the lobby at nine A.M."

The agent asked next, "What is the destination?"

Kathleen hesitated a little and finally said, "I'm sorry, I don't know. He just told me to dress casually and pack a swimsuit."

He said, "Any indication that you might leave the island? He does have the money and the means to do a quick day trip and be back before the festival starts."

She said, "No, I'm really sorry. Would you like for me to call him and get a better idea where we are going?"

After a few moments, Agent Simmons finally answered, "No, it will be fine. I can have a stand by ready, but what I need are a couple of minutes in the lobby to scope out some things. I also want you to arrive sometime after nine ten."

Kathleen looked at the clock and it was 8:30 and said, "Well that shouldn't be a problem, I just got out of the shower."

Before he ended the call he said, "One more thing, stay vigilant about your surroundings and don't go anywhere alone. If you think something is not right or you get into any trouble don't hesitate a second to call.

If for any reason your phone doesn't work, I will need you to signal to me somehow."

Kathleen said, "Well I am wearing a hat with a scarf wrapped around the band. How about I remove the scarf if trouble arises?"

He responded, "That works well, if you take the hat off, just place it somewhere near you at all times."

Kathleen agreed and quickly hung up the phone and ran back into the bathroom to get ready. First she dried her long auburn hair and then decided to pull it back off her forehead with a hairband. She picked up her beach bag off the floor and threw a ponytail holder, clip, and brush inside. Next, she pulled out her makeup bag and began to cover her face with a base that contained sunscreen. Considering the heat, she decided less was better. It only took another five more minutes to cover her eyes, cheeks, and lips. Stepping back into her bedroom, she walked over to the closet and found the outfit she had bought the day before. Removing her towel she reached inside the bags and removed the emerald green halter and white cotton shorts. Trying them on again she walked over to the mirror and decided that she still liked the outfit and removed the tags.

Walking back over to her closet she found the green and orange scarf and walked over and picked up the hat off the coffee table. She took the old scarf off and wrapped the new one on. When she was done she glanced at the time and saw that it was 9:05. Going back into the bathroom, she removed her swimsuit from the hook and packed it in the bag along with sunscreen and a sarong. All she had to do last was find the right shoes for the day and get her beach sandals. When she was walking back toward her closet, she stopped when she heard a knock on the door.

Thinking to herself, "Who could that be—maid service?"

She put down her beach bag and headed toward the door. Unlocking the bolts she opened the door to find Michael Brunson staring back at her with a smile.

He spoke first, "Hi, Trisha, I was on my way to the lobby when I realized that I should tell you to bring a camera."

Kathleen was glancing over Michael's body and trying to catch her breath to respond, "Oh, a camera, well, believe it or not, I forgot to bring mine on this trip." Michael seemed a little surprised but Kathleen continued, "I am a terrible packer!"

Michael returned her smile and asked, "Are you ready? I see your bag packed—did you pack a swimsuit?"

Stepping to the side, to let him in, she said, "Yes, come on in, I just need to throw in some sandals. Do I need a towel?"

Michael stepped inside and said, "No, all is taken care of."

Kathleen left him standing there, went over to her closet, and picked up two pair of shoes. She threw one pair in the bag, put the other ones on, and said, "I'm ready now."

Michael had made his way over to the balcony door and looked outside. He said, "You have an amazing view! Don't you just love this feature of the suite?"

Walking toward the balcony she said, "Yes, and the ocean breeze is so nice in the evenings."

He walked out and tapped the hot tub, "Have you used this yet?"

Kathleen grinned a little and looked down, "No, not yet, but I plan to before this trip ends."

Michael walked up to Kathleen and placed a hand on her chin and slowly lowered his mouth for a sweet, soft, little kiss on her painted lips. She didn't move and just sort of stood there mesmerized by his kiss. He said, "Shall we go now for our little adventure."

Kathleen swallowed and said, "Yes."

Michael motioned her back in the bedroom; he followed her and then turned around to lock the balcony door. With her eyes, she swept back over the room and saw her room key and phone charging on the nightstand. She walked over and grabbed both and stopped only once more to grab her hat and bag by the coffee table. Closing the door behind her they made their way down the stairs. Once they hit the bottom, Michael said, "This way— toward the beach."

Kathleen glanced around and saw that he was pointing at the pathway that led to the beach, and he began to head in that direction. Kathleen stopped walking and looked around. She thought, "Oh no, I told the agent I would be in the lobby."

Michael stopped walking and then turned back around. "Did you forget something?"

Kathleen just smiled and started walking toward him, "No, I'm good."

She thought to herself, "Okay, Agent Simmons, you said you were good. I hope you are because plans have just changed."

They continued along the path and then Michael stopped and bent over to pick an orange flower. He stood back up and took a step toward her. With one hand he pulled back her hair over her ear and with the other, slid the flower inside her hairband. He then took her hand and walked beside her all the way to the beach.

A few more moments passed and they were walking the same path she had taken earlier this morning on her run. At the last resort lounge chair that bordered the property, she saw a small rubber boat with a motor pulled up on shore. Michael began to slowly lead her in the direction of the boat and then stopped and said, "Do you get seasick?"

Kathleen looked at the boat and looked at him and said, "Well, I've been out deep sea fishing before, but the boat was much bigger."

Laughing out loud he said, "We are only going to be in this boat for just a short ride."

She followed his outstretched arm and saw him pointing at a small yacht anchored in the water out ahead. He continued, "That boat is the one we will use today."

Kathleen said, "That is a beauty! I can't wait."

With that she held onto his hand and placed one foot inside the boat and then the other. She didn't release his hand until she had safely sat down with her bag placed on the boat between her legs. Michael then removed his shoes and placed them inside the boat and began to push the boat into the water. With such ease, he was able to hop inside with very little effort.

He turned around toward the back and started the motor. Within a few seconds, they were off toward the yacht. As they were riding across the water Kathleen began to study Michael's movements. He was wearing a white linen button-down shirt and his tanned muscles were flexing as he was steering the boat. Water was splashing up and some was hitting his khaki shorts. She had noticed that somehow he managed to keep his shorts dry with their launch. Turning her focus back to his face she tried to guess his age while studying the small lines around his mouth. Next she looked at his dark hair blowing in the wind and couldn't find any gray. Maybe he was around thirty-three or thirty-six at the most. Her thoughts suddenly ended when the boat rode up a large wave and lunged forward just in time to make it over. Michael glanced back at her and smiled, "I planned that. Don't worry."

She gave a wink back but said, "I'm going to keep holding on just in case."

It only took about five minutes to get to the yacht, and she could tell with each minute that passed the boat was much larger than a small yacht. When they finally arrived she glanced over the vessel and was pleased that it looked healthy and safe as well as big. The bigger the boat, the less likely she was to get seasick if they ran into a short storm. She thought, "Turning green is sure to put a quick end to any date."

She brought her mind back to Michael and watched him as he turned off the motor and grabbed a rope to tie the boat up to the yacht. He didn't know, but this was his first test. Her father had taken her out many times fishing, and he said you could always tell so much by the way a man tied a knot. Growing up on the coast he had always lectured her on getting on boats with men. He would say, "If a man's knot doesn't look like this, don't board the boat."

Michael finished up with the ropes and caught her smiling at him. He asked, "What are you smiling about?"

She simply said, "You just passed a very important test."

Michael looked back at her with a strange look on his face but held out his hand for her bag. She lifted the bag and handed it over and then took his hand and climbed on board the yacht.

Once she was on, he asked, "Was I suppose to know what you meant?"

Kathleen reached up and placed her hand on his head and smoothed back his hair off his forehead. "No, but you should know that I would have stayed on that dingy if you hadn't done so well with those knots."

Michael looked back at his work and then back to Kathleen, "So you have been on boats before?"

Kathleen nodded yes and began to walk around and check out the yacht. "This is quite nice. Did you rent her for the day or for the entire length of the festival?"

Michael sat her bag down on the clean white leather seat and answered, "Neither, I bought it last night."

Kathleen turned around with a stunned look on her face. She knew he had money, but just to drop it on a boat while so far away from home. Just how much money did he have? Walking around some more, she could easily tell this yacht was well over two million, maybe even a little more with more exploring inside.

"Let's take a look inside and see what it looks like," said Michael.

Turning back around she said, "You have not been inside yet?"

Shaking his head no, he motioned for her to continue on inside. "I did have someone give it a test drive and thoroughly check it out before I bought it."

Kathleen could only smile and really didn't have anymore words to offer. She began to make her way toward the living room area and saw that it was decorated very tastefully with dark leather lounges and green and white throw pillows. There was a mounted flat screen TV on the opposite wall with a satellite connection. On the opposite side, there was a bar that was stocked with Brunson wines. She looked back at Michael and smiled, "So what would you do, if I didn't like wine, and I only drank Coronas?"

He walked over to the fridge and opened it up, "I noticed the other day you were holding a Corona at the bar, so I stocked it full."

Taking a closer look she could see bottled waters along with at least twelve Coronas. Playfully she said, "You thought I would possibly drink twelve in one day?"

He grabbed two and shut the door back and said, "I would help. Now let's go check out the rest of the boat."

First he opened the Coronas and then removed some limes from a container and placed them inside. She couldn't help herself and looked at her watch. It was only 9:30 in the morning. He noticed her gesture and laughed, "Come on," he said, and grabbed her free hand and led her down a small hallway.

The hallway opened up to a master suite with bathroom. The bed had a headboard made of white leather and on each side there were windows opening up to the outside with screens. The bed had a chocolate brown and teal blue comforter with large teal blue throw pillows. Lying at the bottom of the bed were two white robes folded up nicely. She looked closely to make sure his and her name was not already embroidered on them. She found no names and wasn't sure if she was disappointed or not.

Moving on toward the bathroom, she found it much larger than most bathrooms she had seen on a boat. This one had a nice shower that would hold up to two people. Thoughts of him and her began to slowly creep up in her mind, and she quickly took a big swig of the cool Corona to try to jump back to reality. She walked out of the bathroom and then took another small hallway that led to a kitchen area. On the table she saw fresh fruit already cut up and croissants with different jars of jelly. Juice was in a container on the counter as well as coffee brewing. She immediately turned and asked, "Are we alone?"

He quickly picked up on why she asked and said, "Yes, the coffee pot is on a timer."

Next they made their way out and found the other bedroom and bath. This room and bath were smaller, but very comfortable nonetheless. It was decorated with a solid red cover with black and red throw pillows. Kathleen spoke, "Whoever decorated the boat did a really good job."

They made their way back toward the kitchen, and they each filled a plate for breakfast. It was Kathleen that offered, "Let's go sit outside and enjoy this beautiful weather."

Michael agreed, and they made their way back outside. Once Kathleen was seated, she reached over and grabbed her sunglasses and hat from her bag, and put them on. Michael had picked up a remote and was surfing for some music. Finally satisfied with some classic rock, he placed the remote down and lifted his Corona up for a toast. "To us, and a great day with a chance to get to know each other better."

Kathleen raised her bottle and clinked it up against his and took another drink. She looked out over the water, and she could see two other boats anchored around them. She thought to herself, "That agent is really good if he is on one of those boats."

CHAPTER 41

The Ranch

It was 7:30 in the morning when Mandy and the girls decided to get up. When they entered the kitchen, they still looked very tired, and the younger ones looked confused with their new surroundings. Butch stepped out from behind the island, walked over and gave each a big hug. Leaning over to get to their eye level, he asked the girls if they saw the horses outside. With a big smile spreading over Feebe's face, she ran toward the living room with the large wall-length window and peered outside. It wasn't long before Shelly and Mandy walked over to join Feebe. Just a few moments later all in the room could hear Feebe scream out, "There, I see one, it is black with white spots!"

Mandy spoke next, "There are three more to your left."

Shelly turned around and asked, "Can we ride them?"

Aileene answered first, "Yes. You can ride as soon as you have eaten some breakfast."

The girls cheered and ran back into the kitchen. Agent Floyd opened up the fridge and asked, "Do you want orange juice or milk?"

Mandy and Feebe wanted juice, and Shelly wanted milk. Floyd opened up the cabinet to get the glasses and began to pour. Kay-Loviett walked back over to the window and gazed out into the morning light. Paula walked over to her and said, "I can ride. I will take the girls out one at a time."

Kay-Loviett stared back at Paula and said, "Well, it looks like the decision has already been made, and I'm not going to tell those girls differently. Is Aileene always like this?"

Paula just smiled and said, "Oh yeah, and she will kick your ass in a courtroom."

Kay-Loviett replied, "Good, cause I'm counting on that."

In the kitchen, Butch pulled out a skillet and got some eggs out of the fridge. It took him a few tries but finally found the right cabinet for a bowl in which he could scramble the eggs. He already knew how each one liked her eggs and didn't even ask. Aileene walked over to the pantry and found some bread. She then took out a few slices and placed them in a toaster. Floyd had already gotten three plates out with silverware. With all the teamwork, it wasn't too much longer before the girls were all seated at the table and eating quietly.

Mandy finished first and looked up and found her dad motioning her over to talk. She got up with her dishes, walked over, and placed them in the sink. Seeing the girls were okay without her, she wandered over to the living room to her dad. Butch immediately gave her another hug and whispered, "I'm so proud of you for being so strong, and I'm so sorry this mess has happened."

Surprisingly, Mandy did not pull away, and she held on tight to her dad. Finally, she slowly pulled away and looked him in the eyes and said, "Tell me the truth—how much danger are we in?"

Butch looked back and could see the fear in her eyes as well as the strength. Butch let go of her shoulders and picked up her hands and brought them to his chest. He finally answered her truthfully, "We are all in danger, and I need you to continue to be strong. Those girls look up to you so much, and I need you to continue to ease their mind but at the same time be vigilant."

Mandy smiled back, "I love them like they are my little sisters. If I can help it, no harm will come to them."

Butch pushed back the tears that were trying to form and gave Mandy a quick hug and then led her over to the large window. Pointing with his hand he said, "There is the arena where we will go riding. It is the closest to the house, and it is fully enclosed. We will go out as a group, and we will come back as a group. Everyone stays together."

Mandy shook her head and agreed. A few moments passed and he said, "I will eventually have to leave you here with Aileene and the girls. We have to put the bad guys away, and I can help them do that."

Turning back toward him she smiled. "Of course you do, you are the best! We will be fine."

Butch was a little saddened. One day he would be able to look at Mandy and say, "I'm done. No more bad guys," but unfortunately now was not that day.

Caribbean Sea

Kathleen had just finished telling Michael about her boating adventures with her dad when a small boat started making its way toward them. Michael stood up and said, "If you don't mind, I have hired a skipper and a cook for the day. I believe this is them now."

Kathleen smiled back and said, "Not at all."

She then got up and made her way over toward Michael to stand. She watched as the men pulled along the side of the boat, boarded, and then the smaller boat pulled away again driven by someone wearing a shirt with the marina logo. The two men introduced themselves as Captain Barnes, the skipper, and Jose, the cook.

Kathleen extended her hand and shook theirs and then they left them alone again on the deck. She took a seat back on the leather bench seat, then turned her head toward Michael, and asked, "So where are you taking me?"

Looking down at her he said, "Why don't you go change into your swimsuit and when you return, I will tell you?"

She didn't answer right away. In the last few days, there been way too many surprises—enough to last her a lifetime. She stood and finally agreed; picking up her bag, she made her way back inside the boat.

Kathleen decided to take the master suite and headed in that direction. Once she was inside, she bolted the door and placed her bag on the bed. Opening up her bag, she pulled out her swimsuit and sarong, and placed them on the bed. She saw her phone. She picked it up and looked to see if she had any messages. She was a little disappointed that she had not heard from Butch or Paula. She thought, "They really didn't seem like the type to not call and say their own good-byes. Something must really be going on back home for them to leave in the middle of the night. I wonder what Agent Simmons is not telling me?"

She had not been introduced officially to either agent and only caught a glimpse of one who was talking to Paula last night at the wine festival but couldn't be certain what he looked like. She had no idea if that one was Agent Simmons, and she couldn't remember the name of the other one. She tossed the phone back inside the bag and then began to remove her clothing. She pulled on her bikini and wrapped the matching sarong around her waist. Deciding to leave her shoes behind she repacked her bag with her clothing and headed back out the door.

As she made her way down the hall she could hear the rattle of pots and pans in the kitchen as the cook was stirring around whipping up something for lunch. She thought, "Good thing I decided to run this morning."

When she entered the living room area, she spotted Michael in the bar making a frozen drink. "That looks good. What is it?"

Michael got two cocktail glasses down and filled them both to the top. Handing her a glass he stated, "Dirty monkey. It has bananas in it."

Kathleen lifted the glass and placed her pink lips on the straw and sipped. "Nice, I like it."

Michael said, "Great, why don't you get the drinks, and I'll get some towels, and we can head up toward the front. There are some lounge chairs there."

Kathleen headed in the direction that he pointed to and carried the drinks as he asked. Reaching the front of the boat she found not two lounge chairs but one oversized lounge bed with a dark blue cushion and one big pillow. Kathleen placed a drink on each table that was set up on the outside for their drinks while Michael laid out the towels. Once finished, Michael settled in on the bed and then pulled Kathleen down beside him. He spoke, "It didn't take long to get you in bed with me."

Kathleen gave Michael a playful punch in the chest and then wrapped her arms around him and gave him a kiss on his cheek. She then removed her arms and snuggled up beside him. As soon as she lifted her drink, the engine started, and the boat began to move forward. Looking over at Michael she said, "So where are we going?"

"It's a deserted island. I reserved it for the day just for us."

CHAPTER 42

Chicago

Officer Lee Matthews was behind the wheel of the black sedan with Agents Kay-Loviett and Bass Floyd in the back, going over some last minute details before they approached the Fernandez home. After a lengthy discussion at the ranch, the decision was finally made to move forward with the fire at Evangelina's restaurant and see what feathers would be ruffled with their inquiry. Detectives McNeil and Williams were following along behind them in a patrol car. After a couple of more turns, they finally reached the end of the neighborhood that housed the Fernandez estate.

Officer Matthews inched the sedan forward and stopped in front of a control panel that had a button for service and a keypad for numbers to be typed in. He lowered the window and pressed the service button. Looking around it was not hard to notice the top-level security that Emilio Fernandez had in place. Kay-Loviett looked out her window and saw what appeared to be a guardhouse just behind the gates to the right. She spoke first, "Well this is over the top. First we have to be announced, then given permission to enter the neighborhood, and now we have to go through the process all over again?"

Floyd said, "Look at the size of these walls—not only are they tall but look how thick they are."

As if someone heard them, the gates began to open and a man appeared wearing a suit and earpieces. Matthews said, "I'm not going to even guess what he is carrying under his jacket."

The man walked slowly up to Matthew's window and said, "Please follow the driveway up to the house. You are expected."

Matthews just responded "Thanks, buddy" and put the car back in drive and began to move forward again. The man in the suit did not stop the detectives, instead he stood back and watched and then saw to it that the gates closed again.

Paula looked back behind her and saw the gates closing. She asked Butch, "Can they close those with us in here like that?"

Feeling a little uneasy, Butch reached inside his jacket and felt his gun. Making sure it was still there and hadn't fallen out during the drive over here he finally spoke, "Well it doesn't matter now, and they are now closed. I don't like it though."

Paula said, "Me neither."

Matthews came to a circle in front of the house and decided to park there. He turned off the car and opened up the glove box and grabbed another weapon and hooked it under his left pant leg. Kay-Loviett just watched him but said nothing. They all got out of the car about the same time and together they walked up the flight of stairs toward the front door.

Before Officer Matthews could ring the doorbell, the door was opened by an elderly lady wearing a navy uniform. She took one look at the group and immediately frowned as she spoke, "Mr. Fernandez is expecting you. Please follow me."

Kay-Loviett said, "Thank you."

They all stepped inside the house and began to look around to get more familiar with the layout of the house. The lady paused only a moment and then headed down a long hallway. Kay-Loviett followed first and then the others slowly joined in as they continued to look around. The hall finally ended at a corner, only to open up to reveal another hallway to walk down. The lady finally came to a stop and then turned around and said, "Mr. Fernandez is waiting for you in the study." She motioned for them to enter the room.

The double oak doors to the study were opened and all could see Emilio sitting behind his very large and impressive desk. Once inside, the lady announced from behind, "Mr. Fernandez, the five visitors have arrived."

Emilio stopped what he was doing and looked up. "Thank you. Please shut the door on the way out." He stood up then and made his way around the large oak desk. He gestured toward the leather furniture for them to have a seat, "Please make yourselves comfortable. How can I help you?"

Butch was surprised at how fast he felt the blood rushing to his face. He wanted so badly to place his hands around his neck and squeeze the living shit out of him until he confessed to the break-in at Aileene's house. Somehow he was able to control it and looked over at Kay-Loviett.

Kay- Loviett reached inside her jacket and pulled out her FBI badge and said, "My name is Agent Kay-Loviett, and this is my partner Agent Bass Floyd. We are with the FBI."

She then turned toward her left and said, "With us are Detectives Williams and McNeil and over there is Officer Matthews all from the Chicago Police Department."

Emilio said, "I'm Emilio Fernandez, but I think you already know that."

Kay-Loviett didn't respond to his comment, instead she asked, "Is Mrs. Vivian Fernandez home today?"

Walking over and taking a seat and once again gesturing to the others to follow, he said, "No, I'm sorry, my wife and three sons left this morning for our vacation home in Madrid."

Butch said, "Isn't it a little early for Thanksgiving holiday at school?"

Emilio smiled and said, "Yes, but my wife has been very busy lately and decided that she just wanted to take some time off to spend with the kids. I suggested she go ahead and leave, and I would follow at the end of next week."

Kay-Loviett said, "Was this decision made before or after the restaurant in her name caught fire?"

Emilio stopped smiling and said, "That was a horrible accident. I lost a chef that had worked for me for fifteen years."

Butch asked, "Did you say worked for you? I thought your wife owned the restaurant?"

Emilio stood up and walked behind his desk to grab some papers. Walking back over he said, "Here is a copy of the title of Evangelina's Restaurant. You can see that it is in her name. It was a gift to my wife as an anniversary present."

No one spoke as Kay took the papers and glanced over them. Emilio continued, "There on the last page is a copy of the insurance company that will handle the paperwork with the fire. Also, I included the names of my lawyers who will be happy to answer any questions that you might have."

It was time to play hardball now. Reaching into her coat pocket, Kay-Loviett produced a copy of the search warrant for the restaurant and gave it to Emilio. She said, "I have a search warrant dated yesterday to search Evangelina's Restaurant. Before my agents arrived, the place was in flames."

Emilio continued to stare at Kay-Loviett without uttering a word.

She continued, "What do you think the chances are of a place burning to the ground on the same day a warrant was produced to search the premises?"

Emilio walked toward the double doors and opened them. He turned back around and stated, "It is an unfortunate situation that we are all in. If there is anything else, please call my lawyers. They are listed on the paper. Now, I have an eleven o'clock conference call, so please excuse me."

At that moment, two gentlemen wearing suits and earpieces arrived. The taller one said, "Please follow me. I will show the way out."

Just like that the meeting was over, and Emilio wasn't going to give any information or talk without his lawyers present. This had turned into nothing but "You see me and now I see you kind of meeting."

Butch opened his mouth and was about to say something when Paula grabbed his arm and said softly, "Stay cool."

Butch almost made it out the door when Emilio spoke, "Say hello to your girlfriend, Mr. McNeil."

Butch quickly turned around toward Emilio only to find the second man in a suit standing right in his way. Not giving an inch, Butch stepped to the side and said, "She will look forward to your visit in court, Mr. Fernandez."

Paula said to the second guard dog, "Easy big man, we are leaving."

With that she patted Butch's shoulder and then he turned around and followed the rest out the door.

The two men never left their sides until all were in their cars, and they started up the engines and began to make their way out of the estate. When they reached the gates, the doors were opened for them, and they quickly turned left and exited. Looking over her shoulder, Paula announced, "The gates are closing again."

With an angry voice Butch said, "He can't hide forever."

CHAPTER 43

An hour later, Kay-Loviett and Bass Floyd were sitting in the FBI office in Chicago waiting to hear back from her boss Gary Fields. Kay had called in earlier and was told to leave a message and Fields would get back to her. It wouldn't do any good for everyone to sit around waiting, so she sent Williams and McNeil to the police department to check in and get an update with the lab techs. Kay-Loviett finally spoke to Agent Floyd, "I think our case is in jeopardy."

Floyd responded, "Not necessarily."

Firing back, "Oh come on. By now Emilio has reviewed all the documents from Aileene's briefcase and has probably moved money around."

Floyd, "I don't think so. It would look worse now if money reappeared or disappeared from any of his accounts."

Kay-Loviett got up and stretched. She walked around to the corner of the room and began to pour some coffee. Looking back she said, "Do you want some?"

"Yeah, that would be great."

Kay-Loviett handed Floyd a cup and asked, "How long did you know Dave Wittfield?"

Floyd shuffled his feet some and looked down before he answered, "Five years. He was a great guy as well as a great agent. He will be missed terribly."

Kay-Loviett said, "How are the wife and kids holding up?"

"Terrible, as you can imagine. The service will be on Sunday. The wife decided to take him home to Washington State."

Kay-Loviett said, "I'll arrange a jet if you will send out a memo that a jet will leave early Sunday morning and return Sunday night."

"Yeah, I can do that. This job really sucks sometimes!"

At that moment, Kay-Loviett's office phone began to ring. She quickly walked over to her desk and said, "Agent Kay- Loviett."

"Hi, Agent Kay-Loviett, it's Gary Fields. How did your meeting go with Fernandez?"

Kay-Loviett walked around her desk, sat down, and grabbed a pen and paper. She spoke next, "Not well, he gave us documents about Evangelina's Restaurant, with nothing new and then lawyered up."

Kay-Loviett could hear Field sighing and then he said, "What we have here Agent Kay-Loviett is a mess. We have a dead agent, a D.A. with her family in protective custody, as well as a witness, and Emilio Fernandez has a copy of our case against him. Am I missing anything?"

Kay-Loviett responded, "The service for Dave Wittfield is on Sunday, and I am arranging for a jet to go to the services in Washington State."

That silenced Fields' rampage. "I am sorry to hear about the agent, and that makes this case even more personal. Do you have a plan yet?"

"Yes, but it is risky."

"Okay, spill it."

Kay-Loviett took a deep breath and then finally said, "We are going to bluff with our witness."

Paula and Butch were seated at a long table reviewing evidence from the crime lab. As expected, no fingerprints were on the briefcase or anywhere else in Aileene Bell's house.

Paula held up a photo of Eddie and asked, "I think the killer put Lisa's finger in Eddie's throat to make us jump through hoops. I don't think it means anything. He just wants to confuse us."

Butch looked up and said, "I think you're right. Look, I think it is time to call Kathleen and see if she remembers anything."

Butch took out his mobile phone and dialed Kathleen's number. After seven rings, he hung up. To be cautious, there was no voice mail set up. He looked over at Paula and shook his head. "There is no answer. I am going to ring Agent Brown."

Another moment passed and Butch said, "Voice mail."

Paula looked a little worried and said, "What about the other agent?"

Butch pulled out a card with Agent Bart Simmons's number and punched a few buttons. On the third ring, it went straight to voice mail. Butch got up and began to pace and said, "Why would all three not answer the phone?"

Paula answered, "I don't know, and I don't like it. I think we made a mistake by leaving her. She was a witness to our crime scene, and we left her in the hands of the FBI."

Butch frowned, "I don't like it either, with everything falling apart with the FBI's case, they could very well make Kathleen a part of their next move."

Paula got up now and picked up her phone. I'm going to call Agent Brown again. I have his number. After the fourth ring she left a message, "This is Detective Paula Williams, and I would like for you to call and give me an update on our witness as soon as possible, thanks."

Butch said, "Thanks?"

Paula smirked, "I'm trying to remain civil until we know more. Why don't you call Kay-Loviett?"

Butch picked up his phone and found Kay-Loviett's number and dialed. It also went to voice mail. "Do these people ever just answer their phone or do they screen all calls first?"

Paula said, "I think its time to call the chief."

Butch put a hand in his pocket and removed a silver coin, "Heads you call, and tails I call."

Paula nodded and Butch flicked the coin in the air. The coin hit the desk but then twirled around till it rolled off the desk and onto the floor.

Both Detectives bent over and peered under the desk to find the coin on heads. Frowning, Paula made her way over slowly to the desk and picked up the office phone and dialed the chief's office. Police Chief Arnie Wallace answered after the second ring, "Chief Wallace."

"It's Detective Williams. There is a good chance McNeil and I are off to meet up with our star witness again."

"Who is paying for this flight?"

"Sir, I think the FBI is toying with our witness, and it might be in her best interest if we get back to her."

Wallace said, "I'm not surprised. I don't understand why you left her and returned in the first place. Let me remind you that you work for the city of Chicago not the FBI."

Paula responded, "Yes, sir."

Wallace continued, "She saw the killer who committed one of the most horrific crimes of this year, and you left her in forty-eight hours."

Paula stated clearly, "You are right. I think McNeil and I should have stayed with her, and we are going to tie up some loose ends here and head back out to the Caribbean this afternoon."

Before hanging up, Chief Wallace barked into the phone, "I want an update as soon as you land and remember you report to me. I will handle the FBI."

Paula placed the phone down and Butch said, "Let me guess? He wasn't pleased."

Paula said, "That is an understatement, he wants us packed as soon as possible and return to the witness."

Butch pulled out his cell phone and said, "I'm going to call and check on the girls. They aren't going to be happy that I am leaving again."

Paula headed toward the door and said, "I'm going home. I will meet you at the airport. Call me when we have a flight time."

Butch said, "Oh, I guess I will make the flight arrangements."

"Yep, I made the call, so you book the flights."

Butch said, "Great, then I get the ass whipping when I turn in the expense report."

Paula winked and then closed the door behind her.

Small Island in the Caribbean

For the last two hours, Kathleen and Michael were relaxing in each other's arms drinking cold drinks and eating various snacks. They had talked about work, family, and vacations they had taken as kids. In her web of lies, she decided to keep her father real and tell of real stories growing up. She justified it somehow to herself that it didn't matter who she was or her job because she had a father.

She was a little worried a few times when she thought "Trisha Abbott" had slipped up. But Michael didn't ask any questions or give her the impression that he thought she was lying. She just found it so easy to talk to him. At times she thought about confiding in Michael about the events in Chicago and her drama over the last few days. Somehow she sensed he would understand and would protect her all the same. She thought, "Oh how I wish I could tell you the truth. I hate all this lying."

As if hearing her thoughts, Michael asked, "What are you thinking? You have that crooked smile on your face?"

Kathleen decided to keep quiet about her identity and reassess the situation tomorrow. So for now, she smiled really big and lied again, "Just wondering what to expect when we arrive at the island."

Michael seemed satisfied with her answer and responded, "Well, look to your left, and you can start to make out the shape."

Kathleen turned and then got up from the lounge and walked the three steps to the side of the boat. She continued to look intently out to sea as the island began to appear closer with each minute.

"So how big is this island? It doesn't look very big."

Michael answered, "The island is only one mile long and about a half mile wide. We will stop soon. There is a reef, and the water is very shallow around the island."

"A reef? Can we snorkel?"

"Absolutely, I have gear. Do you dive?"

"Yeah, but with all this alcohol consumption, I think I would rather snorkel."

Michael laughed out loud and then grabbed her hand and kissed it. "We haven't had that much?"

Kathleen just gawked at him and said, "We have had two coronas and one dirty monkey—all before noon."

At that comment he just smiled and wrapped her up into his arms and kissed her forehead. He finally said, "I will take good care of you today."

Kathleen didn't have to wait much longer. The boat finally came to a stop and she could hear the anchor being lowered. She said, "The island looks amazing."

"It is."

Turning back toward Michael she asked, "What is on the island?'"

Michael didn't answer and just grinned, "A surprise."

It only took a few minutes for the captain to prepare the dingy; Kathleen grabbed some towels and her bag, and Michael refilled their drinks. The captain helped them board the small craft, and in no time they were off gliding over the waves toward the shoreline. Kathleen smiled over at Michael as she held her hat with one hand and had the other hand wrapped around her fresh drink. Michael was sitting very close to her with one arm draped around her waist and the other holding his own drink. Once they hit sand, the captain jumped out and began to pull them to shore.

Michael swung his feet over the edge, jumped out, and then helped Kathleen out with her bag. The only things that managed to get wet were their sandals. Again, Kathleen was impressed! The captain jumped back in and said, "I will bring the chef now" and rode back toward the boat.

Michael took her bag and said, "Follow me. It's not far."

Kathleen matched his steps and made her way around the palms and flora until they finally came to a yellow beach cottage with a blue wrap-around porch. Climbing the steps after Michael, she could fully take in the breathtaking view when she got to the top. Looking back, she could see the boat anchored, and the dingy loaded down with the cook as well as a few baskets and bags. "Wow, I didn't even see this place from the water."

He responded, "Most people don't because their eyes are drawn to the coastline and the few mountainous hills to the left. Come now, I want to show you the inside."

Michael opened the unlocked door and said, "No point locking it." He shifted to the side to allow Kathleen inside. Instantly she fell in love. The inside had wooden walls that were painted a pale pink with dark wood trimmed windows and baseboards. The floors were made of natural stone tile with inserts of dark wood strips. The living room furniture was made of cane with large plush pink and white striped cushions. From there, she continued on into the kitchen area and found dark oak cabinets with wrought iron handles. The appliances looked new and there was a small table for two in the corner. Michael followed her and then placed her bag down on the table and grabbed her hand and tugged her toward the opposite end of the cottage. She could feel her heart beginning to pound loudly as she realized he was leading her toward the bedroom. One step away from the door, he stopped short and turned around to face her and said, "The cottage has only one bedroom, and it opens up to the back porch. Here is the most stunning view of all."

Feeling her heart begin to slow some, she made her way into the bedroom and immediately could see the view through the glass panes. Michael smiled and said, "I told you it was breathtaking!"

He then opened up the double doors and pulled her out on the balcony. Kathleen scanned the area, threw her arms around Michael, and said, "It is so perfect!"

From the balcony you could see the entire island and more water in the background. There were exotic birds in several trees and a small waterfall. Looking down she found a well-manicured garden with a swimming pool and hot tub. Over to the left side, she saw a cabana with a large grill and a table set up for two.

"I thought we could take a walk first while the chef prepares lunch. What do you think?" Michael asked.

"Sounds fantastic," Kathleen said and took his hand this time and led him down the back steps with a big smile on her face.

CHAPTER 44

Michael and Kathleen had hiked for about twenty-five minutes when they finally made it to the top of the hill. Michael was about four steps ahead of her, and catching up with him, she instantly noticed a red blanket spread over the grass and a cooler. At this point of the date, Kathleen was no longer surprised.

Michael walked on over and took a seat and opened up the cooler and pulled out two bottled waters. Kathleen took the water and immediately opened the top and took a big gulp. "Thanks, I really need this."

Michael smiled, reached out, took her hand, and pulled her down on top of him. Part of Kathleen's drink spilled, but it didn't seem to matter as Michael was holding her tight and kissing her. Kathleen felt her body tense, but it slowly began to relax as the kissing continued. At first, her hands were glued to his chest, but she began to feel around and touch more of his body as she kissed him back. She had ached inside to touch his hard, muscular body all over since the day she first laid eyes on him. Now, she was finally getting that chance.

Michael broke the spell when he slowly leaned away, and said, "I'm sorry that was a little fast."

Kathleen came to realize that she was lying on top of him and her sarong had fallen off and she was just wearing a swimsuit. Thinking to herself how easily things could have gotten out of control, she rolled off but quickly leaned up against him in a sitting position. Michael sat back up, straddled her backside, and pulled her inside. He wrapped one arm around her waist and with the other pulled her hair over to one side and then rested his chin on her shoulder. They were now in the perfect position to enjoy the view. Kathleen hadn't really noticed it until now. She said, "You can see for miles up here."

Michael kissed her neck and answered, "This is truly a private island, and the brochure said no one will bother you."

Kathleen slowly turned her face to the side and began to meet his kisses. The touching began again as she placed both her hands around his thighs. Michael was rubbing her neck and shoulder, and his other hand was still wrapped tightly around her waist. As his hand slowly made his way up to her chest, she began to grow warm inside. Whispering softly he asked, "Will you spend the night with me on the island?"

Kathleen released his thighs and moved forward where she could spin around toward him. Michael's green eyes had a touch of blue sea in them, and he had a grin on his face. She placed one hand on his face and the other on the ground and balanced herself until she could reposition. Finally she spoke, "You are right—this is a little fast."

Michael grinned more broadly and wrapped her up in a bear hug and rocked her side to side. He said, "Let's head back. I'm starving."

Kathleen agreed, and she grabbed his hands and pulled him up with her.

Michael took more water from the cooler, handed Kathleen her hat, and then they were back off down the hill. As they hiked back, Michael began to talk about his work some more and the places that it took him. Even though his vineyard was in Sicily, he traveled all over Europe selling and promoting his wines. He probably talked about Greece alone for fifteen minutes because that was one of his favorite places. He went on to describe how each of the islands that make up Greece is unique and different. One could spend years sailing around and exploring. Next he talked about Rome and Athens. With Kathleen's history background she could not get enough of his adventures and kept asking lots of questions.

Michael thoroughly enjoyed her interest and was amused because most people in his social circle had already been to those places and had experienced it themselves. Kathleen was different from anyone he had ever met before, and it was very refreshing. It was when he was talking about the Roman Coliseum that she finally slipped up and never even realized it. Conversation was so relaxed that Kathleen forgot she was supposed to be Trisha. In her defense, Rome was the city that she longed to visit more than any other place in Europe. They were probably about five minutes away from the cottage when she said, "When I teach my students about the gladiators, Rome becomes their favorite place to study. I myself would rather see the Sistine Chapel and the art museums."

Michael stopped and took Kathleen's hand. She gazed up and met his eyes but still hadn't realized what she had said. Thinking he was going to kiss her again, she was slowly pulled closer to him and when he was just inches away he asked, "When are you going to tell me your real name?"

Chicago

Around 12:30 P.M. Kay-Loviett got the call from Chief of Police Arnie Wallace. The Chicago Police Department was no longer playing nice. "My detectives are going after the witness. We have a duty to protect her and—"

Kay-Loviett rolled her eyes and then broke in. "Okay, but as long as your detectives are there with the witness they are going to have to cooperate with the FBI."

Wallace spoke, "Out of respect and to keep the witness safe, I'm sure communication will continue to co-exist."

Kay-Loviett was shaking her head, the last thing she needed was to get in a pissing match with the Chicago PD. "Look Chief Wallace, I want to work together. You are not the only one who lost men—we lost a damn good agent."

Wallace didn't back down, "Okay, if you want to work together, tell me your plan. Explain to me why two FBI agents who are suppose to be watching the star witness are not answering their phones?"

This was news to Kay-Loviett. With all that was going on here, she had not touched based with Brown or Simmons. Looking at her watch, it should be around 2:30 P.M. in Barbados. The last time she spoke with the agents was early this morning sometime around six. She reached inside her jacket and pulled out her phone. There was a missed call from McNeil, but nothing from the two agents. Wallace barked, "Hello? You still there?"

Kay-Loviett said, "I'm here. I have total faith in the agents that are watching Ms. Bishop and—"

Wallace snorted, "I don't need to remind you about your undercover agent or my two patrol officers. Find the agents and our witness and get back to me ASAP. I want to know what my detectives are up against when they arrive."

Kay-Loviett knew he was right; they were not dealing with your average run-of-the-mill criminal. This family was wealthy and ruthless, and used professional killers to do their dirty work. She finally spoke, "I will call them now and report back promptly with or without making contact." She hung up.

Agent Floyd was standing nearby witnessing only half of the conversation. He asked, "With or without contact?"

Kay-Loviett started mumbling and punched a few buttons in her cell phone, while she was waiting she said, "There apparently seems to be some lost contact with Brown and Simmons. Check your phone. McNeil tried to call me, but mine went to voice mail."

Floyd stood and said, "I don't have any messages. Let me check my missed calls."

Kay-Loviett got Simmons's voice mail and then tried Brown's cell. On the third ring, Brown answered, "Brown"

With a sign of relief spreading across Kay-Loviett's face she said, "What is the status of our witness?"

Brown hesitated and then said, "Witness is on a date with Michael Brunson. We are currently out of contact at the moment, but Simmons is tracking her though the transponder in her bag."

"Agent Brown, what exactly does 'out of contact' mean? Do you still have our witness or not?"

Part Three

CHAPTER 45

Agent George Brown was sitting in a small fishing boat about five hundred yards away from the island where Brunson and Bishop were located. According to their GPS, the transponder was sitting in one spot on the island and hadn't moved since they arrived. Agent Simmons had taken a dingy and gone around to the north side of the island to come ashore. He was currently waiting to hear back from Simmons but unfortunately Simmons didn't have any service with his phone. He was a little surprised that Kay-Loviett had gotten through to his cell with the service coming and fading out for the last five miles. He spoke into his cell to Kay, "It's complicated. Ms. Bishop was supposed to meet Brunson in the lobby, but instead Brunson ended up going to her room. They headed out the back toward the ocean and disappeared onto a boat."

Kay-Loviett said, "Who is Michael Brunson, and why does she have a date?"

Brown quickly informed her that Brunson had checked out, and he was the owner of Brunson Winery. Ms. Bishop had met him and had dinner with him last night after the wine festival.

He continued, "We all thought a little fun and relaxation would be good for our witness, and it even might help her remember what Eddie said to her."

Kay-Loviett wasn't pleased and her tone of voice was obvious to Brown. "So if Simmons is out tracking our witness, where are you?"

Brown couldn't help himself, "I'm on the beach stretched out under a cabana having a cold beer waiting on Simmons to check in."

Kay-Loviett was dead quiet. She had never met Agent Brown but already didn't like his style or humor.

After no comment from his superior, Brown spoke again, "I'm on a boat in the middle of the Caribbean, and it seems Brunson has taken Bishop to a deserted island for honeymooners. Simmons is on the island now and checking things out."

Kay-Loviett responded, "Detectives McNeil and Williams are headed back out there so you will have company. Try your best to cooperate, we have a lot going on here, and I don't want the Chicago PD on my back."

Brown was staring out at sea and began to smile with the news of Paula coming back. He said, "No problem, we were working well with each other before they were pulled away. I don't think anything will change when they return."

"Good. Call me when you have confirmation on our witness," said Kay-Loviett before she hung up.

Brown closed his phone and tucked it into the front pocket of his linen shirt. He then pulled out his binoculars to see if he could see any movement at all on the island. Scanning the area, he only picked up a few birds flying around from tree to tree. The place looked deserted except for a path that led to a beach house. Since they arrived, he had not seen any movement coming or going from the house to the boat launched out at sea. There was a small craft pulled up on the shore, but no one was around it. He scanned back over to the boat and looked for movement there but it appeared no one was on board.

Simmons had agreed with him that Bishop must have put her beach bag down in the house somewhere and left it there. Neither of them knew how many people were aboard or if Brunson and Bishop were alone together on the island. Together they had speculated what they would eventually find and placed a small bet as to whether or not Brunson and Bishop would end up staying the night on the island. He said they would stay and Simmons had disagreed. Twenty dollars wasn't a whole lot of money, but he hated the thought of losing more than anything. Brown put his binoculars back down and pulled out his cell phone. He hit a few buttons and immediately heard Paula's voice on the other end. "Williams"

George eased back into his chair and propped his feet up on the side of the boat, "Hey, babe, miss me?"

"Miss you? Butch and I have been out of our minds worrying about our witness. Why have you not answered your phone?"

"So you haven't been worrying about me?"

Paula took a deep breath and then calmly asked, "Where are you?"

George said, "We are out in the middle of the Caribbean following little Ms. Bishop on her hot sexy date with Mr. Moneybag Brunson. It appears he bought a boat and decided to take her to a secluded island for a little fun in the sun."

"What? She left Barbados?"

Picking his binoculars back up, he scanned the area again and said, "Yep."

Paula seemed to be a little calmer now as she spoke, "Butch and I are boarding a plane in about twenty-five minutes, and we should be there sometime late this evening."

George said, "Call me when you land. I have a feeling though I will be here all night."

She said, "What are you saying? They plan on staying there overnight."

"I don't know. It's just a hunch I have. Maybe you can come join me and keep me company, and I'll send McNeil out with Simmons."

"Don't count on it. Now, give me your coordinates in case we lose phone coverage, or we have to come find you." George pouted some but finally gave his location and hung up the phone.

Paula wrote down the information and tucked it in her jacket along with her phone and ran toward the airport entrance to find Butch.

Kathleen let go of Michael's hand and thought about what he just said. "How would he know I have a different name?"

She took a step back with a frightened look on her face. Michael's face tensed with a worried expression, and he said, "Trisha, you just talked to me about teaching when you claimed earlier to be a receptionist. I think I have the right to know who you really are, and why you've been lying about what you do for a living."

Kathleen suddenly realized her mistake and began to relax but it didn't last long because Michael was frowning at her for misleading him, and he wanted answers now. She was confused, and she didn't know what to say or do. She liked this man and was looking forward to the rest of the day and what possibly might unfold later tonight. She had deceived him, and it wasn't fair. What could she possibly say now to fix this and what should she say to keep her safe?

Michael continued, "Trisha? You know it doesn't take a genius to figure out that everything you've said over the last two days just doesn't add up. I knew something was off from hello."

Kathleen looked up and said, "What do you mean from hello?"

Michael put his hands on his hips and said, "When you stuttered your name, I asked you then if it was your real name."

Kathleen thought back to the beach and remembered how he was right. She was just beginning to say Kathleen when she quickly changed her name to Trisha. Kathleen looked down at her feet and closed her eyes for a moment. Michael took a step forward and gently placed a hand on her chin and raised her face to meet his eyes. He said, "Trisha, I know you didn't seek me out for my money. I sought you out. Plus, after spending several hours with you, I know you are not a bad person who would purposely deceive someone."

With his other arm, he placed it around her back and pulled her into a hug. He then stated, "Please, tell me what is going on. I just might be able to help you."

Kathleen finally pulled back and said, "My name is Kathleen Bishop, and I'm a history teacher from Chicago, originally from Florida. I didn't lie about everything, especially not about my father and growing up around boats."

Kathleen paused and tried to judge his reaction before she continued on, "I'm sorry. I would like very much the opportunity to clear this up."

Michael never really lost that downward crease around his mouth but did reach out and grab her hand, and started leading her back toward the cottage. Finally after about three minutes of walking he finally said, "Go on, and I'll listen with an open mind."

Kathleen had been pondering where to begin and what she should say. Finally she started with the beginning when she left her school parking lot on Wednesday. Michael never interrupted; he just listened as they walked. They had just reached the swimming pool when Kathleen spoke of the two slain police officers outside her apartment. Michael finally stopped walking then and looked at her with shock as well as concern. A moment passed without any words, and then Michael continued on around the swimming pool and motioned with his hands, "Let's go have a seat there in the shade. You look exhausted."

They made their way over, and Michael pulled out a chair for her to sit in, and he took the other chair opposite from her. She was about to finish her story when she saw the chef walking over with a tray of food and some drinks. He smiled and placed the drinks and plates in front of them and said, "Did you enjoy your walk? This island is spectacular."

Michael nodded, and Kathleen said, "It is beautiful, and I am having a great time, thank you."

The chef smiled and said, "Wonderful. Please enjoy your meal." Then he left them and walked back toward the grill on the other side of the swimming pool.

Kathleen followed him with her eyes until she was satisfied he was far away not to hear the rest of the story. She picked up her fork and took a bite of the grilled shrimp with some rice. Michael did the same, and they quietly sat for a while, neither speaking as they ate their meal. When she was done eating, she glanced around to make sure they were still alone and continued. "I saw the man who is believed to have murdered my student's family, as well as the two officers. That is why I'm here under a different name. I'm hiding."

Michael took a drink of his lemonade and sat back and looked at her. He finally asked, "Where is the FBI now? Are they here on the island watching you?"

Kathleen looked around and shrugged her shoulders, "I don't know. They knew about our dinner date last night, and they checked you out."

Michael sat up then and said, "They checked on me?"

She closed her eyes and nodded her head, and then glanced back up at him. "I'm sorry for the invasion of privacy, but yes, they cleared you and told me I could spend time with you. Look, you are right, I am exhausted. I'm also confused—how can my heart be bleeding one minute and the next I keep thinking about kissing and touching you?"

He looked back at her with intense eyes and said, "Do you have strong feelings for me, or do you like being with me because I bring back normalcy and I'm safe?"

Kathleen thought for a moment about what he said and then slowly got out of her chair and walked around the table toward him. Without saying a word, she reached out and grabbed his hand and gently pulled him while he rose from his chair. She turned with his hand still in hers and led him up the balcony stairs toward the master bedroom.

CHAPTER 46

Simmons had climbed up a tree and was sitting on a limb with binoculars. He watched Bishop and Brunson eat without saying a word. He thought to himself, "Something is wrong with the happy couple." Ten minutes had passed before Bishop began to speak to Brunson. He watched them as a few words were spoken and took note of the body language that was exchanged between them. It didn't take him long to figure out that Bishop had come clean about her identity. Brunson appeared to not take the news lightly.

A few more moments passed and Simmons watched as Bishop got up and walked around the table toward Brunson. Again he studied their body language and watched as the two of them climbed the stairs that led up to the cottage. Simmons focused in on Bishop's body clad only in a swimsuit and cover-up as she made her way up the stairs. It appeared she was leading him. He watched as Brunson followed her inside and then he turned around to close the double doors behind him. He could make out a bedroom through the open windows. Watching the events unfold he said aloud, "Shit, there goes my twenty dollars."

Kathleen was lying on Michael's chest physically exhausted as he was kissing her neck. He slowly wrapped his arms around her and rolled her off, as he rolled on top of her. Looking down at her face, he couldn't help but smile and kiss her nose. Kathleen blushed and said, "I don't know what happened just then, but I sure would like to experience that again."

Michael laughed out loud and said, "You amaze me as well as surprise the hell out of me. You can experience that anytime you want as long as I'm on the other end."

Kathleen smiled back and with all honesty said, "I really am sorry for deceiving you. I never meant for any of this to happen, and I surely didn't plan on finding myself in your bed after meeting you only twenty-four hours ago."

He kissed her gently and said, "You are safe with me." He moved off of her, pulled her close, and let her snuggle up against his body till she fell asleep.

CHAPTER 47

Victor was on the island, making his way through the palms and trees to meet up with Zane Black. He found him sitting under a palm with bottled water and talking on his cell phone. When Zane saw Victor approaching, he ended his call and got up to face him. Victor asked, "What is the latest?"

Zane said, "Emilio has everything on his end covered. The only thing left now is to find the money and our cargo. He wanted to know if he should send Patch back out."

Victor smiled his most devious smile and said, "No, he is not needed."

Chicago Safe House

It was a little after noon, and Patch was standing in the woods outside the ranch house where Aileene Bell and her family were hiding out. He was wearing camouflage and had blended in very nicely with the forest surrounding him. The place was a little more difficult to find than he expected, but he always enjoyed a challenge and the money that was offered. His mission was clear and simple: kill Aileene Bell, along with her two girls and the babysitter. No federal agents were listed, but it was a given that he was to kill anyone that stood in the way. So far he had spotted two agents covering the front and two agents placed along the back of the property. Taking his binoculars out of his backpack, he put them up to his eyes and scanned the windows of the house. There was no movement inside, and he couldn't see anyone. He wasn't surprised. As a precaution, Bell and her family were probably told to stay away from the windows and move around as little as possible. He decided to make himself comfortable and wait till dark to make his move, so for now, he began to study the agents and make mental notes of their movements.

CHAPTER 48

Kathleen was standing in a dark staircase with a faint light shining from above. She looked around and saw the stair banister and reached out to grab it to steady herself. Looking up she saw a faint light coming from the top of the stairs. She began to slowly climb, watching as she placed one foot in front of the other. Hearing a noise from behind her, she glanced back to see what or who was there. As she continued to look, only silence followed. She slowly turned back around as to not lose her balance and then climbed another step. The sound came again from behind her but this time she could make out the noise. Someone was climbing the stairs behind her in soft-soled shoes. Turning back around she called out, "Hello, anyone there?"

She waited for an answer but received none. The shoe sounds came at a faster pace now, which frightened Kathleen. Quickly, she turned and ran up the remaining few steps to the top. Finally she made her way up the staircase, and she found a long hallway with too many doors to count. Turning back she saw a man emerging from the stairwell. Not understanding why he would not answer she asked, "Who are you, and what do you want?"

Kathleen continued to watch as the man kept walking without answering. Soon his face began to appear from the shining light that came from a small bulb that was hanging by a cord from the ceiling. He looked familiar but she didn't know his name. Suddenly his hand emerged from around his back, and he was carrying a knife. Kathleen screamed, "Someone help me!" and took off down the hallway banging on doors and twisting door handles as she went.

He wasn't running or didn't seem to be in any kind of hurry. He just kept walking toward her with a smile of death. Finally a door opened up, and Kathleen rushed in and slammed the door behind her. With her back toward the room, she never saw the other person coming toward her. An old voice said, "Here darling, let me help you with this latch."

Kathleen turned around but saw no one but a small baby lying in a crib. Confused but remembering the man with the knife, she turned back around and scrambled to lock the bolt and the chain. Satisfied the door was locked, she turned back around and found Lisa standing there gently rocking Mia back and forth. Kathleen said, "Lisa, I need help! There is a man chasing me down the hallway. We have to find something to block the door."

Lisa turned away from her and began to walk away down a small hallway. Frustrated, Kathleen looked around and found a small chair that she could move by herself. She ran toward the chair and began to push it across the floor and up against the door. As she stood back, she could see the door handle twisting and hear someone scraping an object along the wooden door. Thinking it was the knife and the killer wasn't giving up, she turned away and ran toward the hallway to find Lisa. Once she entered the hallway she could see two small bedrooms with a bath at the end. Looking in the first bedroom she found nothing but a small, unmade bed with clothing thrown around the room. Someone had obvious been looking for something important and appeared to not have found it. Moving on, she paused when she got to the other bedroom and was relieved to find Lisa again.

This time she was not holding Mia in her arms, instead she was standing there with her arms covered in blood and outstretched toward Kathleen. Kathleen screamed, "Lisa! What happened?"

Lisa gazed back with a blank look in her eyes, and then turned and started walking around a crib that was set up in the middle of the room. She bent down with blood dripping from her hands to pick up Mia from the crib. Kathleen slowly walked toward the crib to see Mia, but when she looked inside, she only saw splattered blood all over the pillow and sheets with a ripped up baby's nightgown lying in a pool of blood. Kathleen let out a deafening scream and this time Lisa responded, "Look what they did to my baby."

With tears in her eyes she continued, "Eddie is dead, but he left this behind" and she pointed down toward the crib and Kathleen saw movement emerging up from the mattress in the form of a bloody hand.

Kathleen began screaming again and backing away as Lisa continued to talk and point. Kathleen couldn't understand what she was saying, and she was trying to back up from the crib when she tripped and fell backward on something wet. Turning her head she saw that she was lying on top of Eddie's bloody body, and she began to scream again.

Kathleen was still screaming, as she was being poked and pushed around until finally she opened her eyes and found Michael looking down at her with a worried expression on his face.

Slowly she realized she had been dreaming and immediately reached out and hugged Michael tightly. He held her back and calmly said, "Shhh, it's okay now. I'm here, and you are safe. It was just a bad dream."

Looking at her white hands, she saw that they were shaking terribly. She felt dampness on her back and under her hair. She must have been tossing and turning for sometime before Michael came to her rescue. She pulled away and noticed he was fully dressed, and she was still naked wrapped up in sheets from their earlier lovemaking.

Finally, Kathleen found her voice and said, "I was with Lisa and she was talking about the baby. I can't remember what she said, but something about what Eddie left behind. Then, I fell on Eddie, and he was covered in blood. Oh, it was awful!"

She lounged back into Michael's arms, and he held her tight for the next few moments. Michael was rubbing her shoulder with one hand and smoothing her hair with the other. Kathleen spoke, "When is this nightmare going to end? I feel so helpless, and I can't remember anything important enough to help solve this case."

Michael leaned backward where he could look at Kathleen's face. "It will come to you. Don't force it."

Michael leaned back in and kissed her gently on the forehead. "How about you get dressed and come outside with me. We could take a swim and then jump into the hot tub."

Kathleen slowly nodded, "A swim sounds wonderful followed by some Brunson wine in the hot tub."

Michael stood and said, "I will head on down and prepare everything. Take your time."

Kathleen smiled back and said, "Thanks." She watched as Michael stood up and headed back out of the bedroom.

Looking around she found her swimsuit and sarong lying on the floor. She immediately thought back to their lovemaking and began to blush. Never before had she slept with a man she had just met. She slowly removed and unwrapped the damp sheets from her body and made her way to the bathroom. After using the facilities, she walked back over and picked up her bikini and put it on. Again she couldn't help but think about the moment when he untied her straps to her top. She admitted to herself that she liked him—a lot. She asked herself, "What am I going to do? What could this possibly lead to? He is definitely way out of my league."

She walked back into the bathroom and looked in the mirror. She slowly ran her hand through her hair and tried to work some of the tangles out. Her hair was a hopeless mess, so she gave up and walked back into the bedroom; she grabbed her sarong and tied it around her waist. Looking back at the bed, she smiled and then turned toward the double doors to the balcony and then opened them up to the pool below. She could see Michael talking to the cook and drinking some kind of purple drink. Sensing her, he turned, looked up, and smiled at Kathleen. She smiled back and then made her way down the stairs. He walked over and said, "Try this drink, the locals call it purple shit."

She smiled at him and then took the drink. She tried it and said, "Nice, I think I will have one. If you don't mind, I think I will swim a few laps while he makes the drink."

He gestured with his hands toward the water, and Kathleen removed her sarong and dove in. She was instantly submerged and gliding toward the opposite end of the pool. The water felt cool, and it refreshed her body and her mind. She closed her eyes and relaxed as her arms worked and moved her forward. She slowly made her way to the surface and emerged taking a deep breath. She continued on toward the edge extending her arms and kicking her legs. When she reached the end, she flipped over and kicked the side of the pool with her feet. She was now floating toward the other end and repeating the same motion. After about three laps, Kathleen finally stopped and stood up in the shallow end by the steps. Michael was smiling down at her and holding her purple shit.

He said, "Feel better?"

Kathleen climbed the stairs, and reaching the deck, she ran her hands through her hair and squeezed the excess water out. She stretched out her hand toward the drink and said, "Yes, thank you."

She took a sip and then reached out with her other hand and touched his cheek. She took one more step and then wrapped her arm around his neck and pulled him in for a kiss. Michael kissed her back and then pulled back and said, "Follow me, the hot tub is ready."

Holding on to his hand, she followed Michael a couple of steps. When she reached the edge, he stepped in first and then helped her in. The water was quiet warm, but not too hot; it was just right. She settled into the seat and took another sip of her purple drink as Michael slid over closer and placed an arm around her shoulders. At this moment she felt safe and protected, and she laid her head back on his shoulder and closed her eyes. Michael said, "I want to know more about Kathleen the teacher. Please tell me more."

She slowly opened her eyes and gazed into his face and began to tell him all about her life in Chicago.

Over in the bushes about thirty yards away, Agent Simmons was looking on, watching their every move. Simmons thought, "She doesn't even notice I'm here. Obviously she only has eyes for him. Boy, does she make an easy target!"

CHAPTER 49

Vivian was sitting outside on her Spanish veranda sipping a glass of wine and talking to Emilio on the phone back in the States. Watching the setting sun splash colors over the sea, she could hear the children laughing and playing in the distance with their cousins. She loved the French Rivera and spent as much time here as her job allowed. She asked into the phone again, "Emilio, is that everything?"

Emilio answered back, "Yes, thanks, Viv. I will be leaving first thing in the morning and should be there by dinnertime tomorrow. Tell the kids I love them, and I will see them soon."

Vivian smiled into the phone and reported how the kids were happy to be there and play with their cousins. "I'm glad we came on over. We all need this vacation, and the kids are so happy. Hurry up and join us, okay?"

Emilio responded, "Yes, we all need this vacation, and I will be there soon. I love you, Viv."

"I love you too, Emil. Bye now." She closed the phone and walked back over to the kids playing soccer in the lawn.

Her phone vibrated again, and she stopped to look down and view her Blackberry. There was a new message from her bank, and she clicked it to read. It was only a message confirming the transfer she had made earlier, so she closed it out and returned it to her pocket. She started walking again toward the kids. Running the remaining steps, she headed toward the ball and gave it a fierce kick into the goal with the kids cheering her along.

FBI Office, Chicago

Kay-Loviett was sitting at her desk with Agent Floyd looking on as she viewed the reports generated by her computer. Gary Fields had sent her page after page of the latest bank account records for her to view. Looking over them again they could not find any discrepancy. Somehow Chicago Steel had accounted for every dime it spent, as well as money brought in for the last five years. Kay was shaking her head and said, "How can they have another account that just appeared?"

Floyd responded, "They are good. This account clears up any and all questions associated with Chicago Steel."

"Well, Aileene did have our case in her briefcase. Damn!"

Kay-Loviett picked up the phone and dialed Fields. His secretary answered and sent her call straight through to her boss. He answered, "Fields."

Kay-Loviett said, "Its Agent Kay-Loviett. I'm looking over what you sent me, and it's different all right."

Fields asked, "We were afraid of that, especially since our paperwork was handed over to them last night. So, how is it different?"

Kay-Loviett answered, "There is one account that is new that was not in with the previous accounts that we used to build this case."

Fields ran a hand through his hair and said, "Are you sure you didn't miss it earlier?"

Kay-Loviett said, "I'm sure. Floyd and I both doubled-checked, and we have gone back over each account in detail for the last several hours."

Fields pulled up the file on his computer and asked, "Okay, which account are we talking about?"

Kay-Loviett read out, "Nine-eight-zero-zero-four-seven-six-two-nine-three-nine-one CBA."

Fields repeated the numbers and typed them into his computer. As they waited, Kay-Loviett asked, "Can we get information on that new account? I want to know when it was opened and the latest transactions."

Fields said, "It's not that easy. The only information that is available to us at this stage is the location and the name on the account."

Kay-Loviett asked, "Okay that is a start. In whose name is it registered and where is the account located?"

Coming across his screen was the account with the following account name and location. He read it out to her, "It appears the account is in the names of Emilio and Vivian Fernandez, and it's located in Madrid, Spain."

Kay-Loviett said, "What do you want to bet that Vivian has been to the bank today?"

Fields responded, "You are probably right, but we do not have enough at this stage to issue a warrant for the accounts. We have got to have something else before we move forward on these accounts."

Kay-Loviett was frustrated and said, "You think one cut up dead agent with his logs would account for something!"

Fields was more patient and said, "Look Kay-Loviett, at this point you don't have enough for a warrant, and I am not going to risk the backlash from Chicago Steel's lawyers if we proceed on what we got, which is nothing but notes and yes, a dead agent."

It was quiet for a few moments and Kay-Loviett didn't respond.

Finally Fields said, "Agent Kay-Loviett, you are smart and found these inconsistent records to begin with. Don't give up yet—keep at it. With that being said, you don't have long before I pull the plug on this investigation and bring you back home."

Kay-Loviett could only reply, "I'll do my best and keep you posted. Maybe we will get lucky and something will happen with our witness."

Fields ended the call and Kay-Loviett looked at Floyd and frowned as she placed the phone back down on her desk.

She said, "What is the latest with our witness? She seems to be our last hope."

Floyd responded, "Last I heard, Brown reported her still on that island with Michael Brunson."

Kay-Loviett said, "I want contact made with her. I want to know if she has remembered anything, anything at all that could help us."

Kay-Loviett got up and walked around toward the glass wall and looked down on the city below. She said, "We are running out of time. Something has got to happen and soon."

CHAPTER 50

Paula and Butch stepped out of the cab at the front of their hotel in Barbados. This time, Paula packed her own clothes and had more luggage than last time. Walking back up to the reception desk, Paula greeted the petite blond behind the counter and asked, "Do you have any messages for Bob or Mary Jacobs, room ten ten?"

The lady typed in a command to her computer and then shook her head, "No. Is there anything else I can help you with?"

Paula smiled back and said, "No, thank you." She turned back toward Butch and said, "Let's head up to our room and make some calls from there."

Butch agreed, and he placed his free hand in hers, and they started walking down the walkway that led out toward the back. On their way out, they passed by the patio bar where couples were sitting talking and dining. Butch looked their way and stopped to say, "Looks like nothing has changed since we left. Everyone is happy and enjoying themselves in paradise."

Paula looked back at Butch, "Are you all right? I know you were not happy with leaving the girls behind again."

Butch kept looking around and finally said, "I will be a lot better when this case is behind us, and Emilio is sitting in a jail cell."

Paula squeezed his hand and said, "Come on. Let's go make that happen."

They continued on down the walkway passing two swimming pools and many happy guests before finally arriving at Room 1010. Butch reached in his pocket and retrieved the key and opened the door cautiously. Nothing jumped back at them, and they quickly checked out the room. The only difference since leaving was clean towels and the bed had been made. The cleaning staff had left behind fresh rose petals thrown on their bed with a towel in the shape of a swan. Paula made her way over to the bed and immediately began picking up the petals to discard them.

Butch walked passed her and placed the room key on the nightstand and reached inside his waistband under his shirt and removed his weapon and placed it beside the key. Sitting there a few moments, he allowed his mind to wander; unfortunately he couldn't get the girls out of his mind. Frustrated, he got back up and made his way over to the minibar. Opening it up, he was a little more than tempted to grab the cold Corona inside. Mumbling instead, he grabbed the bottled water and opened it up and took a swig.

Paula emerged from the bathroom and was holding her hairbrush. With each step she made toward him she brushed another section of long blond hair. Standing beside him now, she bent over and opened the same bar and gazed inside and said, "Damn, what I wouldn't give for a cold beer now!"

She grabbed a bottle of water like Butch had done and closed the door. Making her way over to the bed, she sat down and then pulled out her cell phone. "I'm going to call Agent Brown first."

Butch and Paula were both a little more prepared this time and had programmed both agents' numbers in their phones. With a punch of a button the other end was now ringing. Brown answered on the second ring, "Brown."

"Hi, Agent Brown, it's Detective Paula Williams. McNeil and I have arrived, and we are back in Room 1010."

He said, "I see. You decided to share the same room again? How cozy for you."

Paula ignored his comment and got down to business. "Do you have anything?"

Brown decided not to push her and responded, "Things are still the same here. Simmons reported in a while ago and said Michael and Kathleen emerged from the master bedroom and are now enjoying themselves in the hot tub with drinks."

Paula said, "Are you suggesting they were in bed together?"

"Yep, and I won twenty dollars off Simmons for guessing that right."

Paula rolled her eyes and couldn't exactly say what she was thinking aloud in front of Butch. Brown was definitely being Brown. Sometimes she couldn't believe she had fallen for this guy and hard, too. Butch interrupted her thoughts and asked, "Kathleen and Michael?"

While clutching her cell phone, Paula nodded her head yes to Butch and said, "What time are they expected to return tonight?"

Brown said, "I'm thinking they're not. Like I said earlier, it is going to be a long night. Why don't you come join me?"

Paula asked, "What about the festival? Doesn't Michael have to get back for that?"

Brown replied, "I have no idea. I just know it looks like they are settling in for a long night."

Paula said, "Have you seen any sign of outsiders?"

"Nobody but us, a cook, and a captain."

Paula thought for a moment and then asked, "Did the cook and captain check out?"

Brown sat up for a moment in the boat and thought about that question. He finally responded after a delay with, "I'm not sure."

"What does 'I'm not sure' mean? Either you did or you didn't?"

Brown relaxed a bit in his chair and said, "Now that I think about it, Simmons said they were all clear."

Paula asked quizzically, "Now that you think about it?"

He said, "All is under control. When we traced them down using the transponder, we called in the boat. The captain and cook were hired out by a local agency that represented the boat sale."

Paula asked, "Are you saying Michael Brunson bought the boat just for the trip to the island?"

"Yep, the man sure has got a lot of cash."

Paula said, "Keep me posted. Butch and I are going to walk around the resort and see if anyone looks new. Let me know when you head back. I don't think they will stay for the night."

Brown laughed aloud and asked, "Do you want to bet twenty dollars on that?"

Paula didn't respond and closed the phone.

Butch looked down at her and then walked over and sat on the bed beside her. He said, "I didn't expect Kathleen to take up with this Michael guy so quickly."

"Me neither," Paula agreed. "She needs to be careful. It seems Michael is trying to impress her with buying a boat, as well as taking her to a secluded island."

He said, "It seems to be working." With that he stood up and headed back over to the minibar and opened it up once again. Paula stated the obvious, "Get me a Corona as well."

Butch reached inside and grabbed two. He twisted the cap off the first one and handed it to Paula. He did the same to his and walked over to the balcony to open up the door. Paula stood up with her beer and said, "I'm going to take a quick shower and then get dressed to go to the festival."

Butch said, "Take your time. I'm going to sit out here and call the girls."

Paula went into the bathroom and closed the door. Butch took a seat on the lounge chair and pulled out his phone. He scrolled down and chose a number. Aileene answered on the second ring, "Hello?"

"Hi, it's Butch. We landed safely, and we are now at the hotel. How is everything going back there?"

Aileene glanced at the girls putting away the dishes in the kitchen. "All is fine here. We just finished up dinner, and the girls are about to make some popcorn for the movies we are about to watch."

Butch looked out over the water at the magnificent view and still felt a little envious about a night in with the girls, popcorn, and movies, regardless of the safe house situation.

"Well that sounds good. What movies?"

"*Wizard of Oz* and then *Lion King*."

"I was envious with the popcorn and company, and now with those movies, I'm really envious."

Aileene laughed, "I don't know, an island in the Caribbean sure competes well."

After a moment of silence, Butch asked, "Aileene, when this is all over maybe we should take the girls on a trip over the Christmas holidays?"

Aileene stopped smiling and twisted her mouth as she contemplated what he said.

"Aileene?"

She said, "I hear you. Let me think about it. A lot has happened, and I don't want my feelings to get mixed up."

Butch said, "No, No, I understand. A lot has happened."

She said, "Yes, but this horrible event has put some things in perspective as well. Let's just commit to a drink when all of this is over, and we will go from there."

Butch smiled and said, "Deal. Can Mandy come to the phone? I would like to say goodnight to her. I don't think I'll have another chance to talk to her tonight."

She asked, "In for a long night?"

"Yes, I'm afraid so."

Aileene said, "Bye now and take care."

"Thanks, you do the same. Oh and Aileene…"

"Yes?"

"I miss you."

She thought for a brief moment and smiled, "I miss you, too" and she walked over to hand the phone to Mandy.

Taking the phone, Mandy stepped out of the kitchen and let Aileene finish up with the popcorn. She walked into the living room and said, "Hi, Dad."

"Hey, darling, I hear all of you are safe and about to start a movie."

"Yes, this place has a nice video collection. Things could be a lot worse, but this place is really nice, and the girls are settling in just fine."

"Great, but what about you?"

"I'm good. Anytime I can miss school, life is great!"

Butch smiled and said, "I don't know if I will be able to call again tonight, but if you need me, call and leave a message if I don't answer."

"Oh, all right."

Butch could hear Feebe running in the background saying, "Popcorn is ready, Mandy!"

Mandy said, "I guess you heard that?"

"Yes, I love you Mandy. Stay safe."

"I love you too, and you do the same. I will see you when you get back."

Butch thought and smiled at that. "I will see you when you get back" was something they always said to each other no matter the dangerous assignments Butch seemed to find himself in.

He said, "Yes Mandy, I will see you when I get back." Butch closed the phone and placed it back in his pocket.

Butch sat back and tried to enjoy the tropical setting and slowly sipped his beer. He knew one beer would be all that he would get for a while, and he wanted it to last as long as possible. He had just closed his eyes when he heard laughter emerging from the sidewalk around his balcony. The talking and laughter got closer with each step the happy couple made toward his room. Finally they emerged and he could see a young woman with a middle-aged man walking hand in hand toward the beach. The lady was wearing a long yellow strapless sundress with sandals. He took a closer look at her face and decided she might be in her midthirties; it was hard to tell now days with all the creams and plastic surgery. Her jet-black hair was twisted up high into a knot with only a few pieces on the side falling around her face. Butch's eyes glanced over to the man. He was wearing white linen pants and a red shirt with white flowers plastered on it. Not many men he knew would wear white linen pants, but looking at this man, he could tell he would wear anything she asked.

Butch continued to watch them until they disappeared along the path. Then his thoughts immediately went to Aileene. He tried to remember why they ended things but got lost backtracking. The only thing that seemed to matter now was how to repair their relationship. He started thinking about some of her favorite restaurants that they had enjoyed visiting and came up with three choices for that special drink. After some more thought, he decided on the restaurant that overlooked the water on Fifth Street. Of course the climate and scenery would be very different from here. The restaurant there would have their covers down on the outdoor patio with their outdoor heater running all night. The view would be lovely though especially with Aileene by his side. He could picture her now in his head; she would be wearing her teal blue jacket and designer jeans with heels. Her blonde hair would probably be worn down hanging just below her shoulders. He smiled at the image he formed in his mind and took the last sip of his beer.

Butch placed his empty bottle down and turned to face the noise coming from within the room. He found Paula emerging from the bathroom wearing a short black dress with a very low neckline. Butch stared. Paula smiled back and asked, "How do I look? Hopefully like a lady still on her honeymoon and looking for a good time."

Butch pushed back his thoughts of Aileene and jumped back into the present. "You look stunning as always. I don't think you could ever look bad in anything you put on."

Paula blushed a little and said, "It's not too much?" and then she turned around for him to see the back.

Paula's blond shiny hair was pulled up exposing her beautiful neck. Butch's eyes followed the base of her neck down to her bare lower back. The dress was backless with only a thin string going across the top to keep it from falling off her shoulders. He watched her as she turned back around and she said, "Well, too much?"

Butch finally found his voice and said, "Perfect, but where are you going to hide your gun?"

She smiled and said, "It will be in my purse."

He then asked, "Um, I think I might need some help with my wardrobe."

Paula turned away and walked toward her luggage. "I picked up something today just for you."

Butch was a little taken back and said, "Really? That was very nice of you."

Paula finally found what she was looking for and pulled out an orange shirt with parrots on it followed by white linen pants. She said, "You go and take a shower, and I will iron these."

He continued to stare at the pants and finally decided this wasn't a joke, and he slowly turned around and made his way into the bathroom. He closed the door behind him, and he couldn't help but think how he was just like the man he saw earlier walking hand in hand with the young lady. He shook his head, and finally smiled and let out a big laugh as he turned the water on for his shower.

CHAPTER 51

Kathleen and Michael were sitting in the hot tub and drinking their second cocktail unaware of the eyes following their every move. To an outsider, they looked comfortable and at ease. Michael had one arm draped around Kathleen's shoulder and the other extended over the side holding his drink. Kathleen was the one currently talking and her drink was on the side table half full. She turned her head as she talked and was slightly leaning into Michael with one hand placed on his chest.

Kathleen had just finished telling Michael about her last trip home to Florida over the summer holiday when she finally stopped abruptly and said, "I need to get out—now. Too much heat and alcohol."

Michael placed his drink down beside hers and then placed his hands on the side of the tub and lifted his body upward. Kathleen just sat and watched as his muscles flexed and the water ran down his taunt body. Michael then stepped out and grabbed two towels from the nearby rack. He walked back to the hot tub and held out his hand to help her out. Kathleen took his hand and allowed him to use his strength to pull her up. Again, she just stared at his near perfect body as she lifted her leg over the tub's rim and stepped down. She was a little shaky, so he let go of her hand, grabbed her waist, and lifted her down and said, "Yeah, I think the alcohol is getting to you."

"Thanks for your help," Kathleen said, as she took the towel from his outstretched hand. Kathleen dried off a little and then wrapped the oversized towel around her body. She then confessed, "I'm not a big drinker, and I usually just stick to beer."

He smiled at her omission and then pulled her toward his warm chest. She placed her head on his shoulder as he wrapped his arms around her. They stood like that for a moment and then she finally lifted her head and said, "I'm better now. Let's go take a seat and see what the chef is making us."

Michael took her hand and led her toward the table for two and pulled out her chair. She stepped in and began to sit down as he gracefully slid her chair forward.

He said, "I will be right back."

Michael then left her and walked over to the chef and exchanged some words. The two talked for about two minutes, and then Michael came back with a basket full of bread with a small platter filled with three dipping dishes. He placed it on the table and said, "Here, this will help."

Kathleen took a piece of bread and broke part of it off and dipped it in the oil followed with a dab in the spices. She was a little embarrassed at her reaction to the alcohol but decided to just go with it. "I guess I know now why they call it purple shit!"

Michael laughed aloud and said, "Yes, we now know. The chef is almost done with our steaks, and you can get some more food in your system."

She looked down at her bread and then took another bite. She then grabbed a second piece from the basket and repeated the process again, "This is good, and I would like to hire him full time."

Michael asked, "Do you like to cook?"

Kathleen nodded her head and said, "Absolutely, I just don't seem to find the time, plus it's not as fun when you are cooking for one."

He put down his bread and said, "That could change you know."

She didn't know quite what to say so she said nothing.

Another moment passed and Michael continued, "I really enjoy your company, with or without the alcohol."

She looked back up at him and smiled, "I normally don't move this fast," and she looked back down and took another bite out of her bread.

When she lifted her face back up, he looked straight into her eyes and said, "I don't either, I am usually more cautious."

Kathleen finished her final bite and asked, "How often do you come to the States?"

An expression crossed over his face that she couldn't quite read. After a long pause, he said, "I'm over there more than you would think."

She was about to respond when she saw the chef making his way toward them carrying a large platter. He stopped at the table and lowered the tray as he lifted a plate with his other hand and placed it in front of her. He then did the same for Michael. The steak looked wonderful and had a cream sauce on top and was served with asparagus and a baked potato. The potato was already opened, and the butter was melting into the sour cream and bacon. Kathleen literally felt her mouth water. She finally was able to reply, "This looks fantastic! Thank you very much."

The chef smiled back and said, "You are very welcome. Please enjoy. But do save room for dessert. I have prepared a very special dish that the locals make."

Kathleen readily agreed, and the chef asked, "Is there anything else I can get either of you?"

Michael responded, "I'm good, Kathleen?"

Kathleen cut open her steak and then said, "No, this is great."

The chef smiled, bowed, and then turned around and headed back toward the grill. Watching him, she said, "I wonder what dish he is going to make with just a grill?"

Michael did not have an answer but said, "Well, I'm going to save room to find out."

Kathleen took a bite of the steak and found it very tender and slightly red, just the way she liked it. She tasted the asparagus and found it seasoned with a touch of butter and sea salt. She went back to the steak and cut another piece when a sudden memory flashed in her mind after seeing the blood. She dropped her knife and then pushed her chair back from the table.

With a worried look, Michael said, "Kathleen, what's wrong?"

She looked back at Michael, and she could also see the chef rushing over toward her.

The chef stood at their table and asked, "Is everything okay with the food?"

Kathleen pulled herself together enough to say, "I'm sorry, everything is fine with the food. I just remembered something, that's all."

The chef gave her a strange look and then looked toward Michael and said, "Let me know if you need me." He walked away toward the grill again.

Michael stretched out his hand on top of hers. "What did you remember? Was it about the murders?"

Kathleen gazed back at him and said, "Yes, I remember everything now. Eddie told me where he hid something. I need to get to my cell phone, and call the detectives I've been working with."

She removed her hand from under his and slid her chair back to stand up. As soon as she stood she felt a wave of dizziness filling her head, and she began to sway. Michael had stood up at the same time as she did, so he was able to catch her when he noticed her swaying back and forth.

Kathleen fell into his waiting arms and she mumbled, "What is wrong with..." she tried to finish her question but couldn't get out another word.

Kathleen closed her eyes and felt her weightless body being picked up into Michael's strong arms. She then realized he was taking her somewhere and then slowly figured out he was climbing up the stairs that led to the master bedroom. A swarm of thoughts went through her head as she tried to put the pieces together. "Am I drunk? No, I know what that fells like. Then what? Am I sick?"

She was trying to open her eyes and form words but couldn't do either. She could hear words around her and thought, "It must be the chef and Michael talking."

She concentrated on understanding what they were saying but couldn't. Once again she tried to open her eyes but couldn't fight the darkness anymore and faded away.

CHAPTER 52

Picking up their act once more, Butch and Paula made their way toward the pathway that led to the main restaurant and bar. They were smiling, laughing, and holding hands as they entered the bar area. Lots of men stopped what they were doing and took a long look at Paula. Paula, feeling their eyes on her, snuggled up to Butch a little closer. Butch couldn't help but notice their bluntness as they stared and then gave him a second glance. He took it all in stride and smiled back at the gentlemen until they continued on with whatever they were doing.

They walked around a bit more before they finally settled down at a small table in the corner. They adjusted their seats where it appeared they wanted to sit closer, but in reality, they wanted to sit with their backs against the wall where they could check the place out. Butch picked up a menu as Paula scanned the area. She then picked up the other menu and said, "Does that couple on the far right seem odd to you?"

Butch glanced up and said, "Which ones?"

Paula's eyes never left the menu as she said, "Long brown hair with hot pink dress on."

Butch took another moment to glance at his menu and then waved a waiter over as he looked over the couple. The waiter appeared and Butch ordered two waters with limes and a plate of cheesy nachos with beef. The waiter asked, "Would you like jalapeños as well?"

Butch looked at Paula and then nodded his head, "Yes, please."

The waiter disappeared as quickly as he arrived, and Butch said, "I remember seeing them at the beach. She looks a little different wearing clothing."

Paula smirked, "Oh yeah, I remember them now. Her swimsuit didn't leave much to the imagination."

Butch continued, "Why did they appear strange?"

Paula couldn't pinpoint the reason, so she just said, "I have no idea. It was just a feeling."

The waiter arrived again carrying their waters with limes and said, "The nachos will arrive shortly."

Paula thanked him, picked up her glass, and took a sip. She continued to glance around until she saw a man walk by quickly with a young lady wearing a pale pink dress. They were holding hands and were leaving the bar area together. She didn't get a good look at their faces, but something about them looked familiar. She couldn't place her finger on where she saw them before and decided to push the issue aside for now.

"Paula?"

She looked over to Butch and said, "Sorry, did you see that couple that walked by quickly, she had on a long pale pink dress?"

Butch placed his drink down and said, "No, I was busy watching this guy over here, the one to my left sitting alone."

Paula slyly looked over and then said, "He is with the petite brunette that got up earlier to go to the ladies' room."

The waiter made his way over to them carrying a platter that held their nachos. Paula said, "Wow that was fast, thank you."

The waiter placed a napkin in Paula's lap and asked if there was anything else. Butch said, "Just some more water for now, thanks."

The waiter left and then came right back with a water pitcher. He filled their drinks and walked away toward another table to do the same. Butch picked up some nachos and placed them on his plate and then switched it out with Paula's. "Why thank you honey bun!"

Butch smiled back as he made his plate and then took a chip and ate it. "This is good."

Paula tasted a bite and said, "Yeah, too bad I can't eat like this everyday."

Butch looked at her funny and said, "Paula, you eat everything I eat everyday on the job, and it doesn't seem to phase you like it does me."

Paula looked up and said, "Working with you has made me work out twice as much as I used to."

Butch finished another chip and said, "Really? I didn't realize it."

Another couple walked by and both of them glanced over at them and said nothing.

Butch asked, "What time does the wine festival end tonight?"

Paula looked at her watch and saw that it was a little after nine and said, "Ten thirty. We have another hour and a half. We should probably head over soon."

Butch agreed and picked up another chip. It took another five minutes to wax off the nachos and Butch called over the waiter and said, "Charge this to room ten ten, name Jacobs."

The waiter wrote down the information and said, "Have a nice night."

Butch stood up and walked around and slid Paula's chair back as she stood up. He glanced down right at the perfect moment to see her reveal her very nice thighs. Butch saw her notice and said, "What? I'm doing what any sane man would do on his honeymoon" and he bent down and placed a big kiss on her lips.

Paula allowed the kiss and decided to throw her arms around his neck. When Butch pulled back, Paula pulled him back down and gave him another kiss and slapped him on his ass. She smiled at him and then took his hand and turned around to head out toward the festival. Once again, Butch could see the men drooling at Paula as she made her way out the door. He couldn't help it, but he literally felt his chest swell with pride.

Together they walked hand in hand through the outdoor patio that eventually opened up to the large room that held the wine festival. They were both greeted at the entrance with a small bag each. Paula looked inside and saw the wine of the night was from Brunson's Winery. "That's odd. I would have thought Michael would have wanted to be here on this night."

Butch said, "Why is that odd?"

She pointed at his bag for him to look inside. Butch opened it up and found a bottle of wine with some literature about Brunson's Winery. "I see what you mean. Maybe this man makes enough money not to care."

Paula said, "Maybe. I don't know."

He looked at her and said, "I know what you mean. I like Kathleen, and I think she is a swell girl, but it seems he has gone a little overboard for someone he just met."

Paula immediately took his hand and pulled him into the festival in search of Brunson's Winery. After about four aisles, they finally found his display set up with his merchandise. They took a few more steps toward the set up, and Paula froze. Standing in front of her was Michael Brunson with his beautiful assistant wearing a long pale pink dress. She immediately turned to face Butch, "If this is Michael Brunson, who is with Kathleen?"

Butch appeared shaken a bit but made himself to the front of the people gathered at Brunson's Winery. When he finally reached the table, he asked, "Are you Michael Brunson?"

The guy pointed to his name tag and smiled, "Yes, I am. What can I help you with tonight?"

Paula ignored the question and asked, "Have you been here all day?"

The man didn't seem offended and answered, "Why yes. Tonight is a big night for us since we are the specialty wine featured. I haven't been here at the booth, but I've had several meetings with business vendors. Why? Have you been looking for me?"

Butch ignored the glance over Paula's body that he made and he said, "Thank you. Sorry to have bothered you."

Butch grabbed Paula's elbow, and they worked their way back through the crowd gathered at his display. He could hear Brunson in the background saying, "Wait, did you want to set up a meeting?"

Butch never turned around but he could hear Paula saying, "Not at this time, maybe later."

He finally reached the end of the long aisle and said to Paula, "We have got to find a boat and fast. Did you bring the coordinates with you?"

She opened up her purse and found her cell phone and her little notepad. She opened up the pad and read off the latitude and longitude of the island, and then Butch said, "Let's go to the front desk. They will find a boat for us."

They walked as fast as possible without drawing attention to themselves and finally made it to the front desk. Surprisingly it was not crowded, and he said, "Call Brown and see if he answers, and I will get us a boat."

Paula nodded her head in agreement and walked to the corner of the reception room and touched a number in her cell phone. After three rings, Brown answered, "Hey, babe, change your mind? The water is nice, and there is a full moon with—"

Paula cut him off and said, "Who the hell is with Kathleen when Michael Brunson is here at the wine festival?"

Brown stopped playing with a paper football and said, "What are you talking about?"

She answered, "Butch and I are at the hotel wine festival, and we talked to Michael Brunson. He has been here all day!"

Brown said, "Then who the hell is with Kathleen?"

Paula wanted to scream but kept her voice quiet, "When is the last time you talked to Simmons?"

Brown answered, "About an hour ago, he said they were having dinner out by the pool."

She said, "Something is not right. Get on that island, find Kathleen, and stay with her until we get there."

She could hear Brown turning the boat on as she was speaking. He finally said, "Call me when you get here, if I've not gotten back to you first," and he hung up.

Paula placed the phone back in her purse and watched Butch make his way toward her. "There is a boat waiting on us at the marina. Let's go." He walked toward the exit, held the door open for her, and then quickly followed out behind her.

Outside they could see a line of taxis waiting under the covered driveway for the hotel guests. Butch ran up to the closest one and shouted in the window, "How fast can you get us to the marina?"

The attendant opened the door for them and they quickly got in as the driver said, "Five minutes if I don't get a speeding ticket."

Butch shouted back, "I will give you an extra twenty if you can do it in five minutes without hitting anyone or getting a speeding ticket."

The driver smiled and nodded as he peeled out of the driveway. They made it in four minutes and fifty seconds without any incidents. Butch threw the driver two twenties and pushed the cab door open before it came to a complete stop. Paula had already removed her heels, so she was able to run and keep up with Butch as he jogged down the pier toward the service booth. Butch held up his badge and the young man just pointed to the far end of the pier and said, "They are waiting on you."

Paula could hear the man saying behind them, "Have a safe trip" as she met each step Butch made.

Butch boarded first and then turned around to help Paula, but he was too late—she had already jumped in. He turned back around to the captain and said, "Do you have the coordinates?"

The captain nodded his head yes and yelled over the engine, "Have a seat. It will be rough."

Butch took the seat by Paula, and they both held on. It was at this moment that they realized exactly what kind of boat they were on, or if you want to call it a boat. Paula beat him to the punch, "What kind of boat did you request?"

He said, "I didn't. I just said I needed to rent one fast."

They appeared to have boarded a small eighteen-foot day cruiser with an open bow and were headed out to sea. They went up and down over some big waves and water splashed on both of them. Soon the waves seemed to flatten out, and they came to realize they were not going to die after all. Paula shouted, "Under different circumstances, this would be pretty cool."

Butch looked out at the full moon with thousands of stars that lit up the seas and said, "Yeah, it would be."

Paula reached into her handbag and checked her weapon. Seeing her, Butch pulled out his and did the same. He opened up the chamber to make sure he still had a full round and then clicked the safety off and then back on. Satisfied, he put his gun back into his waistband. He glanced down and looked at his clothing. His white linen pants were soaked through and he was leaving nothing to the imagination. He glanced over at Paula, and she had tucked her short dress under her butt as best as she could. Noticing him she said, "Hey, at least I'm wearing black."

Butch snorted and said, "Real funny. I will get you back for this, don't worry!"

Paula laughed out loud. "You know, I bought those pants as a joke. I was real surprised you didn't say anything. I didn't take you for a white-linen-pants guy."

He continued to shake his head and said, "I hope that tiny string holding your dress up breaks!"

Paula's facial expression looked shocked, "Why Butchy, all you had to do was ask, and I would have shown you a long time ago."

The breeze was blowing hard across his face, but he could still feel himself blushing, exactly as Paula had hoped to accomplish. He just smiled at her and said, "I'm glad you are my partner. You always know just when to lighten the mood."

She gave a more serious look and said, "We need to be careful. We don't know how many people are on that island."

He said, "Yeah, when this is all over, I am going to have some choice words for those agents."

Paula frowned and then said, "I was the one who checked out Brunson. It was my mistake."

Butch said, "Don't go there. That was a well-designed plan that neither of us could have seen coming."

Several minutes had passed by and Paula didn't respond, and he finally said, "It's the agents I'm worried about."

Paula looked up at Butch and asked, "Why is that?"

"Well, we know there is a leak. Who is to say it's from the Chicago PD?"

She thought that over for a minute and was about to explain to Butch her relationship with George, but decided against it. Too much was all ready going on without adding her love relationship with an FBI agent to the mix.

The guy behind the wheel said, "The island is up ahead. What do you want me to do?"

Butch looked out at sea but couldn't see the island. He asked, "Are there any lights, electricity?"

The man shook his head and said, "Just a generator running some lights but not many."

Butch asked next, "Have you been to the island before?"

The man nodded his head yes.

Butch said, "Okay, tell me everything that is there."

The captain had a worried expression on his face but went on to explain to Butch the cottage, pool, and general geographical layout of the island. When he was done, Butch said, "Good, now I want you to get me on that island without being heard or seen."

The man nodded his head like before. A few more moments passed without any words, and then the boat became quiet as the captain shut off the engine. They all coasted for a while, and then the captain leapt from the boat and began to pull them to shore. When the boat finally reached as far as it would go, he held out his hand to help Paula get out. Butch jumped in behind her, and they made their way through the water and up onto the beach. Once on shore, Butch whispered, "Which way is the house?"

The man pointed to the right and said, "About a half mile."

Butch then said, "It's not safe. You need to go back."

The captain did not wait to be told again and waded toward the boat, pushed it back out into the sea, and then jumped in. Paula watched him go and then looked at Butch. "With all this light, I still don't see Brown's boat. I am going to call him."

Butch was about to make another suggestion when he realized she had already hit the send button.

Brown answered on the first ring and whispered, "I'm outside the cottage, and I haven't been able to get in touch with Simmons."

Paula said, "We will work our way to you. Have you spotted anything?"

Brown whispered again, "No, nothing. Come to the left of the front porch. I will be waiting."

Paula agreed and hung up the phone. "There is no sign of anyone, and he is to the left of the front porch."

Butch took a step closer to where he was just inches away from her face, "Stay behind me, and let's move very slowly. With the moon, there is too much light."

Paula nodded her head and motioned for him to move forward. As they began to make their way toward the cottage, a man was watching them through binoculars and then he slowly picked up his gear and began to follow them.

CHAPTER 53

It was dark and now time for Patch to do what he does best—kill. He knew the habits of all four agents and their positions. They were calling in on every hour and then remained silent there after. He waited until the call was made and then set his watch for forty-five minutes. He always gave himself an extra fifteen minutes for the unknown. He had never needed it before and didn't anticipate needing it tonight. To him, four FBI agents was a medium-sized challenge, but he would approach this with high risk. The payout was going to be his last, and he wanted to make sure he got the highest amount possible from the Fernandez family. After tonight, he was done and on his way to Mexico. With this hit, he was sure to never have to work again; he would live out his life sailing and lying on the beach somewhere on the coast of the Yucatan Peninsula. Pushing Mexico out of his thoughts for now, he tucked his belongings in a bag, stood up, and zeroed in on the first agent who was farthest from the house.

Agent Mark Billings was standing by a tree and looking at the ranch house through his night-vision binoculars. He was sweeping the house once again for any movement and was pleased to find none. So far, Aileene had kept the girls inside and out of view, just like they had asked. He checked his watch and then sighed; it was going to be a long night. His wife of two years was pregnant and was due in about two weeks. He was thinking about how much he was looking forward to his time off to spend with his wife and baby when his throat began to cave in, and he slowly began to loose consciousness. He dropped his binoculars and tried to break free using his hands and kicking with his feet but nothing worked. Soon his body began to slow, and he quickly faded into darkness with his last thoughts of his lovely wife, Jill.

Patch bent over and removed the agent's small radio from his waist. Staying in a crouched position, he listened to make sure there was no chatter or warning of him being seen. Satisfied, he stood up and turned the radio off and clipped it to his hip. He looked at his watch; he had thirty-nine minutes left.

Patch began to backtrack some and then made his way over to the opposite side of the field and found the second agent walking around in a small circle. This agent was different; she was a female. After studying her movements throughout the day, Patch had decided she was probably in her late thirties but with a very athletic and fit build. He continued toward her despite her gender. He didn't care who he killed. When he was about twenty yards away, he slowly removed his knife from his sheath and continued his final few steps.

Agent Ginger Villilema heard a noise and stopped walking. She looked around without moving to try and determine where the noise came from. As a precaution, she picked up her radio and was looking off toward the house when a hand wrapped around her mouth and something shiny flashed before her eyes. She never knew what happened as her body collapsed to the ground with blood flowing from her throat. Again, Patch bent down and listened to see if there was any movement or sound coming from the radio. Once again, he was unnoticed.

Patch reached over and grabbed the radio that had fallen to the ground and turned it off. Looking at his watch again, it read thirty-three minutes remaining. He leaned over and wiped the blood off his knife on her pant's leg. He stood and then placed his knife back into the sheath. He now set off around the house toward the front, where the remaining two agents were stationed. These agents were only fifty yards apart, which added a little more challenge to his mission.

Agent Gregory Minks had just finished a phone conversation with his mistress when Patch found him and eased over behind him. The agent opened up his jacket pocket and then glanced down before placing the phone inside. He never saw Patch standing behind him with the heavy blunt object aimed at the base of his skull. As the agent turned, Patch raised his arms and shifted his shoulder in a baseball stance and then fired away. The sound was crushing as it made its connection to the agent's head. The agent stumbled forward and then fell to the ground. Somehow he landed face up and was able to meet the eyes of his killer. Minks blinked his eyes once and then blood began to bubble from his mouth as Patch stood there smiling down on him. A few more seconds passed and Minks' eyes finally closed for the last time.

Not caring if the radio made a sound, he quickly made his way over to the final agent. Agent Jim Minnows was walking toward the woods on the side of the house to take a leak. When he found the edge of the brush, he turned around behind him to make sure he was out of anyone's sight and then looked forward again as he undid his fly. With the sound of his urine splashing on the dry leaves, he never heard Patch come from behind with the same heavy object. He fell forward into the wet leaves and never moved again. Patch looked at his watch and saw that he had twenty-four minutes remaining. With all four agents out of his way, Patch turned toward the house to start his last mission.

First, Patch circled the house and checked all doors and windows carefully. He wasn't surprised to find the place was locked down tight. Making his way back over to the third dead agent, he bent over and searched his pockets for some keys. In the second pocket, he found a single key with a tag marked house. He pocketed the key and then made his way over to the right side of the house. Placing his hands along the brick, he found the wires that he discovered earlier. Taking out his knife again, he slid it under the wires and then pulled upward. All lights in the house went out followed by some sparks and smoke that filled the air. Raising his arm to his face, he pressed his light on his watch and it read twelve minutes remaining. Just enough time to finish this and be on his way.

Aileene Bell was sitting on the living room couch watching *Lion King* with the girls when the power went out, and the house turned completely dark. Feebe moaned aloud, and Shelly quickly said, "Mommy, what's wrong?"

Mandy was sitting on the loveseat beside the couch that held Aileene and the girls. Getting up, Mandy walked over and said, "Feebe jump into my arms. Ms. Bell, you get Shelly and quickly follow me, I know a place we can go until the power is back on."

Not having a plan of her own, Aileene grabbed Shelly's hand and said, "Come on girls, be quiet now and let's follow Mandy."

In return, Mandy said, "Everything is fine. Just think of this as the sneaky mice game we play."

Feebe giggled a little and then finally got quiet. Mandy was holding Feebe tight with one arm and with the other she was feeling her way toward the hall that led to the bedrooms and baths. Aileene was gripping Shelly's arm and was holding on to Feebe's foot as she followed closely behind.

Once they made it in the hallway, Mandy banged into the hall table but quickly recovered and guided Aileene around it. She counted the doorways and mentally pictured each room or bath as she went. Finally, she reached the master bedroom doorsill and reached for the doorknob but quickly realized it was already opened. She shifted over to the left side where she would not run into the bed and then held out her free hand and walked until she felt the bedroom wall. She told herself, "I am almost there."

Mandy continued feeling along the wall until she finally felt another doorsill. With a sign of relief, she quickly opened the closet door and pulled everyone inside. Everyone shuffled in as quietly as possible and Mandy shut the door and whispered, "Over here, come on."

Mandy reached behind some hanging clothes and found the hidden door. Opening it up, she stepped inside with Feebe and Aileene soon followed in with Shelly. Once everyone was safely inside, Mandy reached out and pulled the clothes back over the rod and shut the door. Mandy then felt around for the bolt and turned it slowly as to not make a sound. Aileene began to feel her way around the enclosed area and found that the room wasn't as small as she anticipated. Mandy spoke quietly, "I found this room earlier today. I brought a blanket and two pillows in here along with some water and crackers. I'm sorry, but I didn't think to bring a flashlight."

Aileene reached out and squeezed Mandy's hand and said, "Thank you."

Mandy just said, "Let's get them settled in the corner, and then we can talk."

Patch went to the back door that led to the kitchen and placed the key in the lock and turned the key. The knob turned, but now he needed to unlock the deadbolt. He worked the key into the bolt and found that it did not work. Realizing what the agents had done, he smiled. This was going to be a bigger challenge than anticipated.

Patch never really seemed to get upset; he found that was only wasted energy that he could have used somewhere else that would have improved his situation. So, he carefully made his way back toward the far side of the house to the dead agent who was taking a leak. He bent down and began to go through all of his pockets to find the matching key. He was not disappointed. Taking the key he found, he made his way back over toward the back door again and walked right up and placed the key in the deadbolt. The key turned easily and the door was now open.

Aileene tucked Feebe in under the blanket and gave her a kiss on her forehead. She did the same to Shelly and noticed that she was trembling and her sweatpants were wet. She knew then that Shelly knew the real danger they were in. Aileene felt a wet tear slide down her cheek as she continued to touch Shelly. Her little darling was trying to be a real trooper as she played along for Feebe's benefit. Shelly had agreed to keep quiet and continue on with the sneaky mice game and urged Feebe to do the same.

Standing back up, she moved over with Mandy to the door with the bolt. Aileene said, "Did you discover anything else?"

Mandy said, "Yes, under the carpet here is a door that leads to somewhere. I never got a chance to check it out. I wished now I had."

Aileene placed a hand on Mandy's face and said, "You've done a lot. Now let's see what both our minds working together can come up with."

Patch entered the kitchen and quietly shut the door back without a sound. He stood there a few moments and just listened. Not a sound was coming from any direction. He slowly lifted each foot and made his way out of the kitchen and into another room that he guessed was the living room. He could smell popcorn and he felt around until he found a coffee table with a bowl that contained some. He kept feeling around until he found the couch. Making his way around toward the front, he then began to run his hand along the cushions. In the center cushion, he found a bowl flipped over and popcorn scattered around. A smile crept across his face as he picked up a piece of popcorn and put it in his mouth knowing without a doubt, they were still in the house.

CHAPTER 54

Kay-Loviett was driving her sedan on the interstate heading back out to the ranch house to see Aileene Bell again. Agent Floyd had decided to go with her at the last minute, so there he sat riding shotgun. When they were about ten minutes away, she asked Floyd to call Agent Minks to give him the heads up. The last thing she needed was to get shot by other agents. That would definitely seal the deal as the worse day of her career.

Kay-Loviett had talked to Minks at seven o'clock, about thirty minutes ago but didn't know then she was going to head back out. Floyd closed his phone and said, "No answer. I am going to try the radio."

Floyd reached down and pulled the radio that matched the ones the agents were using out of her bag. He turned it on, pressed the button, and said, "Agent Floyd here, do you copy?"

They waited about twenty seconds but heard no sound. Kay-Loviett stepped harder on the gas pedal and said, "Try again."

Floyd checked to make sure he was on the right channel, then pressed the button down, and repeated, "This is Agent Floyd, does anyone copy?"

Again, no sound came back and Kay-Loviett began cussing aloud and driving her sedan even harder. As she peeled off the interstate toward their exit, she said, "Go ahead and call in backup to the address. I don't care if it is a safe house, something is not right. Damn it! Damn it! What the hell is going on!"

Floyd made the call and help was now on its way. Speeding, they were now only about three minutes away. Kay-Loviett had to slow down when she took the last turn off a paved road or she would have ended up hitting a tree. The entrance to the estate was hard to find in the daytime, let alone nighttime. When she was about a half mile away, she cut the engine and turned off the lights. She said, "From here we go on foot."

Aileene finally convinced Mandy to stay with the girls and take them under the carpet and through the trap door. Feebe was already tired from the long day and had already fallen asleep. Shelly was a different story. Mandy wrapped her arms around her and said, "Shh now, I'm not going to let anything happen to you. This little hole will keep us safe."

The door was finally lifted and Mandy stepped down first and then held out her hands for Feebe and the blanket she was wrapped up in. Feebe opened her eyes and lifted her head as she was moved, but quickly closed them again as she was placed in Mandy's arms. Aileene looked toward Shelly and said, "I need you to stay strong for me and your sister. I love you. Go now."

Shelly whispered, "I love you too, Mommy" and then turned with the pillows and made her way down into the hole.

Aileene closed the door as quietly as she could and then placed the carpet back down on top. She stepped away from the door and walked backward until her back hit the wall. She reached into her pocket and removed her pistol and turned the safety off. She then slid her body down the wall into a sitting position and waited.

Patch searched behind the couches and chairs and even looked behind the drapes hanging against the living room windows. He finally concluded they were not hiding in the living room. So, he slowly made his way back into the kitchen without a sound. He would search every square inch of this house if needed to find them. He found the kitchen pantry and opened the door, but no one was hiding inside. Knowing the kids were little, he checked all the cabinets as well. He walked back into the living room and then worked his way over to the study. Glancing around, there was nowhere to hide except under the desk. Patch walked around the desk and then bent over and stuck out his hands in search of someone. As his hands moved around, he only found open space. Standing back up, he decided they must be in one of the bedrooms. Leaving the study, he paused to listen for the tiniest of noises but heard nothing.

It didn't take him long to find the hallway that led to the rest of the house. He found the first bedroom and cleared it quickly. It was when he was heading toward the second bedroom that he hit a piece of furniture in the hallway. Silently cursing, he never could quite figure out why people put furniture in the hallways; it was such a stupid idea.

Aileene heard a noise and immediately raised the pistol toward the door. She was planning on shooting first and asking questions later. There was no doubt in her mind that she and the girls were all alone. There was more than a fifty-fifty chance whoever cut the power had already killed the FBI agents guarding the safe house. She was now the only one left to protect her girls. She silently vowed, "I will kill or be killed trying to save their lives."

She continued to stay focused with her gun pointed toward the door and then said a prayer, she finished with, "Oh God, please help us!" Aileene closed her eyes and whispered, "Butch, I need you here with me."

Opening her eyes back up, she slowly came to the realization of how much she and the girls needed Butch McNeil in their lives. Placing her free hand over her heart, she decided when this was all over, she was going to do everything possible to get him back. Suddenly, she remembered she had her phone. She thought, "How stupid of me to forget." Realizing the pressure she was under, she just shook her head. She fumbled around trying to get her phone out of her jean pocket while still pointing the gun at the door. Finally she dug it out and decided to text instead of phone. She found Agent Kay-Loviett's number and instantly began texting a message: "Help. The power has been cut, and we are hiding in a safe room built off the master closet. Someone is in the house. I have a gun, and I will shoot."

Satisfied that was all needed, she texted Butch: "Call Agent K-L. I love you!"

She doubled-checked to make sure her phone was on vibrate and then stuck it in the side pocket of her sweatshirt. The only thing now to do was wait. So, she aimed the pistol straight ahead and waited, hoping it wouldn't come down to a shooting match.

Agents Kay-Loviett and Floyd were about five hundred yards away from the house when her phone beeped to let her know she had a text. She held up her hand to alert Floyd to stop and then she removed her phone from her jacket pocket and opened it up. She felt the blood drain from her face as she read Aileene's text. She showed it to Floyd and he nodded in return. She said, "I think it will be a waste of time to check for the agents. We need to move on the house as soon as possible. We won't have long before she is discovered."

Floyd shook his head and then said, "We don't know how many there are. I am going to call and see how much longer for backup."

Kay-Loviett checked her guns while he made the call. He quickly alerted all to the current situation and then closed his phone. Kay-Loviett continued to lead the way toward the house, and he followed in behind her, constantly checking around him.

Patch cleared another bedroom and two baths. The only thing left now was the master bedroom at the end of the hall. He gently stepped inside as to not make a sound and then walked around the bed and into the master bath. He pulled the shower curtain to the side and felt around; he even bent down to make sure someone was not lying in the tub. Nothing. He stood back up and opened the bath closet only to find nothing again. He carefully made his way back into the bedroom and then walked over toward the windows to check behind the curtains. The only thing left was the bed; he walked over and then quickly raised the bed skirt and felt around. He moved over and then around the bed until he was sure no one was there. Standing back up he tried to adjust his eyes to see what else was in the room. There was very little light shining in from the windows since the blinds were closed tightly. He sat on the bed to gather his thoughts. Soon he could make out various objects in the room and noticed the master closet off to the right.

Patch stood up with a smile and then removed his knife from his side. He walked over and placed a hand on the handle and quickly jerked the door open. At that moment, he heard a sound coming from the end of the hallway. Someone had hit the same piece of hallway furniture. He quickly stepped inside the closet and closed the door. There was no light, and it was impossible to see. He felt his way around and found only clothing hanging up. He decided to slide himself behind the clothing and wait.

Kay-Loviett, was rubbing her thigh, and again silently cursing. She and Floyd continued on until they cleared the rest of the bedrooms and finally made it to the master bedroom. Kay-Loviett stepped inside and did a full sweep but found no movement. Floyd stepped in after her and walked over to the window and opened up the blinds. It allowed very little light in, but it did seem to help some. When they were satisfied the room was clear, they made their way over to the closet. Kay-Loviett motioned to Floyd and she opened the door and stepped aside as Floyd stepped in to clear.

Floyd had made only two steps when he saw something shimmer and felt his insides turn into fire as it was ripped opened. He screamed out and reached with his hand and caught some hanging clothing and ripped them down on top of him as he fell to the ground. Next, he heard three shots fired and then his mind slipped away into darkness. Kay-Loviett had made one step in when she heard the first blast. Quickly she stepped back out and yelled, "It's Agent Kay-Loviett, cease fire!"

Kay-Loviett heard a muffled voice and eased herself to the edge of the door and peered inside. There was just enough faint light to see Agent Floyd lying on the floor and another person lying to his left side in a crumbled position. Again she yelled, "Cease fire, it's Agent Kay-Loviett, and I'm coming in!"

She kicked the leg of the other person and got no reaction. She pointed her gun at him and slowly lowered her body down to get a closer look. It was a man wearing dark clothing and holding something shiny in his hand. She reached out and moved his arm to reveal a knife lying beneath him. She slid her hand over his wrist and felt a jarring pain hit her shoulder. As she felt no pulse from the man, she slowly realized that she had been grazed by one of the bullets.

Kay-Loviett ignored the pain, and then crawled back over to Floyd. His pulse was weak so she felt around to find the wound. It didn't take her long to feel the gaping hole left in his stomach by this dead mad man lying beside her. She took both hands and pressed down to stop the bleeding and said gently, "Bass, can you hear me?"

She felt tears roll down her face as she felt him slip away. She felt for his pulse again, but she already knew the answer. Hearing sirens in the distance and quickly approaching, she carefully stood back up and yelled, "Aileene! All is safe now, open the door."

Kay-Loviett heard a clatter from the latch being opened and then she heard "Kay?"

"Yes, Aileene it's me."

Kay-Loviett reached down and moved the unknown man to the side and leaned in to greet Aileene.

CHAPTER 55

Kathleen was lying in bed with the covers tucked around her with her face being the only thing left exposed. She was coming around. At first she felt a dull thumping pain vibrating in her head. She slowly lifted her eyelids and looked around. The moon was shining brightly through the glass windows, and she quickly realized where she was, the master bedroom. Her first thoughts were of Michael, and him lying in bed beside her. She turned her head over to her right but saw no one. She was alone. Feeling a little self-conscious, she felt her body to see if she was wearing anything. The texture felt like cotton to her fingers and she could tell it fit her body snugly. She carefully lifted the covers and looked under. It appeared she was wearing a cotton T-shirt that was not her own. Pulling the covers back down and pulling them closer to her neck she looked around again and tried to put the pieces together.

The only memories that kept flashing through Kathleen's head were of Michael beneath her. She smiled at the memory but quickly frowned when a sharp pain radiated through her skull. She reached up and grabbed her head. "What the hell happened to me? Did I fall, and Michael carried me to bed and tucked me in?"

Slowly Kathleen lifted up onto her elbows and slid upward to a slight leaning position. She moved her legs and arms, and nothing else seemed to hurt except her head. She continued to pull herself up until she was completely sitting up now. Gazing around, she looked at all the furniture and noticed that nothing was out of place. When she saw the chair in the far corner, she noticed some clothing folded up that looked like her swimsuit.

She pulled the covers off her body and saw that the T-shirt was long enough to cover her naked body, just barely. She gently swung her legs over to the side and then stepped off the bed. As she stood her head began to pound harder and her vision blurred. This time she felt around her head in search of a knot of any kind. She found none. Still confused and hurting, she made her way over to the chair and found her bikini bottoms. She leaned over with one hand on the arm of the chair for balance and then lifted one foot and stepped into her swimsuit. She slowly did the next foot, and then gently bent over and pulled them up and onto her body.

Feeling a little better that she was somewhat dressed, she slowly walked over to the glass windows and peered outside. She could see the lap pool below and steam rising from the hot tub beside it. Her eyes continued to look around until she spotted the outdoor kitchen with grill and then the table for two on the opposite side. No one was in site. She said, "Where is Michael? Wasn't there a cook?"

Kathleen vaguely remembered the cook's face but nothing more about him. She took a step toward the door that led to the balcony and the pool below. She found the knob and turned it to find that it was locked. She found the button on the knob and then turned it clockwise. She tried the knob again but the door would still not open. She moved her hand upward and found that there was a deadbolt at the top. There was a keyhole, but no key was sticking in it. She looked over toward the nightstand and then the table by the chair but saw no key. She thought aloud, "Why is this door locked?"

Walking away and leaving the balcony door, she moved toward the master bedroom door that led to the hallway. She placed her hand on the knob and twisted. It was locked also. She thought, "Why? Did I lock myself in here?"

A sense of panic began to work its way up from her chest when she found the button and twisted it and the door opened as she pulled it to her. She took a deep breath then and realized she was not trapped. Pulling the door all the way open, she could only make out a few objects in her path from the moonlight. Feeling the walls, she searched for a light switch and found none. She wanted to call out to Michael, but some gut feeling told her not to. She took her first step into the hallway and didn't see or hear anyone jump out. Again she thought, "Am I all alone? No, Michael would not have left me here. But why was I locked in the bedroom?"

Old memories of Eddie and Lisa began to fill her head and she began to breathe harder now as fear really began to set in. She decided, "This isn't right. Something is wrong. Maybe I should go back and relock the door, and rethink this?"

As Kathleen slowly turned around and made one step with her foot something grabbed her elbow and a hand quickly pressed down over her mouth. Instinct kicked in and she began to push and shove. She connected with something hard, and she heard a small moan escape from the perpetrator. A voice called out, "Kathleen, shhh. It's Agent Simmons."

She twisted and turned and then immediately went still when she realized he was an agent. Simmons pushed her on into the bedroom and then quickly closed the door behind her and relocked it. He was holding a gun. Kathleen saw the gun and took a few steps back and said, "What is going on? Why do you have your gun out?"

Simmons ignored her and took a few steps over to the window and looked out. He motioned for her to back away toward the dark corner in the far side of the room. Kathleen did as she was told. All was quiet for several moments and then Simmons pocketed his gun and made his way over to Kathleen. She said, "What happened? How did I end up in here?"

He looked at her and said, "You don't remember?"

Kathleen shook her head.

Simmons said, "I was watching you have dinner with Mr. Brunson and then you collapsed in his arms. He picked you up and carried you into the bedroom with the help of the chef. Do you not remember anything?"

Again Kathleen shook her head no and then closed her eyes to try to remember her last waking thoughts. Finally she spoke, "I remember being in the hot tub with Michael, but I don't remember eating dinner."

An embarrassing thought crossed her mind and she asked, "How long have you been watching us?"

Simmons didn't seem to mind saying, "Since you arrived."

Kathleen felt her face warm, and her head pound harder. She tried to quickly push the thoughts aside. There were bigger issues here than her fling with a complete stranger.

Simmons asked, "Do you remember anything about the case?"

Kathleen thought hard and finally said, "I had another dream, but nothing important or new that would help. Where is Michael, and why was I locked away in this bedroom?"

"I don't know. After you were carried away, I stood by and watched until I saw the chef leave and come back outside. I followed him a few steps and then decided it was best to come back here and keep an eye on you."

She said again, "So where is Michael?"

Simmons simply said, "I don't know, when I came back, you were the only one left in the house. I've been waiting now for over an hour for someone to make a move."

Kathleen said, "None of this makes sense, why would Michael leave me, and why did I pass out?"

Agent Simmons had no answers. "We need to get you off this island and back to the resort safely. Can you walk?"

Kathleen slouched down into one of the chairs and put her hand to her head and closed her eyes. Her head was pounding so hard she felt dizzy. She tried to think past the pain but she was still very confused. Finally she said, "Okay."

Simmons walked over and said, "I need you to listen carefully to my directions and stay as quiet as possible."

She agreed, and they made their way over to the door that led to the hallway. Simmons pulled out his gun and then turned the knob and carefully opened the door without a sound. They made their way quickly through the cottage and out the side kitchen door. Once outside they ran across an opening and then ducked behind a palm tree. They were in the shadows now hidden from the moonlight. They stayed there a good while as Simmons lifted his night-vision gadget and continued to sweep over the area. There was no sign of anyone.

Through the pounding of her head, Kathleen still concentrated on the events leading up to her waking up. Still nothing. She couldn't understand why Michael had just disappeared. "Did I say something to drive him away?" she wondered. She remembered his smile and some of his kind words to her. "No, he wouldn't just leave me. But he did, and he locked me up in the master bedroom before he did."

Simmons whispered, "Let's go. Stay close."

They had walked for about twenty minutes when Simmons placed his hand up and then came to a complete stop. The pounding in her head had subsided some but she still didn't feel anywhere near 100 percent. She watched as Simmons pulled a phone out of his pocket and held it up for a signal. He must have gotten one because he motioned for her to sit down. She looked at the ground and then thought about what she was wearing and decided to continue standing.

Kathleen continued to watch Simmons as he punched a few buttons and then read the screen. She noticed how his facial expression changed, and she knew immediately something was not right. Quickly she looked around her surroundings but saw no movement. She could only hear the faint sound of the ocean waves and some palms rustling in the wind. There was plenty of light thanks to the moon, but there were still many shadows hidden behind the many palm trees and brush. A cold shiver went down her spine as she was hit with the sudden realization that she remembered everything.

Wave after wave of memories began to flood Kathleen's head, and she instantly felt nauseous. She bent over and then slowly sat down on the ground shaking her head slightly. Simmons asked, "What's wrong?"

"I remember everything. Eddie told me where he left a note right before he grabbed my arm and pushed me away telling me to run."

Simmons put his phone down and asked, "Did you tell this to the man you were with?"

"Michael? I don't know. Dinner is still a little fuzzy. I remember sitting down, and the chef bringing us dinner, and then my memory just gets lost. It is almost like I was…"

Simmons finished her statement for her, "Drugged."

Kathleen wrapped her arms around her, she felt so cold now. "Who would have drugged me?"

Simmons placed a hand on her shoulder and said, "I just got a text from Williams and McNeil."

Kathleen's eyes met his and he continued, "Michael Brunson has been at the resort all day. The man that took you out here is not Mr. Brunson."

Shock filled her mind and spirit. She shook her head and said, "No, you are wrong! Paula told me he checked out, and I was safe with him."

"I'm sorry, but he isn't Michael Brunson."

Still trembling, she blurted out, "How, how did this happen?"

Simmons took a deep breath and then let it out. "I don't know. But what we need to do now is get you off this island before anyone knows you are missing."

Kathleen felt sick, "Who was the man that I shared a bed with? Is he responsible for the murders of Eddie, Lisa and Mia?"

Waves of nausea hit her stomach again, but this time it quickly made its way up. She pulled away from Simmons and leaned over her other side and began to vomit. Simmons reached into his bag and grabbed a bottle of water and a small towel. He knelt down beside her and put his hands on her shoulders. When she was finished, he held out the water and towel. She quickly took both and drank some water. She poured some on the towel and then began to wipe her face with the damp cloth. She no longer felt cold but hot and sticky. She slowly got up with the help of Simmons and said, "Get me off this damn island! Now!"

Simmons's phone vibrated, and he nodded his head yes and then walked away a little to take the call. Kathleen watched him and then looked around again to try to figure out where they were. She really had not been paying attention when they left the cottage. After a few moments she was able to put some pieces together and soon realized they were near the hill that she and Michael or whoever the hell he was, had climbed. A bad taste filled Kathleen's mouth, and she took another sip of water. Looking over toward Simmons, she saw him close his phone and walked back over to her. He said, "We are not far from the boat, maybe about ten more minutes."

She said, "I'm fine. I can walk."

He then asked her, "Where is Eddie's note hidden?"

Kathleen didn't even hesitate as she said, "In Mia's clothing."

Simmons gave a funny look but said nothing and gently grabbed her elbow and started leading her off toward the boat.

They climbed the hill and walked right over the spot where Kathleen had sat with Michael earlier that day. Tears began to flow down her face with each step she took as they worked their way back down on the other side of the hill. She noticed Simmons taking out his phone several times and reading his screen, but he explained nothing to her. At the base of the hill, she could hear the faint sound of the ocean again and knew it wouldn't be far now. She desperately wanted off this island and a very hot shower to wash away everything; she felt so dirty and used. She thought, "What a fool I've been."

Kathleen shook her head as she pictured Michael and all the agents laughing at how easy a target she was. She mumbled aloud, "I'm so stupid. What was I thinking?"

More tears began to flow as she and Simmons finally reached the edge of the brush that gave way to sand. She wiped her face with the towel that Simmons had given her and then took another sip of water. Simmons set his bag down, then leaned under some brush, and pulled out a small inflatable boat that had been well hidden. He tugged at the boat and said, "Pick up my bag and follow me."

Kathleen began to follow him but froze after two steps. There in front of them stood Michael. Simmons had apparently seen him as well but didn't stop walking. In fact, he never went for his gun. Slowly she began to realize that he wasn't afraid of Michael. She thought, "Who are these people? Simmons must not be an agent here to protect me. I've been set up."

Panic immediately took over Kathleen and she began to tremble. Michael saw Kathleen's face and said, "Kathleen, everything is okay now, I just need to…"

Kathleen threw the bag toward him and turned around and started to run. She faintly heard Simmons cuss. "Go after her. I will find George!" he said.

CHAPTER 56

Angrily, Simmons picked up the boat and dragged it back toward the bushes. Once it was well hidden, he looked around and found his bag that Kathleen had thrown. Reaching down he unzipped it and pulled out a paper. Holding it under a small penlight he began to read. A few seconds passed, and then he put the paper away and pulled out his phone. He hit a button and said, "Where are you now?"

He listened and then closed the phone and placed it back inside his pant's pocket. He rearranged a few things in his bag and then checked his weapon. Satisfied, he stood up with his bag and began to walk along the coastline in search of Agent George Brown.

Paula and Butch had been walking for about twenty minutes when they stopped. Butch pulled out his phone and said, "Damn, no signal. Check yours."

Paula did and shook her head, "Nothing."

He said, "We can't be far now."

Butch remained still and just listened. He could only hear the sound of the ocean waves. The island seemed to be shrouded in a deadly calm;

it was an eerie feeling. Paula must have felt it as well because she said, "Something doesn't seem right."

Butch nodded in agreement and sighed, "Come on, we have got to find Kathleen."

She nodded and they headed off again toward the cottage that was still well hidden behind the brush and palms.

Kathleen was running back up the hill, but knew he was fast approaching. She saw a patch of palms off to the side that would make a good place to hide from the moonlight. She quickly turned and headed in that direction. She had just made it into the shadows when she saw Michael appear running up the hill. Her heart was pounding so loudly that she just knew it would give her location away, but he kept running forward, and she closed her eyes and slumped toward the ground. She had to catch her breath, she was safe for now, but knew it wouldn't last. Her mind told her to get back up and run, run like never before. She willed herself to move but the pounding in her head and the empty queasy stomach kept her on the ground.

The man known as Michael ran a few more steps and stopped at the top of the hill. He knew she was fast, but not that fast. He looked around along the edge of the hill and noticed how one area was all dark and shaded by the palms. He knew now where she had gone and headed back down the hill in that direction. He knew she was smart, and he always knew his game was going to be short-lived before she found out the truth about his identity. Now he had to find her and find her fast.

Simmons didn't have to walk far before he spotted Agent Brown sitting on a stump along the beach. When Simmons came into sight, George stood and walked over. Immediately George said, "So what the hell is going on? Where is Kathleen?"

Simmons relaxed his stance and said, "Kathleen ran off when she spotted Michael. I had told her earlier that he wasn't Brunson."

George asked, "So does she know who he is?"

Simmons said, "I never got a chance to tell her. She remembers everything about that night, and she is an emotional wreck. I was just trying to get her to the boat and then tell her. I didn't realize Agent Frost would be there waiting on us and scare her off."

George said, "So she is running now from Agent David Frost because she thinks he is 'Michael the bad guy."

"Exactly"

George looked around out toward the ocean and then said, "So where did Eddie hide the goods?"

It was something about George's demeanor that made Simmons hesitate before answering. This whole assignment had been screwy from the beginning. Why did they bring in another agent and hide his identity from everyone? He decided to play it safe and say, "She didn't actually say, she just said she remembered."

George glanced around again and said, "I don't believe you, Bart."

Startled a little, he looked straight into George's eyes and said, "Come on man, I'm telling you the truth, why would I keep it from you."

George stepped closer and said, "I don't know. You tell me."

Bart shifted his weight and held his ground, "Look, George, this case is screwed up. Why would the Agency bring in another agent without telling you or me about it until now?"

George stepped back and put his hands in his pockets and said, "Does the Agency think one of us is dirty?"

Several moments passed and then Bart said, "Maybe, they know there is a leak."

George looked around again at their surroundings. He finally said, "Shit, fine, don't tell me. Let's go meet up with Williams and McNeil."

George turned and started up the hill and Simmons followed in behind him.

With each step Simmons was second-guessing himself. He had worked with George for a while now and nothing indicated he was dirty. Should he really keep this information to himself? He still didn't know who was here, and who drugged Kathleen. Just when he was about to say something, George stopped and pulled his phone out of his pocket. Bart halted and waited. He pulled out his own phone to check his messages, but there weren't any. When he looked back up, George was facing him and pointing a gun straight at his face. Bart reacted on instinct, but it was too late. The smile that spread across Agent George Brown's face was his last sight before his world faded away forever.

Agent Brown pulled his phone back out and then dialed a number. "It's Zane. Simmons is dead. Close in on the girl, and let's finish this."

Paula stopped when she heard the bullet. It was coming from far away.

Butch said, "They aren't at the cottage. Didn't Brown say there had been no activity there?"

Paula nodded yes and then stated, "We are headed in the wrong direction let's go."

Both detectives began running in a full sprint away from the cottage and toward the area where the bullet was fired. Paula had long thrown down her shoes and was only holding her gun as she ran directly behind Butch.

Butch said, "I just hope we find her before it is too late."

Paula only nodded as she continued to run toward the sound made from a shot that she prayed wasn't for Kathleen.

CHAPTER 57

Kathleen opened her eyes when she heard the bullet. She carefully looked around without making a noise. The shot sounded close, too close. She stood up and began to run again straight into the darkness of the bushes.

Agent Frost stopped when he heard the bullet and silently cussed. They were closing in fast now, and he had to find Kathleen. She would not make it out of here alive without him. He heard a noise up ahead that wasn't too far and began running toward it. After about a minute of hard running another opening appeared and light shone down and revealed Kathleen running just ahead about thirty yards. He sprinted ahead and when he was about ten yards from her he said, "Kathleen, stop! I'm an FBI agent."

Kathleen slightly turned her head but kept running. She was tired, and she knew she could not out run him anymore. She willed herself to continue but couldn't make her legs run any faster. She heard him but couldn't process what he was saying. She turned back again just in time to see him dive on top of her and slam her into the hard ground. He quickly covered her mouth to keep her from screaming and whispered, "Don't make a sound, they are close, and they will kill us both."

She looked into his eyes and tears began to flow. He saw the tears and his expression changed drastically. "Kathleen, I'm not the bad guy. Please trust me."

He was so close to her face, so she turned her head to the side and tried to close off the tears that continued to fall. He could feel her heart pounding beneath her and knew she needed more air. He said again, "Please Kathleen trust me" and then he took a leap of faith and removed his hand from her mouth.

Kathleen immediately inhaled a deep breath and regulated her breathing. She heard what he said but didn't have the energy to scream anyway if she wanted to. He rolled off of her and pulled her in close and wrapped his arms around her. "I thought I lost you. I'm so sorry. I never meant to hurt you."

Kathleen didn't respond; she just listened. Slowly she pulled back away from him and stood up. Agent David Frost stood up as well as she looked straight into his eyes, "I don't know who you are. I—"

There was a sound that came from behind them, and they both glanced in that direction. It was Detective Paula Williams holding a gun out and pointing it at them. "Don't move Kathleen, and mister, I want you to step away very slowly and put your hands into the air."

Agent Frost let go of Kathleen and stepped away. Butch appeared from nowhere and grabbed Kathleen. He asked, "Are you okay?"

She shook her head yes. Agent Frost put his hands in the air and said, "I'm FBI Agent David Frost, and I was sent here undercover by FBI Director Gary Fields."

No one spoke, and Paula continued to hold out her gun. Agent Frost continued, "There is a major leak in this case, that is why I was sent in."

A shot rang out, and Butch went down with a moan. Agent Frost dove on top of Kathleen and rolled her into the bushes. Paula ducked down when another shot was fired that whizzed by her head. She crawled over to Butch to check his wound. Shots were still being fired, and she realized Agent Frost was firing back above her head to some unknown gunman. He was protecting her as she tended to Butch.

Paula's partner was lying on his side and not moving. She ran a hand over his throat to find a pulse. She felt one and then turned him over on his back and found the bullet hole along his left side of his body. Butch's eyes were half opened, and he spoke, "Don't worry about me. Turn around and shoot the bastard."

She took both of his hands and placed them on the wound and pressed down. "Hold on, Butch."

She looked back over at Agent Frost and saw that he was reloading his gun. She made a gutsy call and quickly spun around toward the gunman and jumped up and started shooting as she walked. With the last pull of the trigger she caught a glimpse of him as her heart stopped beating about the same time as his. Catching her breath, she walked over to make sure her eyes weren't deceiving her.

Paula walked about five more steps into the bushes and found him, her lover, Agent George Brown lying on his back with her bullet pierced through his heart. Confused, she bent down and said, "Why?" as tears began to fall down and wet his shirt.

More bullets started flying, and she dove to the ground and made her way back over to Butch. She glanced over to find Agent Frost, but he and Kathleen were gone. She caught a glimpse of a man running through the bushes but she wasn't able to get a shot off. Looking down at Butch, she noticed his breathing was shallower. Picking up her phone, she got a signal and called for help. Butch opened his eyes and looked at Paula. She knew he was trying to talk and she leaned down close.

In a rasp voice he said, "Tell all my girls that I love them so much."

Paula was about to respond but knew that he had already faded into unconsciousness. She continued anyway, "Butch McNeil, you've been shot at before. This is nothing—don't you die on me now!"

She looked at the wound and saw that he was losing too much blood. She moved down to his legs and began to rip at his pants legs. The linen gave away easily and she was able to get a long enough strip to use to tie around him. She carefully lifted him to the side and placed the linen under him and rolled him back over. Lifting his shirt, she carefully tied the strip of cloth tightly over his wound. She then unbuttoned his shirt and made more strips to tie around him. She placed a hand over his forehead and wiped away the moisture that had formed. She spoke softly, "Butch, please hang in there!" and then she curled up beside him and reloaded her gun.

Paula gazed up at the sky and prayed they would pick up her phone's GPS signal and get here before it was too late.

CHAPTER 58

Agent Frost was dragging Kathleen through the palms and brush as fast as he could go. Kathleen seemed to get a second wind after shots were fired in their direction and was able to almost match his every step. When they rounded a corner, Agent Frost finally saw an opportunity to lose the gunman. On the left was a small ditch that ran down the hill that carried rainwater. Frost let go of Kathleen's hand and quickly sidestepped the ditch and then jumped over it with Kathleen right behind him. Once over the ditch, they headed back up the hill toward the unknown gunman.

The move worked because just as the man came down the hill he looked left at the ditch and then continued on toward the right down the hill. Frost was sitting in a crouch position with his gun aimed and Kathleen kneeling down behind him. When the tiniest of openings appeared, he was able to identify the gunman but couldn't risk the shot. The last thing he wanted to do was give their location away if he missed. It was only a matter of time before Kathleen finally collapsed from the exhaustion and the drugs still in her system.

When the man was far enough away, Kathleen whispered, "Was that the captain?"

Frost stated, "Yes, I'm surprised. I thought it was the cook that the Fernandez family had sent."

She asked next, "Who is the Fernandez family and who drugged me?"

Frost wasn't sure and just said, "When we get to safety, we can sort everything out. For now, keep your eyes open for the cook as well as the captain. We don't know for sure who we can trust."

Frost didn't know for sure if the cook and captain were working together. He had not seen the Cook since Kathleen collapsed at dinner. Until now, he had assumed the cook was the one who had drugged her. He looked over at her sitting down; she seemed so weak and fragile. Not at all the woman he had met at the resort. He spoke softly, "Not too much longer now, and I will have you to safety."

Frost stood back up and then helped Kathleen off the ground. They continued on down the hill but more to the left side instead of the route the captain had taken. Kathleen continued to keep up and didn't ask any more questions. Every now and then, Frost would turn around to check on her but she never once looked up to acknowledge him.

Agent David Frost felt like a total jerk. He didn't enjoy the role the FBI had given him. Pretending to be someone else was always the hardest assignment for Frost. He knew it was going to be risky when he was told to get close to Kathleen and convince her that he had feelings for her. Frost had never intended to cross the line with her but he had. When and if the Agency found out, they were not going to be happy. Shaking his head, this situation wasn't as cut and dry as everyone expected. He did not intend to fall for Kathleen during the process. Thinking back over the last two days, he tried to pull away but just couldn't. He then thought, "Who am I fooling? I was the one that made the first pass up on top of this hill."

Frost tried to block it all out for now because he had to get Kathleen to the boat, so he continued on down the hill and tried to focus on each step and his surroundings. After taking several more steps, he stopped suddenly and Kathleen ran into the back of him. She moaned, "Hey, what the—" She stopped abruptly when she saw the body crumbled up in the grass.

Frost had to turn around quickly to cover her scream, but she still got a small sound out. Thinking quickly he grabbed her and began to run again dragging her behind him. After about three minutes of running, they finally reached the coastline. Frost looked around and then he found the boat partially hidden in the shrubs. It was then that he finally let go of Kathleen and pulled the boat out. He walked around it quickly to make sure all was intact with the paddles and then said, "Kathleen, we need to move fast across the beach. It will be dangerous because of the light."

She nodded but said nothing. He was sure Agent Bart Simmons's body was the only thing on her mind now. He walked over and placed a hand on her face. She raised her face and met his eyes. Her green eyes looked dark and cold. He said nothing and then he let his hand slid down her neck and arm. He stopped at her hand and then pulled it to his face and then gently kissed it. He spoke softly to her, "No matter what happens, my feelings are genuine for you." He let go of her hand and said, "We need to hurry now."

There was still no response from her, so he lightly touched her elbow and guided her over to the boat. "On the count of three, we are going to run as fast as we can and push the boat out as far as possible before jumping in. We can use the water for protection, but we will lose the boat if it is hit." He didn't wait for a response, and counted "Three, Two, One, Go!"

Each of them had one side of the boat, and together they were making for the water without any shots fired. They splashed in and swam with the boat as far out as possible. Luckily for them a cloud started to roll over the moon and some relief was finally given from the light. Frost said, "Get in" and he made his way over to her side and helped push her in.

When Kathleen was settled, he grabbed hold of the strap and lifted himself up. Soon he was paddling them away from the beach. Kathleen looked around and finally spoke, "Where to?"

He said, "Don't worry. I have a plan."

But she was. Nothing he could say or do would change that until she found the nearest police station. She tried to picture herself surrounded by policemen in some tiny Barbados police station. The thoughts soon led to the killer. This wasn't working; the men that were after her had already killed two policemen in Chicago and now possibly Detectives McNeil and Williams. She asked next, "What about the detectives? We just left them there on the island."

He stopped paddling and rested the paddles across his lap and wiped his face with his sleeve. "They won't be there for long. Help is on the way."

And just like that, the sound of a helicopter emerged. He smiled at her and said, "That is the good guys. We just need to stay low for a while until they can get to the injured detectives."

He took out his phone and made a few strokes with the keys. He was communicating with someone and that alone made her feel relieved. He said, "They just dropped an agent off at the boat we were on today. As soon as it is secure, she will bring it over to our location."

No more words were spoken between them as they listened to the sound of the ocean waves. Frost had a pained expression on his face as he continued to stare toward the island. Occasionally, he would glance over to Kathleen, but she would not face him. Several minutes passed, and the sound of the helicopter became louder again as it lifted off the island and flew over their heads. His phone vibrated in his hand, and he opened it up and read the message.

The detectives are still alive, and they are headed to the Barbados Hospital.

Kathleen finally allowed herself to look at him and said, "I want to go there if we can. If it wasn't for me, they would still be back in Chicago."

"Kathleen, none of this was your fault. You witnessed a murder and were forced to go on the run."

She said, "I remember what Eddie said to me. Did I already tell you at dinner?"

"No, you were beginning to and then you passed out. I think they put something in your food that made you lose consciousness."

He was going to ask her how she felt now, but he heard the engine of the boat making its way toward them. He pulled out his gun and checked it and then looked at his phone. A message was exchanged, and then the boat got closer. "All is clear. The boat is safe."

It didn't take long to tie up the boat and board. Kathleen was then greeted by Agent Erin Devinshire. She was polite and offered her the suite to make herself comfortable. Not much more was exchanged, and Kathleen made her way toward the bedroom. It all looked a little different this time. She imagined the room was bugged since it was a government boat instead of a personal craft that Brunson Winery owned. She shook her head and closed the door behind her. She thought for the tenth time, "How could I be so stupid? Why did I think a multimillionaire would come looking for me at a beachside resort? Obliviously he hadn't."

Kathleen walked over to the closet and found a few items hanging up that she could wear. She settled on the long sundress that had a smock bodice and tied at the neck. She took it off the hanger and then headed toward the bathroom. The shower stall for two now looked cold and uninviting but she didn't care. She quickly turned the knob and waited on the hot water. Satisfied at last, she removed her swimsuit bottoms and T-shirt and stepped in under the water. She stood there for several minutes and never moved. The water felt great, and it helped her aching head and stomach. She ran her hands through her hair and then wrapped her arms around herself and slowly began to slide down the wall until she was sitting at the bottom of the shower. Tears began to flow again, and she didn't care to try and stop them.

Frost was talking to Agent Devinshire and explaining the events that unfolded at the island. He revealed that Kathleen had remembered and as soon as they reached safety they should be able to get this case wrapped up. The sooner the Fernandez family was in jail the better for everyone, and Kathleen could get her life back. He settled some more things with Devinshire and then decided it was time to check on Kathleen. Making his way toward the suite, he could hear the water running in the bathroom. He carefully opened the bedroom door and then shut it behind him. He walked over to the bathroom door and gently rapped on the door. There was no sound. He said, "Kathleen?"

He waited for a response but got none. He rested his hand on the door and then leaned his head down until it rested on the door as well. "Kathleen, please."

He heard her crying and more pain ripped through his chest until he couldn't stand there and take it anymore. He slowly opened the door and saw her crouched down in the shower crying. She looked up at him with red eyes but made no sound. Stepping in the bathroom, he ripped off his shirt and opened the shower door and climbed in behind her and straddled her. Water soaked through his shorts but he didn't care. He just held onto her tight and kissed her neck. Time stood still and neither said a word.

Agent Erin Devinshire was behind the wheel and driving the boat back toward Barbados when she got the call. She looked down at the number and saw that it was Gary Fields. She answered, "Devinshire."

"Fields here. How far out are you from the harbor?"

Devinshire read the coordinates on the GPS and said, "Twenty minutes or less."

"Good. There will be a swarm of agents there to greet you. How is the witness?"

Devinshire thought about Agent Frost and Kathleen down below for the last thirty minutes and said, "Good. She remembers everything."

"Yeah, that is what I heard. If she doesn't need immediate medical attention, take her to the airport at once. I have arranged for a doctor to make the flight back with her."

She said, "Understood. I will call you when we board the plane."

Fields replied, "Perfect, I will be waiting for your call."

Kathleen reached out and held onto Frost's arms. The embrace felt good and brought her so much comfort. She pushed all thoughts aside and just allowed herself to feel the moment. Finally the water began to turn cold and both were forced to let go and get out. Frost reached up and turned off the knob, then stood, and stepped out. He grabbed a towel and then bent over and covered her naked shoulders. Next, he put his hands under her arms and gently helped her stand. Frost then reached behind him and grabbed another towel and wrapped it around her. He allowed himself to touch her once again and gently led her to the bedroom, picking up the sundress as he went. Kathleen sat on the bed and let Frost run the other towel through her hair. He squeezed her shoulders and whispered, "I am going to check on everything. Are you all right?"

She turned to face him and said, "Yes, once you walk out that door, I don't want to see you ever again."

Frost sat there dumbfounded and all words were lost to him. He could see the pain in her face so he touched her hand briefly and then quickly stood up and headed for the door. Placing his hand on the knob, he thought about turning around and kissing her and begging for her to give him another chance. The agent inside him said, "No, she is a job, and you have done enough damage. So leave and just finish this assignment." Frost opened the door and never looked back as he walked out and shut the door behind him.

Agent Devinshire saw Frost walking toward her with wet shorts but said nothing.

Frost asked, "How much longer?"

"Soon. Fields called."

Frost looked down at his dripping shorts and grabbed a towel that was nearby. He then asked as he dried off, "What did he say?"

"We would be greeted by agents and then escorted to the airport."

Frost said, "She will want to visit the detectives that were shot."

Devinshire just smiled back, "Not going to happen."

For the remainder of the trip, Frost didn't say anymore and Devinshire didn't push. Soon they arrived at the marina, and Frost was first off the boat and greeted the other agents. He walked on down the pier with one as Kathleen emerged and was quickly escorted by four agents to a waiting nearby car. Following her wishes, Frost stepped in a different car and followed her to the airport. It was a quick ride as he described the events of the night to the agents. One of the agents held up his hand for him to stop talking when he received a text message. He replied back and then stated for everyone in the car, "Kathleen wanted to go and see the detectives, and she was very uncooperative when they denied her request."

Frost frowned at the comment and then said, "Yeah, she is worried about them. But you're right—the sooner we get her off this island and into the air the better."

Three cars pulled into the airport and several agents stepped out and made a barrier for Kathleen as she boarded the waiting aircraft. Once she was inside, they all boarded the plane as well, and then the door was closed behind them. Frost decided to take the first seat available, so he could continue to avoid Kathleen. In a matter of minutes, the flight was airborne and headed toward Chicago without another word spoken between Frost and Kathleen.

CHAPTER 59

Paula continued to hold Butch's hand as they made their way through the night sky to the Barbados Hospital. After a very short flight, they landed on a helicopter pad and were immediately greeted by a doctor and nurses. It was at this time, Paula was blocked by the hospital staff, and Butch was whisked away ahead of her. Paula just sort of stood there and watched but couldn't protest or even move. Finally a young staff member walked over to her and gently guided her off the landing pad and through some double doors.

"I will take you to the waiting room, and you can wait there for the doctor to give you an update."

Paula turned to the young lady but couldn't make a sound, so she just followed in behind her.

It had been two hours since Paula saw Butch. Now, she just paced back and forth among the chairs and couches in the emergency waiting room. In the meantime, she had talked to Agent Kay-Loviett and heard the news of Aileene Bell. Butch was going to be so mad when he found out. She was reassured by Kay-Loviett that all were safe and sound except for Agent Bass Floyd who had been killed in the line of duty. Paula sent her condolences and secretly hoped the same fate would not happen to her partner.

Just then, the doctor emerged from the double doors. "I will have to call you back," said Paula quickly, before she hung up the phone. She hurried over to the doctor and braced herself for the worse.

Kathleen was repeating her story for the third time now and was thoroughly exhausted. "Eddie said, look inside Mia's nightgown. Everything is there. I'm sorry."

No one responded so she continued, "That's it. I don't know what is hidden inside Mia's clothing, that is all he said and then he pushed me away, and I saw the man with the knife and began to run."

A female agent who had identified herself as Diane nodded her head and said, "You've done real well, Kathleen. Why don't you rest now, and we will wake you when we are about to land."

Kathleen quickly agreed to the idea. She got up and walked toward an area in the back of the plane that contained a small bed. She lay down and closed her eyes. Immediately Frost's face appeared. She shut her eyes more tightly and shook her head side to side. She thought, "I have got to forget about him."

Kathleen then turned her head and opened her eyes and found a window. Everything was still dark outside. Nothing was visible. She repositioned herself and then reached down and found some covers and then pulled them over her body and closed her eyes. It didn't take long before she was sound asleep with no more thoughts of Agent David Frost.

Inside the Barbados hospital, Doctor McGaven removed his hat and mask and spoke frankly, "He is alive for now, but he lost a lot of blood. I think he is a fighter."

Paula let out a deep breath and asked, "May I see him, please?"

"Yes, but keep it short. I'm sorry, but I'm needed elsewhere. Let the nurses know if you have any questions."

And just like that, he walked back through the double doors. Paula looked around and saw a nurse approach from behind the counter. "I can take you in now if you would like, but remember to keep it short," the nurse said.

Paula just nodded her head in agreement and quickly followed the nurse through the same double doors the doctor had used. She followed the nurse around a few more turns and then down a long hallway. Finally the nurse stopped at a door. "Let us know if you need anything," she said, and then turned and walked back down the hallway.

Paula took a deep breath and then opened the door. Butch was straight ahead lying very still with a tube in his mouth. His arms were beside his side and the covers were pulled up to his chest. On his right arm an IV had been placed and there was tape holding it securely in place. She walked over and noticed right away how pale he was—too pale. She gently placed her hand on top of his and said a quick prayer. Then she blurted out, "Oh, Butch, I'm so sorry. I had no idea George was capable of doing such a thing." A tear rolled down her cheek, and she carefully wiped it away. "You are a fighter Butch McNeil, and there are people counting on you, me being one of those people. Please, please hang in there. I need you and so does Mandy."

A door opened behind her, and the nurse approached her and quietly said, "I'm sorry, but you will have to leave now."

Paula continued to hold Butch's hand and stare at his face. "Please, forgive me and come back." She slowly pulled her hand away and took a step backward while continuing to keep her eyes on Butch. He never moved or twitched. She turned around and looked at the nurse and said, "Please let me know if his condition changes. I will be in the waiting room."

The nurse nodded and then ushered Paula out of the room, closing the door behind them.

CHAPTER 60

Chicago

Kay-Loviett and several agents were back at Eddie's apartment. The room was still roped off and under police surveillance—thank goodness for small wonders. Kay-Loviett showed her badge to the officer and then was allowed back into the apartment. She quickly walked past the kitchen and small living room, and made her way back to the bedroom with the crib. This was not your average nursery. An old wooden crib with lots of scratches was in the far corner. She walked over and glanced inside. There were two articles of clothing lying on top of the bedding. She picked up each piece and then turned them inside out looking for something, anything that would give credit to Kathleen's previous statement. Nothing.

Next, Kay-Loviett walked over to the chest of drawers and began tossing through the items looking for baby clothes. Nothing was sorted. It appeared that Lisa kept her clothing mixed in with the baby's. Kay-Loviett thought to herself, "How odd."

Gently, the FBI agent worked her way through all the clothing turning each piece inside out and carefully examining it—still nothing. Not giving up, she walked over to the closet and started the process all over again. When she was finally feeling this whole search was pointless, she found it.

In the far right corner of the closet was a pile of dirty clothing. It appeared someone had already tossed them, but given the messy state of this room, she wasn't so sure how much was the killer or Lisa just being a poor housekeeper. She saw a pink onesy with some kind of yellow stain on the front. She unsnapped the first two buttons and immediately saw writing. She yelled out to the other agents, "In here. I got it!"

Kay-Loviett quickly worked her fingers unsnapping the rest of the clothing until the onsey was laid out flat in one piece. She stood up and walked over to the single bed that stood beside the crib. She laid the garment down and then began to read aloud.

> "Lisa,
>
> I am in trouble again. I am sorry that I will not be here for Mia. I love you. Go to the corner of Fourth Avenue and Gentry Street and find the public locker number twenty-two. The code is fifty-six-ninety-eight-thirty-seven. Take the stuff to the cops. Make sure you are not followed.
>
> Eddie."

Kay Loviett looked up with a smile on her face and said, "Well, what are we waiting for? Let's go!"

Barbados

A yellow taxicab pulled up in front of the only hospital on the island of Barbados. Aileene Bell paid the driver and then opened up the door and stepped out followed by her girls and Mandy. They were all really tired, but no way was she leaving the girls behind. As soon as she heard that Butch had been shot, she booked four tickets on the next flight out of Chicago. There wasn't any packing and no bags were checked at the airport.

Aileene decided that until the Fernandez family was behind bars, she would never feel safe again. It didn't matter if she had shot and killed the man who had killed five agents and two police officers in the course of a few days. The Fernandez family was still out there and walking free, and she thought it was best to keep the girls close at all times. Looking around as she exited the cab, she thought, "Surely walking into a public hospital surrounded by lots of people wouldn't be my downfall."

Aileene held the two younger girls' hands and walked along the sidewalk as Mandy followed closely behind. She was worried about Mandy. She was too quiet during the plane trip from Chicago to Barbados. She turned around and gave Mandy a wink as they entered the emergency room. As they made their way through the sliding doors, Mandy smiled slightly.

Paula was sitting on a white leather couch flipping through a magazine for the third time. She really wasn't reading; she was just turning the pages. When she heard the doors open she stopped turning the pages and looked up. When she saw Aileene Bell and the girls, she stood immediately and tossed the well-thumbed magazine on the couch. Aileene's eyes scanned the room until she saw Detective Paula Williams walking toward her. She made her way over, released her girls' hands, and reached out to hug Paula. "How is he? Is there any change?"

Paula glanced at the girls and then said, "No, he's still resting. The doctor said he could tell that he's a fighter."

Aileene chuckled a little, "Yes, he is." She stopped talking and turned toward Mandy, only to find her heading toward the nurses' station. Aileene followed her and was only able to hear part of the conversation. The nurse was saying, "Yes, but only for a few minutes."

Mandy turned back toward Aileene and said, "They're going to let me see him. I'll be back soon."

Aileene reached out and touched Mandy's hand, "We'll be right here."

It didn't take long for Mandy to reach her dad's room. She waited for the nurse to leave and close the door, and then she made her way over to his bedside. She simply said, "Dad, it's time to wake up now."

The only sound that was made in return was the humming of the ventilator that was on the other side of the bed. She said again but more sternly this time, "Dad, it's Mandy. It's time to wake up now!"

Again no sound was made. She opened her mouth to speak again but this time no sound emerged.

CHAPTER 61

Kathleen woke up in her own bed in her own apartment. It was Sunday morning. Tomorrow was a school day, and she was determined to go back to work. No one had told her of the status of the case or what Eddie had left behind. She only knew that the FBI had someone stationed outside of her apartment. Kay-Loviett did inform her that Detectives Paula Williams and Butch McNeil were still in Barbados. Butch had made it through surgery but had slipped into a coma and as of last night had not emerged. Kathleen prayed hard last night for God to bring him out of his coma and for this nightmare to finally end. Now, she made no effort to get out of bed. She only lay there and thought about the last several days. No matter how hard she tried, she couldn't get Michael/David Frost out of her mind.

She asked herself, "Why had the FBI sent in a man to wine and dine me? Why did I fall so hard for him?"

And the last question that drove her nuts was the fact that she couldn't understand why she had slept with a man that she only knew for two days. Never had she given herself so freely before. As hard as she thought and tried to piece together the puzzle, the more frustrated she became. Finally, she jerked the covers down and got out of bed. She made her way toward the kitchen and began to make coffee. As the coffeemaker started doing its thing, she left the kitchen and went back into her bedroom to grab her housecoat. She had already decided she wasn't going to get dressed anytime soon. As she reached her bedroom, the doorbell buzzed. She hesitated only briefly, grabbed her housecoat, and threw it on. Next, she slid her feet into her cozy pink slippers and then made her way toward the front of her small apartment. Before opening the door, she gazed into the peephole and saw two officers standing side by side. Still unsure, she just said, "Yes?"

One of the officers said, "Ms. Bishop, a gentleman has arrived with some flowers. We checked it over, and they are fine."

Kathleen undid the latch and then twisted the deadbolt to open the door. She pulled her housecoat close to her chest and said, "Flowers?"

The officer said nothing and just held them out for her. She took them and said, "Thanks." She closed and relocked the door.

Kathleen walked over to the kitchen counter with the flowers and then set them down. They were roses—eighteen pink and yellow roses. She picked up the card that was positioned in the front and took it over to the other counter by the coffeemaker. She set it down and then pulled out a coffee cup and poured her a cup of coffee. She settled on just black and then picked up the card and walked over to her favorite lounge chair and sat down carefully so as to not spill her coffee. After taking two sips, she sat her mug down and then opened the card. It didn't take her long to realize her suspicion was correct—it was from David Frost. She slowly read the message:

Dear Kathleen,

Words cannot express the pain that I have caused you. When the smoke finally clears and this case is finished, please have it in your heart to forgive me. I hope to see you again one day, if only just to talk.

Yours for the taking,

DF

Kathleen read it twice more and then questioned aloud, "'Yours for the taking?' Just what did he really mean by that? Surely he didn't expect me to just say, 'Okay, you are forgiven, David. I would love to be your girlfriend!' Wonder why he signed it DF instead of David Frost?"

Kathleen closed the card and glanced back over at the roses. Pink and yellow were the colors that were used at their table out by the pool on the island. Was it a coincidence or did he carefully pick those colors instead of the more typical red? Pushing all of the questions out of her mind, she put the card down, picked up her mug, and headed back toward her bathroom. She desperately needed a hot bath.

CHAPTER 62

Kay-Loviett was seated at a large conference table with her boss Gary Fields, and several FBI agents, including David Frost. They had gathered today to watch the video that was found in locker number twenty-two. It was as if they were on pins and needles as they watched the video. Everyone had a notepad and pen and was ready to make notes as they plotted to bring down the Fernandez family. Once the video was started, the message was clear, Eddie was afraid for his life, as well as for Lisa and their baby. Not knowing whom to trust and feeling the undercover agent was a setup, he took the money and ran. Sometime later he decided to make a video and rent a locker to hold both. He continued, "I didn't know he was an undercover agent until it was too late. You see I work for a very powerful and dangerous family. They will kill me before anyone gets too close to the family. They don't know that I know who they are, but I do. It is the Fernandez family. I have worked for them almost a year now, and I know they will kill me when they find out I slipped up. I sell drugs for them and turn the money over to another man who reports back to them. Why should you believe me? They own a restaurant called Evangelina's. If you go into that restaurant you will find a hidden camera. They aren't the only ones who think they are smart. Just because they are white and rich, doesn't mean this poor fool is stupid."

Gary Fields stopped the tape, "Was their anything salvageable at the restaurant?"

A man sitting by Frost said, "No, nothing. Someone wanted everything burned. The fire marshal has declared it an accident due to a grease fire."

Kay-Loviett said, "The chef died as well."

Gary Fields said nothing and hit a switch, and Eddie's voice filled the room again.

"The videos show the brothers talking about everything, man. You will see for yourself when you find the videos." It was at this point that Eddie sat back in his chair and smiled. "I'll tell you where they are. I have this history teacher named Ms. B. She be a real good teacher. Well, one day when she wasn't in her room, I snuck in and replaced a disc in one of her history DVD collections." He smiled again and even laughed a little. "I chose the video about the Opium Wars. I thought that would be the most fitting place to put the video collection."

David Frost watched the video and then noticed all laughter and smiles were gone. He saw Eddie lean forward and stare directly into the camera. Eddie continued with a softness in his eyes, "I won't see my baby grow up. When you count the money, some will be missing. I put it in an account for Mia's college. Please don't take that from her. It is all I have left to give her." Eddie's eyes turned moist, and he quickly got up and turned off the camera, and the screen went blank.

The room got noisy fast as chairs were pushed back and agents quickly got to their feet. Fields said, "Agents Kay-Loviett and Frost, stay. We need to talk."

Kay-Loviett looked around and wanted to protest. This was her case, and she wanted to be one of the agents who went to the school to get those videos. Looking at Field's face she decided it was in her best interest just to sit back down. So she placed her hands back on the chair and pulled it forward and sat. Frost had already taken a seat. She didn't have long to contemplate what he wanted because he said, "George Brown—who the hell is he?"

Aileene was sitting in a chair pulled up close to Butch's side when she saw his fingers and then his hand move. She reached out and grabbed his hand, "Butch, it's Aileene. Can you hear me?"

Butch turned his head toward her voice and then slowly opened his eyes. He tried to make a sound but his mouth was too dry. He saw her smile and watched as she bent over him and kissed his forehead. She turned and headed for the door but quickly came back inside. Soon a lady dressed in white entered the room.

He knew then, he was definitely in a hospital. "Shit, I got shot again," Butch thought.

EPILOGUE

Eight Months Later

It was in the middle of July on the island of Cozumel when Aileene Bell was walking along the sand with all eyes on her. She was wearing white and was walking barefooted toward Butch and the minister standing behind him. She glanced around and smiled as she saw Mandy, Feebe, and Shelly standing to the left of Butch all dressed in emerald green. The girls were her bridesmaids. This was truly one of the happiest days of her life. When she thought back to how close she came to losing Butch, her heart stopped, and she caught her breath. Butch must have noticed because a look of concern flashed across his face. She took a deep breath and then looked into his eyes and mouthed, "I love you."

Paula was sitting in the front row. With time, the pain and confusion that she felt toward George began to diminish. It was determined that Agent George Brown was a man named Zane who worked for the Fernandez family. She was not the only one fooled. When the case was finally wrapped up, two leaks were discovered in the Chicago Police Department, but it was never determined how the Fernandez family knew their location in Barbados. It wasn't until the past month that Paula had finally learned to forgive herself. Now as she looked ahead, she was happy for Butch and Aileene as they said, "I do."

Through all the meetings and interrogations about her relationship with George, Butch and Aileene had supported her and believed in her every step of the way. She knew without a doubt that they would continue to be there for her in the months that lay ahead. She smiled at them and then looked down and placed a hand on top of her very round belly and said, "Look little one, your godparents just got married."

The Fernandez family

Emilio Fernandez was sitting in a jail cell serving a life sentence for ten counts of willfully plotting murder, drug trafficking, and fraud. His wife Vivian had since filed for divorce and was living with her boys in Madrid, Spain. The Chicago Steel Company was now in the hands of the court until all money laundering had been sorted through. The other brother was sitting at a table in Rio sipping a glass of wine with a beautiful South American beauty that he easily picked up from a bar. Victor had never resurfaced after Barbados and was now on the list of America's Most Wanted.

Ft. Lauderdale, Florida

Kathleen walked along the pier beside her father, James Bishop. They were laughing after a good day during which they caught the limit on snapper and mackerel. Her mom, Joyce, was waiting at the end of the dock as they made their way toward her. She smiled and said, "So, do we have enough for dinner?"

James happily said, "Yes, and David has the cooler to prove it."

Kathleen turned around and saw Agent David Frost struggling a little, but he was managing by himself. It had taken her a while to realize she wasn't going to be able to get him off her mind. She tried—boy did she try. After the school memorial services were held for Eddie and Lisa, she jumped right back into school and tried so hard to block him out, but he just wouldn't go away. After spring break, she finally picked up the phone and called him. It took him twenty-two hours to get to her apartment; he was in Spain with Agent Kay-Loviett trying to hunt down Victor Fernandez when she called. Now, four months later they were still making it work. David had taken two weeks off for a vacation, and Kathleen had decided to take him home to Ft. Lauderdale to meet her parents. David knew this was a big step for her, and he had no intention of disappointing her ever again.

Here is a sneak preview...

Just For You

COMING SOON

LATE 2011

PROLOGUE

7:15 pm

Wednesday, September 22nd

Central University of Arlington, Texas

Robby Singleton left his last class of the day and was headed home on foot. He shared an apartment with another guy but technically there was a third roommate, his girlfriend. Becky did not pay rent, at least not to his apartment. Becky's parents dished out over five hundred dollars a month to an apartment shared with another girl where they thought she lived. Both apartments were in the same complex just one building over.

The walk from campus back home normally took about ten minutes, but tonight a few students lingered after class and now he wasn't going to get home until around seven thirty. He was in no hurry. Becky's class did not get out until nine o'clock.

As Robby walked along the pathway, he noticed some areas were darker than normal. He stopped, looked up and around until he saw the reason for the darkness. There was a street light out and he quickly made a mental note to call someone. Becky made this same walk, and he didn't like her making it alone and in the dark. Tonight she would be walking home with Jamie, her pretend roommate. Both girls were in the nursing program and Wednesday night was their lab night that ended late.

Robby continued on down the path for another minute or so when he felt his cell phone vibrate in his pocket. Stopping for a moment, he pulled it out and read the text.

Got out early. Leaving class now.

A big smile spread across Robby's face. He thought, "Becky is going to be in a good mood tonight maybe I'll get lucky."

Robby picked up his pace, he wanted to get home to shower and download his assignment from class before she got there. Placing his phone back in his pocket, he then switched his backpack over his other shoulder and began to jog the rest of the way home.

Rounding the last corner, he stopped quickly when a dark SUV pulled up beside him. He stopped jogging and turned to look who it was. A voice said, "You look like you are in a hurry. Would you like a ride?"

Robby recognized who it was and said, "No thanks, I just live over there."

"Are you sure? It's no problem."

Robby was thinking of Becky and decided at the last moment, "Sure, why not."

Robby reached for the door, opened it and then climbed in.

Becky and Jamie were walking and talking along the path and never once noticed the street light out. Becky was explaining to Jamie how to approach their homework that was just given to them at the end of class.

Jamie said, "I'm so tired. We work so hard and then they throw an additional assignment our way to complete in just three days!"

"I hear you. At least we have the weekend."

Jamie stopped, "I thought you and Robby were going to Houston to visit his parents."

Becky shook her head, "No, his dad got called away on a business trip. We are going to try another weekend."

Jamie started walking again and Becky met her pace.

Jamie asked, "So do you think he will pop the question in May when we graduate?"

It was Becky's turn to stop walking. She hesitated but then answered, "I sorta hope not."

"What? Why?"

Taking a step forward she said, "I'm not ready. I want to get a job first and work at least a year."

"I don't understand. He has plenty of money to support both of you, with or without your salary."

Becky giggled and said, "Yes, and I look forward to spending it one day."

Jamie squeezed her arm and said, "I think I know what you mean. We worked so hard to become nurses and it's going to be so exciting when we get that first job."

"Exactly! I'm afraid if I rush into marriage there will be pressure from his parents for us to start a family right away."

"Did Robby's mom ever work?"

"Nope, I think she only went to SMU to snag a rich husband."

Jamie laughed aloud, "Don't let Robby hear you say that!"

"No kidding, his mom can do no wrong" said Becky.

Glancing around, Becky took in her surroundings. She said softly, "This pathway is a little creepy. I'm glad we are almost home."

Jamie nodded and both girls crossed the last street and headed toward their driveway that led to their apartment.

Becky said goodbye to Jamie and then turned left and made her way over to building B. Climbing the stairs quickly, Becky made it to the third floor and then walked down the hall that led to Apartment B32. Becky pulled out her keys and opened the door to darkness.

"Hello?"

Becky hated coming home to a dark apartment and both Robby and his roommate Derrick knew that. Turning on a light first and then closing and locking the door behind her, she made her way into the apartment. Becky placed her books down on the kitchen table and then walked over to the notepad by the phone. Derrick had left a message that he wasn't coming home until tomorrow afternoon. Looking around some more, she didn't find any messages from Robby.

Becky decided to go and check the bedroom just in case Robby decided to lie down and somehow had accidentally fallen asleep. As she made her way toward the hallway turning lights on as she went she remembered how tired Robby was this morning. When she was just a few steps away she called out, "Robby?"

There was no answer so she kept walking until she found the light switch at the doorway to their bedroom. Turning the light on she glanced around the room and then let out a pierced scream that would have woken the dead.

Robby was lying in bed with blood splattered all around the sheets and walls of the bedroom. Knowing he wasn't alive, Becky turned around and ran to the front of the apartment screaming the entire way.

Finding the front door, Becky struggled with the deadbolt and finally got it opened and landed right into arms of their neighbor Jackie before finally collapsing into a sea of darkness.

CHAPTER 1

Monday, September 27th

Five days later

Dr. Lindy Ashley just finished writing her last notes on her latest case file when Erin her secretary buzzed in.

"Lindy your husband is on line two."

"Erin, he is my ex-husband now, remember?'

"Sorry, I'm still trying to break that habit."

Lindy rolled her eyes and placed her pen down on the file and then pressed two.

"Hello George. What can I do for you?"

"Hi Lindy, sorry to call you at work but I wanted to stop by around six o'clock to pick up Parker and keep him through the weekend."

"George, we decided Parker stays with me. All this running back and forth is confusing the shit out of him."

"I know Lindy. It's just that I didn't realize how much I would miss the little fellow."

"Well George, have you decided about getting your own little fellow."

"What? This coming from you Miss Sensitivity."

"Yeah, Parker stays with me and no you can't come pick him up."

"Lindy please, I just can't go out and replace him."

Lindy sat back in her brown leather chair and closed her eyes. George was still carrying on with the speaker phone on full blast. Slowly she opened her eyes and scanned her desk until she found the photo of her and Parker at the beach. George had taken the photo just as Parker jumped up and caught the frisbee. Parker was six in the photo but according to the lifespan of Jack Russells, he had several more good years ahead of him. She silently asked herself, "Am I being fair?"

Erin popped in the doorway and broke her train of thought. "Sorry to interrupt but your four o'clock appointment is here."

"Thanks Erin, give me two minutes and send him in."

George suddenly sounded louder, "Am I on speaker phone? You know I hate when you do that Lindy."

"Well apparently there are other things you hate about me or you wouldn't have left our marriage AND our dog to begin with."

Silence followed.

Fifteen seconds passed by and then Lindy spoke, "Okay George. You can come and pick up Parker Saturday morning around ten o'clock but this is the last time. So say your goodbyes."

"Can I assume you still run at eight o'clock with him?"

"What is your point George?"

"If Parker runs with you, he is not going to run again with me."

Flabbergasted, Lindy quickly sat back up and said, "Enough George! Take it or leave it. I have to go now."

As she reached for the end button she barely caught the last words "Take it" before the line went dead.

Lindy pushed back from her cherry wood desk, stood up and then straightened out her pencil black skirt. She then walked over to her private bathroom and took a quick look in the mirror. Glancing at her lips, she noticed they needed another coat and picked up her pink tube of lipstick off the sink counter and reapplied. She continued watching in the mirror as she moved her lips up and down. Satisfied, she left the bathroom and closed the door behind her. She had just enough time to grab a new folder and notepad before her new patient arrived.

As she watched the door open her breath immediately caught in her throat. Stunned a little, she looked down at her folder and read the name.

"Agent Matthew Blake? Hi I'm Dr. Ashley. Please come in and have a seat."

Agent Blake walked forward shook her hand and then took a seat on the brown leather couch as directed. Lindy could see Erin smiling big and mouthing the word "G-O-R-G-E-O-U-S" as she turned and closed the door behind her.

Composing herself, Lindy walked around the sofa and took a seat across from him in her pale yellow chair. She was about to ask a question when he spoke first.

"Look, you know why I'm here and I know why I'm here. This is not the first time I have shot a man. Lets have our talk and then you can bill the agency for your astronomical fee and then I am out of here."

Lindy tilted her head and spoke, "Actually Agent Blake, I have no idea why you are here."

Matthew frowned, "The agency didn't send you any paperwork?"

"No, I only have your name and the paper you filled out when you arrived."

Matthew leaned forward and then spoke with his hands, "Well shit! Okay Doc, here is the drill. In my line of work, you shoot someone dead and they send you off for a-"

"Excuse me Agent Blake. I know the drill. I have counselled many lawmen over the years."

"Great so lets-"

"Excuse me again Agent Blake." She paused and smiled. "Before we begin, I want to be very clear with you that I will not sign off on any document until I've had a chance to talk, listen and discuss the issue at hand."

Matthew looked at her with a hard stare and a scowl on his face. She smiled back and then set her folder down on the coffee table between them. Looking at her closely for the first time he realized she wasn't some knucklehead shrink. She was self confident, polished and very easy on the eyes. Her appearance was different as well. She wasn't wearing a white coat or jacket. Instead she wore silk and her arms were exposed for full view. She wore her jet black hair down and it fell across her blue blouse. His eyes continued to flow down her body and met her long legs. They were crossed at an angle and her black skirt exposed her lovely mid thighs. Slowly his eyes left her and he took in the room. It wasn't black and white. The room had color, charm and style. He took a double look at the walls and asked, "Are your walls painted pink?"

Lindy sat back and smiled again, "The color is called rose petal."

Blake nodded as if all made sense now.

Lindy spoke next, "Agent Blake do you mind if I call you Matthew and you call me Lindy?"

Matthew looked at her blue eyes and swore they were twinkling back at him. He only could nod as he was mesmerized and quickly falling into some kind of weird spell.

She sat back up and recrossed her shapely legs and spoke, "Matthew tell me what happened the day you pulled the trigger that ended a life."

An hour later, Matthew was behind the wheel of his shiny black '69 Chevy Camaro and speeding down interstate 20 to the FBI field office in Dallas. Cars, trees and buildings were all flying by as his thoughts continued to reflect on his session with Dr. Lindy Ashley. He asked aloud, "How the hell had she gotten me to talk about my mother?"

Matthew was trying his best to sort through the hour long session and trying to pick away at when and how it all began. He looked at himself in the windshield mirror and thought, "What the hell? I look exhausted." Glancing down at the radio, he hit a button and it went to his 80s rock and roll station. ACDC's Back in Black was playing and it immediately brought a sense of relief as he began singing away and pounding the steering wheel to the beat. Just as the song ended, he thought he had broken free of her spell until he came to the crashing realization that he set up another appointment for later in the week.

"Damn her!"

Matthew turned down the radio and took out his cell phone and called the office. On the second ring, someone picked up and he said, "Blake here. I'm just checking in. I'm about twenty minutes out."

A female voice on the other end said, "Hi Matthew its Janet, you have a meeting at six o'clock with the boss man. I will let him know you will be here."

"Yeah, thanks Janet."

Janet asked, "So how did your appointment go with Dr. Ashley?"

"I went and that is all you need to know."

Janet snorted, "Touché!"

"Yeah well, it's only the fourth time I've been sent" and then Matthew closed the phone.

Matthew continued on down the interstate and thought about what he had said to Janet. "Was it the fourth or fifth time he had to draw his gun that ended someone's life?" Oh well, the latest victim, Ned Fry, would be one he would never loose sleep over in a million years. Ned was a child abductor and Matthew was forced to use his gun when Ned held the seven year old boy hostage during a shoot out last week.

Slowly Matthew's thoughts wandered back toward Lindy Ashley again. What was it about her? He remembered the way she tilted her head with her red nails holding a pen to her painted lips. She was down right sexy as she crossed her legs and talked with her hands. She would ask questions and Matthew responded to all of them like a pistol whipped puppy dog.

Matthew was a little frightened by Lindy. No one has had that effect on him since Cynthia was alive. With the thought of her name, memories came crashing back inside his head. He could still see Craz Numez with his bulking arms wrapped around Cynthia's neck just as if it was yesterday instead of four years ago. Matthew spoke aloud, "Burn in hell Craz" and then he leaned forward and cranked the radio back up.

Singing along with Bon Jovi, Matthew shook his head and tried to knock loose the cobwebs as he exited off the interstate in search of a new diversion.